DECENNIAL

MAX FORTUNE

Published by:

Fortune Publishing Group

E-mail: info@fortunepublishinggroup.com

www.FortunePublishingGroup.com

For Large Book Orders Contact Fortune Publishing Group at: (443) 256-3400 ext. 1900

ISBN13: 978-1-955358-03-3

Printed in the United States of America

For more info about Decennial visit: www.decennialbook.com

Book cover designed by Max Fortune

DEDICATION

This book is dedicated to George Floyd, Breonna Taylor, Eric Garner, Daunte Wright, Freddie Gray, Rayshard Brooks, Atatiana Jefferson, Philando Castile, Alton Sterling, Ahmaud Arbery, Janisha Fonville, Jacob Blake, Stephon Clark, Botham Jean, Aura Rosser, Akai Gurley, Michelle Cusseaux, Oscar Grant, Andre Hill, and the other countless Black men and women who have senselessly lost their lives because someone saw the color of their skin; and determined instantly whether they were good or bad, friendly or foe, right or wrong.

No one can control the color of their skin when they are born into this world. We can only control the content of our hearts, minds, and attitudes in hopes that they can paint our country in a way that adds brilliant colors to the fabric of this great nation we call America.

ACKNOWLEDGMENTS:

I would like to thank God for choosing me as a vessel to share this vital message. This has been a very challenging book to write because of the subject of race and the complexity of the story itself. I thank God for giving me the strength, courage, and wisdom to write this book.

I'm eternally grateful for my wife, Nicole Fortune, who is the true embodiment of helpmate. Her love, understanding, and support daily and especially while writing this book has been invaluable.

To my children, Byron, Kristan, Jabria, Kasim, and Samiyah, thank you for your individual and collective contributions to this book. Without your input, this book may have never been written.

I would like to thank Jamillah Nasir for her input and for always being available to help make my writing better.

I would like to extend a special thanks to the team who assisted me with this book:

I would like to thank Carol Sawyer for her dedication and commitment to helping me sort out all of the main ideas I wanted to touch on in this book. Your creativity is exceptional.

I want to thank Elexis Gibson, a fantastic intern who just seemed to handle whatever tasks I threw her way. Her creative talents helped me flush out the characters and details of the story.

I would also like to thank another amazing intern Emma Stinson for her creative talents and attention to detail. Her ability to shape the major events and, more importantly, focus on the minor details was instrumental.

I began writing "Decennial" as a movie script and quickly realized I need to write and publish it as a book first. I would like to thank intern Megan "Lee" Shaw for working with me on the movie script for "Decennial."

Last but certainly not least, in any way, I would like to thank my editor Cristen Martin who committed to helping me focus on this story, tighten it up, and who attended Zoom calls with me every other day for six weeks to work on this story to get it to completion.

CONTENTS

CHAPTER 1

CIVIL UNREST

APRIL 2015 CHARLOTTESVILLE VIRGINIA

The scarlet and crimson inferno scorched the molten tar on the city streets. Buildings were ablaze throughout the city. Police cars were being torched and left to burn like the scene from an apocalyptic war zone.

News of Freddie Gray's brutal death at the hands of police officers spread rapidly. Initially, as a small bonfire on the west side of Baltimore and ultimately amplifying throughout multiple cities across the United States. For far too long, the African-American community had been negatively impacted by the merciless arm of the law, and the injustices doled out by the very police sworn to protect and serve them. Black Americans wanted their bruises acknowledged. They'd felt unheard and unimportant for far too long, and they were now ready to give their collective statement.

Charlottesville, Virginia's city streets were overrun with protesters fueled by rage and righteous indignation, many of whom transformed into rioters within hours. Virginia, the nation's tenth state to enter the union, had a centuries-old history with bigotry and racial unrest. On the night of Gray's death, a thunderous crescendo of their pain-filled voices arose from every corner of the nation. Their cries permeated the country's borders and reached the hearts and sensibilities of people throughout the world.

In response to the rioters, armies of police officers swarmed the streets like a gang of killer bees buzzing as they gathered into formation. In an effort to contain the massive crowds that formed, the police began firing rounds of tear gas, one after the other. The metallic taste of tear gas filled the air as people scattered to find relief from the burning sensation in their eyes and nose.

Officer Robert Whitmore could not seem to tune out the distinct sound the canisters made as they pinged against the ground. His uniform, usually meticulous, was now torn and smudged from all the smoke and debris in the air. He was indistinguishable from the other officers, apart from his long nose and narrow dark eyes. Robert was a sizable man with a ruddy complexion and an authoritative aura. He was used to being in control without even trying; this was different. His mere presence alone was not enough to quell the rioters' chaos. He nervously inhaled deeply as he scowled with disapproval, trying his best to dispel his feelings of frustration at the mayhem hindering his need to be in control. He couldn't help but think that he and his fellow officers needed to be using *more* force, not less.

Out of the corner of Robert's eye, he saw a protester approach him screaming, "Justice for Freddie Gray," as they set fire to a police car with a Molotov cocktail. Robert stumbled backward as the heat from the blast seemed close enough to melt his skin.

Simultaneously, the plate glass windows of several nearby businesses exploded in unison from fire, with noise so loud Robert's ears began to ring. Robert covered his ears briefly before bending over to gather himself and springing into defense mode. Within seconds, his fellow officers joined him, pushing and shoving the protesters back in an attempt to regain order.

Robert and his fellow officers' attempts to quell the chaos proved futile, as the rioters, fueled with frustration, pushed back the group of officers. Robert's heart began to pound rigorously as the crowd of rioters overpowered his team. Robert suddenly panicked as he is thrust backward, and his body slams onto the hood of a moving car.

Dr. Andre Langston slammed on his car's brakes and gripped the steering wheel tightly as it threatened to jolt out of his grasp. He was forced to deviate from his routine drive to his lab because of the riots. Dr. Langston coveted his routines, the predictability of his patterns brought him a sense of comfort. As he glanced out of his front windshield, he realized that the man on the hood of his car was a police officer. Robert rolled off the hood of Dr. Langston's car and fell to the ground. Dr. Langston watched in horror, wondering if he just killed a man.

He instantly visualized tomorrow's news headlines: *"Angry Black Man Kills White Police Officer With His Car."*

Before he could go in full-on panic mode, the officer climbed gracefully to his feet and began ruthlessly yelling insults and cursing at any protesters within his earshot. Robert barely glanced at Dr. Langston as he motioned to him with his hands to keep his vehicle moving away from the mob of people in the streets.

As Dr. Langston calmed down and continued driving to his destination, he gazed out of his car window and watched as the city he called home; was torn apart with violence. He was taken aback by all of the violence he witnessed that night. Acknowledging in his mind that this wasn't the first time he had seen the police act in such a threatening and animalistic manner but not recalling ever seeing it so widespread. As Dr. Langston continued to gaze out of the windows of his car, the windows illuminated, reflecting the fires' orange and red blaze. He tapped hesitantly on his car's brakes as he turned the corner, hoping that all of the chaos would come to an end soon.

His car speakers crackled with the sound of a radio broadcaster at the scene of the riot, which he could barely hear over the chants and screams outside. Dr. Langston struggled to fight off his disappointment with what he saw and heard that night. It wasn't that he was surprised by the chaos and outrage; as a Black man, he knew that Black people were tired of injustice. With pain, confusion, and a lack of knowing what else to do, rioting was their only cry for help, but the destruction he viewed was striking.

"This shit has got to stop," he muttered to himself as he attempted to navigate, more slowly than ever, through the tumultuous mobs in the streets.

MAY 2015 POLICE HEADQUARTERS CHARLOTTESVILLE, VA

The Charlottesville police headquarters turned into a chaotic command center or more like a war zone. Men and women from different departments and organizations of law enforcement scrambled about, shouting over one another. Each person fiercely debated what action should be taken next, even as violence was turbulently burning through the city, crumbling it to the ground. Every officer argued that their plan was the best for getting the situation under control; meanwhile, no measures were put in place as unbridled violence rolled through Charlottesville and city streets across the country.

The brutal and ruthless death of yet another Black man had threatened to go unpunished, igniting riots and division everywhere, and the police headquarters was no different. Many of the officers argued that their comrades accused of Freddie Gray's death acted appropriately and that the officers shouldn't be reprimanded in order to satisfy the public's appetite for justice. Others squabbled about what meaningless disciplinary action they could enact to calm the rioters down. What started as a civil discussion had turned into an aimless, heated dispute.

The chaos was interrupted abruptly by a large man whose figure took up the entire doorway.

"Quiet down," the man bellowed. His voice was harsh and authoritative. A hush quickly fell over the room as everyone's attention turned to Officer Teigan.

"This petty back and forth won't get us anywhere," he addressed the entire room with a frown. "Everybody, out! I have a call to make."

While the officers cleared out, Teigan walked over to the conference room window and surveyed the city below. Even though the conference room was on the police headquarters top-level and far removed from the sounds on the streets, the chaos was still apparent. The city streets were still cast in a red haze. With a sigh, Teigan dialed the police captain.

"Jenkins would have a better idea of how to handle this mess." He muttered to himself.

"Captain Jenkins, I have a city burning to the ground and a roomful of officers who can't get their shit together, and it's all over the death of another Black man," Teigen belted out.

"This will fade away just like the others," Captain Jenkins' voice emanated clearly through the receiver, quietly chuckling. "Sooner rather than later, I hope."

Teigen, humored by the joke, closed the blinds and turned his back to the window and the scene unraveling in the distance.

"I need you to be present at a meeting in about an hour. I need all the help I can get containing this mess." Teigan sighed heavily. "Law and order ain't as easily maintained as it used to be," he added.

"Nowadays, our men gotta be worried about getting caught on camera," Captain Jenkins said, agreeing with Teigan.

"Back in the day, nobody batted an eye at a little beating. That's why I worry about E.J.; it's hard to be a cop these days," said Captain Jenkins.

"Ahh, your boy is tough as nails. He'll be alright," Teigan assured his friend. "See you in an hour," he said, hanging the phone up with a click and striding back to his office.

As Teigan exited the conference room, he called gruffly to a young black officer sitting at his desk right outside.

"I need you to set up a meeting of all of the department heads for me, have them all back here in one hour. Got that, um-uh," Teigan stuttered and snapped his fingers, trying to remember the officer's name.

"My name is Darnell, Darnell Bradley, sir," the young officer replied. "I'll get right on it," he said as he masked his annoyance with a tight smile.

Darnell waited impatiently for Teigan to close his

office door shut behind him. Then he sneakily glanced around the precinct, making sure no one was listening. He hummed under his breath as he dialed a series of numbers on his cellphone.

After a few rings, Darnell heard a beep on the opposite end. He sighed in relief. " Dr. Langston," he said in a hushed voice. "You're still looking to get funding for your project, right?"

"I'm always hunting for funding. You've got something for me?" Dr. Langston asked.

"Look, man, just thought you should know there's gonna be a meeting here in an hour. Big department heads talking about how to handle the officers who killed that guy," Darnell whispered. Darnell quickly scanned the room with his eyes, worried that someone was watching him or, worse, listening to his conversation.

"This might be a great opportunity to pitch them your program," he added in a hurry as he noticed someone approaching his desk. "Gotta go. Remember, the meeting starts in an hour."

An hour later, a group of police officials and department heads fill the largest conference room at police headquarters. The men and women sit around a large table, leaning forward in their swivel chairs as they begin to quarrel back and forth about the best course of action to take to bring the city back to order. Their raised voices clamber on top of one another. At the head of the table, Teigan massaged his temples in frustration.

"This meeting is going as horribly as the first one--

perhaps even worse," he thought to himself.

He had gathered the heads of all the departments to discuss hopes of creating a collective solution to the violence the city was facing. Instead, the meeting became an intense battleground of debate that was far from an amicable solution. The tension in the room was so prevalent that it felt like the air in the room was escaping making it harder for Tiegan to breathe with each moment.

Darnell sat outside the conference room and ignored the raised voices that emanated from it, rubbing his forehead distractedly. Eventually, he glanced up from his desk to see Dr. Langston striding into the precinct; a Black briefcase gripped at his side.

"You're late," Darnell angrily snapped under his breath. "The meeting started 10 minutes ago."

"If you only knew the day I've had," Dr. Langston said, shaking his head, as he brushed by Darnell on his way into the conference room.

The commotion in the conference room made it easy for Dr. Langston to slip in undetected. Everyone was so preoccupied with shouting over one another to notice another person joining the meeting. Dr. Langston quickly took a seat in the back of the room, placed his briefcase in his lap, and observed all of the chaos as he waited patiently for a moment to jump in.

"How about mandatory anger management classes?" a high ranking lieutenant offered.

Even from his seat across the room, Dr. Langston could see the frown lines on Captain Jenkins' forehead—

it was apparent that Captain Jenkins would rather be anywhere else than in that meeting having that discussion.

"We did that last time. We need something better than that, or we're going to have an all-out war on our hands." Teigan countered. "Commissioner Jameson, please tell me you have an idea." Teigan beckoned.

"Alright, I've got it," Jameson said, pushing his chair back away from the table to stand up." Anger management classes, leave without pay, and have them sit down with one of our psychologists."

Dr. Langston shook his head in disagreement as he noted several others around the table had nodded in approval of the commissioner's suggestion.

"Yeah, give em' a little mark on their records, the departments happy, and the riots stop. It's a win-win." Captain Jenkins said agreeably.

"The victim doesn't win," Dr. Langston finally interjected. Twenty heads turned to face him where he sat at the back of the room. Silence fell as he continued, now standing up himself. "In fact, nobody wins if there's no justice." He asserted.

"Who the hell are you?" Jameson asked, making his way across the room to confront Dr. Langston.

"This is a classified meeting. Who let you in here?" Teigan shouted in anger.

"My name is Dr. Andre Langston, and I have a proposal for you that could very well solve all of these problems," he uttered.

"Look, um-uhh, Mr. Langston, was it?" Jameson

asked, condescension coloring his voice.

"*Doctor* Langston," Dr. Langston said as he corrected Jameson and held out his hand for a handshake. Jameson glanced down at Dr. Langston's hand and turned his back on Dr. Langston as he walked in the direction of the door.

"You're not needed here," Jameson said as he walked away.

"Oh, but I believe I can be of great service to your department," Dr. Langston said as he placed his briefcase on the table and opened it. No one in the room had taken their eyes off Dr. Langston.

"Imagine if officers convicted of using excessive force against African-Americans were required to virtually walk in the shoes of an African-American citizen of our city. How would their policing practices differ if they had to experience life as a minority in America?" Dr. Langston eagerly expressed.

"I believe if officers had the opportunity to experience what it's genuinely like to be treated the way they treat citizens of color they would develop greater empathy and gain a level of understanding that would prevent more unnecessary beatings and killings of Black civilians, here's what it would cost which is a small price to pay to achieve peace and civility?" Dr. Langston continued to explain.

Dr. Langston made eye contact with several of the shocked-looking officers seated at the table as he produced several pages of research and reports from his briefcase. He then tossed his proposal and research onto the table with a gesture like he just won a hand of Poker.

"Yeah, right," Captain Jenkins said with an uncomfortable laugh.

"What kind of hoodoo voodoo bullshit is this?"

"It's a highly researched and fully developed alternate reality program that could change the way policing is done across America," Dr. Langston countered confidently.

"Yeah, okay, Houdini. Your little program isn't needed here. Please see your way out," Captain Jenkins huffed a laugh as he walked to the door and opened it with a broad motion directing Dr. Langston to exit.

"All we need is-" Dr. Langston began.

"See your way out!" Captain Jenkins interjected.

"Before I have one of my officers remove you."

Dr. Langston grimaced as he gathered his papers from the table and placed them back in his briefcase. All eyes followed him as he walked to the door and out of the room. Dr. Langston left the conference room, trying his best to take his pride and dignity with him.

As soon as Dr. Langston left the meeting, Teigan shook his head in disbelief.

"Who the hell let that nut in here?"

"I don't know, but if I find out, there's gonna be hell to pay," Jameson warned, obviously irritated.

"Teigan, have someone prepare the paperwork for those anger management classes. That's the route we're going to take." Jameson concluded.

"We don't need no goddamn simulation bull-crap. No white man wants to be Black for a day," Jameson scoffed.

Jameson's mocking tone was met with approval by the laughter that erupted around the room.

CHAPTER 2

BLOOD IN THE STREETS

MAY 2020 MINNEAPOLIS, MN

Five years passed since Freddie Gray's death. Despite there being no justice served, the riots had stopped; the media shifted focus to other topics, and, for the most part, most police departments throughout the country had been able to put the event behind them.

That is until the slow and painful death of George Floyd, played on national television, on repeat for all of America to see. George Floyd's death caused a resounding outcry for justice, and once again, protestors took to the streets. This time was much different than the riots after Freddie Gray's death.

After George Floyd's death, the protests that took place spread to more than just a handful of cities in America. The protests spread like falling dominoes to almost every major city in America. The protests were not just an outcry from Black America; people from all walks of life joined these protests. Amongst the Black faces, there was a sea of white faces and other minority groups present. There was also a significant representation of young people who poured into the streets in solidarity with the Black Lives Matter movement.

The most significant factor was primarily due to the dynamics of what was happening in the country at the time. The Covid-19 pandemic had brought the entire country to almost a halt. Most Americans were confined at home with more time than usual to watch television.

Millions watched in horror and disgust as Officer Derek Chauvin knelt on the neck of George Floyd and held viewers transfixed by the horrifying scene for a little over 9 minutes. The video of George Floyd's death depicted him dying slowly by asphyxiation at the hands of a man sworn to protect and serve the public.

George Floyd's death created an immediate uproar of protests, mainly because Officer Chauvin received no reprimand or punishment initially for what seemed to many as a crime and, at the very least, an inhumane act.

Once again, riots and protests spilled into the streets. The frustration, pain, and desire for racial justice fueled the protests, making them even more volatile than before. The resentment caused by centuries of racial oppression and the unjust murders of Black people came boiling to a head.

The protests began peacefully. Many protesters, who were perfect strangers, quickly found themselves bonding to one another like family.

Going out into the streets, day after day, marching, praying, keeping vigil. Chanting at the top of their voices, "Black Lives Matter!"

JUNE 2020 CHARLOTTESVILLE, VA

Many protestors poured into the streets in droves, disgusted by the blatant racism seemingly prevalent in law enforcement. This time, the people, not just Black people, were determined not to be silenced.

However, the peaceful aspect of the protests was interrupted by a surge of police officers' who established an aggressive presence. Their full-on body armor, shields, weapons, and tear gas did not display peace officers nor a posture of cooperation. They no longer resembled officers of the law but a militia at war with its own people.

As police officers swarmed the areas where protestors gathered and attacked the crowds of protestors, chaos ensued. The once peaceful protests turned into violent riots very quickly. Many of the protestors were trampled in an attempt to escape the horde of officers determined to clear the streets.

Officer George McDuffie prepared his mind for battle mode as he got suited in his black body armor. As he exited the transport vehicle with his fellow officers, all he saw was turmoil. He had chaos erupt before in these situations and despised it. He dedicated his life to preserving law and order, and he felt like the protestors were determined to defy that. His rage was blinding, coloring his vision with red. He grabbed the collar of the nearest protestor who had been pushing at him.

The man tried to pull away, and in a fit of rage, George's rage repeatedly whacked him with his nightstick until he fell to the ground. "Stay down!" he screamed at the protester, continuing to strike him.

George's rage narrowed his focus. He was oblivious to his fellow officers' actions as well. The officers fired rubber bullets as hard as steel into the massive mob of people. The bullets struck several protesters, with the velocity and force of a real bullet knocking many of the protestors over instantly, leaving them motionless on the ground, suffering from concussions, broken teeth, and fractured eye sockets.

Like many police battalions across the country, George McDuffie and his team met the largely peaceful "Black Lives Matter" protests with excessive force. It's as if police departments across the country coordinated their efforts and shared the same play book. The plan was simple, meet all protests, peaceful or not, with force. The message was seemingly coordinated by the messaging heard daily on television, and the message was to use power, not to show weakness or even empathy for a segment of the country that was hurting.

For weeks there was story after story on television documenting just how rampant the use of excessive force had become in law enforcement. These were no longer isolated events that could be ignored as an individual police officer's error in judgment. When it came to the "Black Lives Matter" protests, many law enforcement departments decided to view and treat them like rioters.

JULY 2020 CHARLOTTESVILLE, VA

Dr. Langston, at home in his office, was intently focused on his computer. He found a glitch in his code and had been frantically typing for the last hour to fix it. Out of the corner of his eye, he saw the television flashing with breaking news. Momentarily, his attention shifted away from his computer, and he glanced at the broadcast.

"Following the nationwide protests, pressure from citizens calling for police reform has caused a widespread crackdown on police brutality. As a result, officers involved in the most blatantly vicious acts of violence against their citizens will immediately be convicted of indecent conduct toward a citizen. This is a conviction that carries a minimum sentence of ten years. If the act is motivated by racial discrimination, they will receive a mandatory minimum of twenty years in jail with no opportunity for parole," the news reporter disclosed.

Dr. Langston raised his eyebrows, surprised that the courts had started to take action against officers, who abused their power. He never thought he would see the day that justice would be served for so many Black victims of brutality at the hands of officers charged with protecting and serving them.

He leaned back in his office chair and pondered to himself about whether this could be the perfect opportunity he'd been waiting for to pitch his program again.

"Maybe Captain Teigan and the other officers would take the Decennial Program more seriously now that these offenses are being addressed in the court of law," Dr. Langston thought to himself.

"Yeah, it's time," he whispered out loud as he gazed at the television.

CHAPTER 3

OFFICER GEORGE MCDUFFIE

AUGUST 2020 CHARLOTTESVILLE, VA COURTROOM

The scattered whispers of the jury bounced off the walls in the windowless, dim courtroom and died suddenly as the fierce and well-dressed prosecutor stood.

"The people vs. Officer George McDuffie on the count of aggravated assault case: 20-0755," the bailiff said to the Judge"

"Your honor, the people call Officer George Mcduffie to the stand." said the prosecutor.

George instinctively loosened his tie just a bit before he stood up from his seat and took the longest walk of his life toward the witness stand. He felt the sting of everyone's eyes on him like a thousand needles in the back of his head. His footsteps seemed to echo at a deafening volume, reverberating in a strained staccato throughout the courtroom.

Despite the cool air being pushed around the room by an antique-looking ceiling fan perched above his head, a bead of sweat trickled down George's forehead. George swore to tell the truth, the whole truth, and nothing but the truth. It shouldn't be a problem, he thought. He was quite sure of his innocence. His piercing blue eyes darted around the courtroom, trying to look at anything except the victim and his family. Instead, George found himself looking squarely into the worried eyes of his wife, Pam.

She looked so frail these days, so frightened, like a kid who had just seen a monster beneath their bed. He wondered if she thought of him as the monster.

He thought to himself how he'd turned her quiet, soccer mom life into a real shit show for the last few months. She couldn't go anywhere without someone making subtle, accusatory remarks that were aimed at her but veiled in conversations so general that if she addressed these slights, she could be made to feel as if she was giving credence to their scorn. He felt sorry for her as he imagined what these past few months had been like for her. He tried his best to bury the lump of emotion swelling in his throat for her. Their eyes remained locked, and he was trying to read the emotion in them, but all he saw was pain and fear.

George didn't want to think about the possible outcome of his trial. He didn't want to notice the fragility of his wife and his marriage, and he definitely didn't want to think about what would happen if he couldn't go home with her at the end of the day. George swallowed audibly, bringing his attention back into the room, and turned his eyes away from his wife's haunting stare.

The statuesque prosecutor, who was meticulously dressed, stood up and approached the jury. She had a reputation for taking on tough cases and for being thorough and convincing to jurors. George, knowing this, swiped at the sweat beading on his forehead and reminded himself that he didn't have anything to hide.

The prosecutor began to lay out her case, making eye contact with each juror.

"Officer George McDuffie responded to a robbery call on Friday, June 5th at approximately 8:13 pm. He approached a group of young Black teens, and they all ran, all except for Avery Brooks, who was listening to music and couldn't hear the officer. When Avery reached into his jacket pocket to turn down his music, Officer George McDuffie fired three shots into his midsection, one of which struck his spine and permanently paralyzed the young man," she stated dramatically.

George lost his breath as the prosecutor spoke. Although he was there on the scene, the prosecutor made the incident sound so much worse than he remembered it playing out that night.

"Now, Officer McDuffie, you grew up in a pretty rural area, correct?" The prosecutor questioned as she turned and faced George directly, her dark eyes seeming to pin him to the wall.

"Yes, Ma'am," George replied, nodding his head nonchalantly in his usual baritone voice, tinged with a southern drawl.

"Would you describe your hometown as racially diverse?" The prosecutor asked him with a bit of a smirk on her face.

"Umm, No, Ma'am, I don't think so," George responded.

Ok. How many African-Americans did you grow up around? She continued.

"Well, umm, I never thought about it." George answered.

"Think about it now," she added.

"None that I can recall," George replied with a bit of agitation in his voice.

"Did you have any African-American friends? How about buddies? How about teammates?" She rapidly asked.

George hesitantly responded, "I am sure I would've had one if they were around...perhaps." George fired back as he shifted uncomfortably, and wondered where she was going with her interrogation.

The prosecutor doubled down on her line of questioning, pushing George to explain his childhood and upbringing. George's stomach flipped uneasily as he shared his lack of experience with Black people. With each question, his answers became less sensible.

After leaving George tongue-tied and sweating, the prosecutor expertly shifted her focus from his childhood to his career. She pressed him about his involvement in a case when he served in the narcotics division. "George, tell the court why you chose to go into the narcotics division in the first place."

Having thoroughly researched everything about Officer George McDuffie, she asked the question and already knew how he would answer.

"I went into the field because I would see all these thugs on the streets dealing drugs whenever I drove through the city. They're too lazy to get up off of their ass and get a real job. Any idiot can sell drugs. It takes a real man to pay the bills the right way. All those criminals do is rely on tax-paying people like me for their food stamps and health insurance. Living for free on my people's dime, I mean, hard-working people's dime." he ranted angrily.

"Who are 'your people'?" the prosecutor asked as she raised her eyebrows, knowing she had him exactly where she wanted him.

"You know..." George began, his voice trailed off in an attempt to beat around the bush. "People like me... white people."

Disapproving murmurs hum through the court as jury members shook their heads and took note of George's unintentional, inflammatory language. George glanced over to where his lawyer was seated. He noticed that his lawyer had buried his head in his hands in disbelief as to what he heard. George rubbed the back of his neck, thinking quickly.

"W-Well in the city, there's just more Black people committing crimes," George articulated, attempting to explain himself. "They'd rather sell drugs than get a real job like the rest of us. Then they get on welfare and use our tax money to pay for all their stuff." George ranted frantically. George hearing those words out loud instead of thinking it, sounded ridiculous even to himself.

The audience sat in silence and disbelief as George continued to unmask his biases. The prosecutor stood back, wearing a slightly satisfied, sly smile on her face as George did all of her work for her. George, finally aware that he had put his foot in his mouth, stopped talking.

The prosecutor became more sure of herself by the minute and continued to layout incidents showcasing how George's racial bias played out while he was in uniform. She revealed his lengthy record of complaints and write-ups for excessive force.

"Officer George McDuffie has racked up quite the record of write-ups during his time on the force. Especially in this past year—he had an astonishing 11 incident reports citing excessive force in one year. That has to be a record," the prosecutor expressed convincingly to the jury.

"The latest incident was just a few months ago during the Black Lives Matter protests. There is an incident report here in your file claiming that you battered a civilian during those protests."

"I object. That statement is speculative," George's lawyer yelled.

"Withdrawn," the prosecutor quickly retorted, accomplishing her objective of showing recent behavior of excessive force to the jury.

"Those weren't my fault!" George snarled. As he refused to take the blame for any of it. "I acted the way anyone else would if they were in my shoes." George went on to say.

"But you're not 'anyone else.' You are supposedly a highly trained officer, and yet you didn't utilize any deescalation tactics in any of these incidents." The prosecutor countered swiftly.

"That's bull." George snapped, his frustration winning out against reason.

"Order!" yelled the judge sternly as he banged his gavel, as he became visibly agitated. George gritted his teeth as he felt that even the judge seemed pitted against him.

A hush fell over the courtroom as George shifted in his seat and folded his arms in annoyance. He couldn't see why everyone was so upset with him. *"My actions were justified!"* He blurted out.

The prosecutor let her argument sink in for a moment before moving on. She paced, surefooted, in front of the witness stand. George gritted his teeth, trying to mask his frustration.

The prosecutor once again shifted her line of questioning.

"Would you consider yourself a pretty big guy, Officer McDuffie," she asked, looking directly at George. "What are you, 6'3, about 250lb?"

"Yes. What does that have to do with anything?" George grumbled, still irked from the earlier line of questioning.

"How does a tall, muscular fella like yourself get intimidated by a high schooler?" The prosecutor asked, calmly.

George clenched his jaw in irritation as he growled, "He looked like a thug."

George purposely avoided the gaze of Avery's parents, who shook their heads in disgust.

"Oh, I see! A high school quarterback wearing his team's jersey resembled a thug to you." The prosecutor noted, voice dripping with sarcasm.

George ran his hand over his blond buzzcut hair style as he sighed. He couldn't understand why he seemed to keep saying the wrong thing--or how the prosecutor kept twisting it to make him seem guilty. He felt that he had to tell his side of the story to make the jury understand what happened.

"Look, here's what happened that night." He began, deciding to remain calm and get out of the grave he'd dug himself.

"I was on patrol, as usual, when I got a call about a robbery in the area, so I went to check it out, and that's when I saw a group of kids walking. They looked like they were up to no good," George insisted.

"For the record, this group of kids...what race were they?" The prosecutor inquired with a knowing tone.

"They were Blacks," answered George, hesitant. "Anyway," he rolled his eyes inadvertently.

"I went to question them, but they ran because they knew they were up to no good."

"Except Avery. He didn't run, did he?" The prosecutor's voice became soft, cajoling.

"No," George admitted, "but I yelled at him to get on the ground, and he didn't. He reached for a weapon, and I defended myself. I did what anyone would do!"

"You shot him three times in the stomach," the prosecutor stated coldly.

"Is that what anyone would do?"

George's attorney objected, and George breathed in relief as the prosecutor backed away from her line of questioning. Instead, she chose to go down another road: "So, you didn't notice that Avery Brooks had headphones on?" The prosecutor asked rhetorically.

"Avery reached into his pocket to turn down his music," the prosecutor clarified. "And that's when you shot him. Not once, but three times, hitting his spine and instantly paralyzing him from the waist down."

George's gaze landed on Avery at last, and he regretted it immediately. A tear ran down Avery Brooks' cheek, and his eyes looked haunted as he remembered the night he almost lost his life. Avery's parents had tears of their own in their eyes as they rubbed his back and shoulders.

George averted his gaze instantly, resolving not to look in their direction again. He kept his eyes trained straight ahead so he didn't have to see their pain. The prosecutor turned her back to George and addressed the entire courtroom.

She allowed a melancholy smile to linger in her eyes and tug at the corners of her mouth when she saw Avery sitting there in a wheelchair. His powerful figure looked somehow diminished, slumped slightly to the left in his wheelchair. His once intimidating, athletic frame now sat inanimate, almost lifeless, in a chair that he would possibly be bound to forever. Avery seemed to shift his eyes periodically, looking down at his legs.

Avery's face was stoic, noticeably agitated, and somewhat bewildered to find himself in a courtroom. Taking slow, deliberate steps that matched her speech's pace, the prosecutor approached the area where Avery Brooks and his parents were seated. This case was a reminder to her of why she became a prosecutor in the first place.

She knew she had one shot at making the jury see her client as a human being, and she refused to miss it. The prosecutor spoke, using her words to paint a picture of Avery Brooks, a star quarterback, beloved son, and friend. The jury needed to understand what Officer George McDuffie took away on that fateful night, when he put three bullets in Avery Brooks.

She allowed her hand to rest briefly on Avery's shoulder. Startled by the hand on his shoulder, Avery looked up, his eyes connected with the prosecutor's, and they shared a momentary tender glance. Remembering that she had to appear somewhat impartial, she stood tall again, bringing herself back on task.

"This is Avery Brooks," the prosecutor stated. "He is a loving son, a straight-A student, and valedictorian at his high school. He received a full-ride scholarship to Virginia

Tech for academics, not football, although he lettered in that sport."

"His school principal can't say enough great things about him. She said he's always been a gem, one of her best students, and that he doesn't have so much as one tardy mark on his entire high school record. He's liked by everyone at school--not easy to do because, well, you know how high schoolers can be. But not Avery. He never smoked. He never drank or did drugs. He always did his homework. He stayed out of trouble. He never even had to be punished, his father told me."

"What teenage boy do you know for whom that is true?" The Prosecutor asked as she took a brief pause, letting the jury digest Avery's story.

"He went to parties like any All-American, popular high schooler would, but he made sure he was the designated driver for anyone who needed a ride."

She took a few steps toward the witness stand, then continued, "Outside of school, he's the same way, it seems. This is a young man who volunteers at a homeless shelter every month. Avery helps his parents run their floral business on weekends. He takes his grandmother anywhere she wants to go, and he goes fishing with his grandfather and a group of older gentlemen on the fourth Saturday of every month. He loves to cook for his friends, and he loves to play and watch football."

She began to approach the stand and stopped directly in front of George. "Avery Brooks had a promising future ahead of him, but all of that was stolen from him, in an instant, by Officer George McDuffie," she declared.

"Officer McDuffie changed Avery Brooks' life forever, the moment he decided that Avery, the honor-roll athlete, was nothing more than a thug and shot him down like a dog in the street."

The prosecutor looked intently at George. His exterior didn't show a shred of remorse, and his voice unrepentantly replied. "How was I to know who he was? I made a quick decision at that moment, and at that moment, he looked like the kind of kid who would have a weapon."

An audible murmur erupted across the courtroom, and the jury's faces were masked with shock and rage.

It was evident to the prosecutor that everyone present was aware of the enormity of George's act. Everyone, that is, except for George himself. His eyes darted nervously around the room as he began to grasp the gravity of the moment.

Suddenly George's stomach jumped into his throat. He looked to his council in desperation, but once again, his attorney had his head in his hands. How was he supposed to convince a jury when his own lawyer wasn't on his side? George thought to himself. Frantically, he glanced around the room and unintentionally made eye contact with Avery Brooks. Avery's eyes reflected his pain and distress, and his cheeks were wet with silent tears.

George slowly lowered his head, determined to avoid showing emotion.

The moment seemed to go on forever, each second of near-silence incriminating George further. The courtroom became filled with the painful sound of Avery's mother's sobs. The silence mixed with her sobbing filled every crevice of the room and made George's throat constrict. His heart heaved painfully in his chest.

The more Avery's dad tried to console his wife. Her cries grew louder. Avery's mom, thick with emotion, blurted out, "That monster should've never had a badge! Look what you did! You took away our dreams. Our hopes! How could you be so cruel? You paralyzed our baby!"

The judge, moved by the moment, called for a fifteen-minute recess so that everyone could compose themselves.

George deliberated whether he should say something else to defend himself. Still, it was impossible to concentrate--the sound of Avery's mother sobbing pierced through his every thought. When they returned from recess, George wanted to speak up, but instead he bit his tongue. He knew that there was nothing he could say that would get him out of the situation, he found himself in.

He stared at the prosecutor, awaiting her next attack.

She simply said, "The prosecution rests; we have no further questions, Your Honor."

George shuffled off the stand and returned to his seat. He glared at his council and sighed impatiently.

For George, the moments before the jury returned their verdict felt like they dragged on for a lifetime. The jury finally returned, and a single juror stood to deliver the final verdict.

George's hands were now sweating; his mouth dry, and he felt like his heart was beating out of his chest.

The juror finally began, "We the jury find the defendant officer George McDuffie guilty of assault and reckless endangerment."

George's heart fell into his stomach. Everything moved in slow motion, and his hearing became muffled as if he was underwater. The spectators clapped as the Brooks family embraced each other and rejoiced that justice was served. George, in utter disbelief, couldn't help but feel like he had just watched a scene from someone else's life, not his own.

Once the initial shock wore off, George stormed out of the courtroom in awe of how unfair the verdict seemed to him. He was a police officer, and now they're sending him to prison? he thought to himself as he desperately felt like he needed to get some air. He crashed through the doors of the courtroom and into the lobby, breathing heavily.

His path was interrupted when he collided with a well-dressed, gorgeous woman smoking a cigarette.

"Sorry," he mumbled under his breath as he continued to rush past her, pushing through the double doors of the courthouse.

CHAPTER 4

OFFICER EMILY CAMPBELL

AUGUST 2020 CHARLOTTESVILLE, VA COURTROOM

Officer Emily Campbell ran her fingers through her wavy blonde hair as she tapped the ash out of her cigarette. Then she brought the cigarette to her well-painted red lips and inhaled deeply. She closed her eyes and allowed the nicotine to soothe the edges of her nerves.

Emily was well dressed today in a white pantsuit. A thick, red belt cinched her trim waist with matching shoes and accessories. Her mother always said that if she didn't feel great, she should at least look great. She looked extra good today; because she felt extra horrible.

She paced outside the courtroom, trying to think about anything other than what led her to be there. She focused on smoking her cigarette and making sure her hair looked perfect.

Her pensive moment was rudely interrupted by Officer George McDuffie pushing past her in a rush to leave the very courtroom that Emily was waiting to go in. She instinctively became defensive and then noticed that George McDuffie was clearly under duress. Emily quickly observed that his breathing was labored, and sweat was visible on his forehead and upper lip. Emily decided to brush it off, and she quickly gathered her thoughts. She realized she had enough problems of her own to deal with.

She took another long drag from her cigarette when she heard someone call her by her full name.

Emily then saw a woman running towards her, shouting, "Emily Renee Campbell, you absolutely cannot smoke in this building!"

Not realizing where she was, Emily took the scolding good-naturedly and snuffed the cigarette out quickly on the bench. She smirked slightly once she realized who it was and took a seat outside of the courtroom. Lindsay was always so fussy, but Emily was friendly with her because she was a fellow female detective on the Special Victims Unit.

Lindsay plopped herself down on the bench beside Emily. She pulled out a stick of gum from her purse and shoved it into Emily's hand.

"Here, take this. You smell like a freakin' ashtray." Lindsay jokingly said as she hooked her arm through Emily's and smiled warmly while looking into her eyes.

Emily smiled back, holding her gaze before she averted her eyes, staring into space. Emily tapped her heel on the wooden floor as she started biting her lip, which was her subconscious reaction to being in a nerve-racking situation.

"Hey. You okay?" Lindsay said more gently. Emily smiled at Lindsay gratefully.

"I just don't know how I got here," Emily sighed slowly, as she remembered the moment her life took such a horrible and sudden turn.

"Aggravated assault!" Emily screamed, her voice almost a shriek. "I'm being charged with aggravated assault?" She repeated, still in total disbelief.

Emily never thought that she would end up defending herself from such serious charges. She was always the one helping convict other people.

"How is this happening to me? I mean, I'm an SVU detective! I wasn't even supposed to be at those damn riots," she explained to Lindsay.

"The patrol unit was completely overwhelmed, and I went to *help*. They were calling officers from every department! All I did was help control the delinquents who were trying to take over the streets," Emily explained.

Emily popped her gum nervously as she glanced up at the clock. It was almost time for her hearing, and she wanted to be done with it.

Emily and Lindsay sat shoulder to shoulder in silence as they waited for Emily's name to be called. She forced her anxiety down but could not help the rapid beating of her heart. Her eyes glossed over as her mind wandered to that day. Emily found herself in a daze involuntarily as she revisited the events that led up to her trial. Losing time was something she struggled with every day since the incident occurred.

Emily recalled being dressed in protective gear from head to toe when she reported to the center of the city in Charlottesville —the riots' epicenter. She recalled staring out the window of the police van, dreading their arrival at the scene. Eventually, they arrived at the site of a burning building. The smell of burning wood permeated the vehicle. She sighed before climbing out of the van. She landed on the pavement and heard the crunch of plate glass beneath her combat boots.

Emily was annoyed that her captain had ordered her to serve on this task force. She secretly believed she had enough seniority and rank as an SVU detective that such tasks were beneath her. She figured she would wind up directing traffic and helping old ladies avoid the fray, not landing in what seemed like a war zone.

She was in the middle of cracking a tough case and was very close to closing in on a suspect. However, she knew when the captain appoints you to a team, you just show up, whether you like it or not. So, Emily found herself helping with the barricade in the inner-city. To make matters worse, she was already in a foul mood because of what had happened to her son, James, earlier that day at school.

Emily recalled being momentarily distracted by her thoughts. It was only a few moments, but while she looked the other way, her team had seemingly disappeared. Emily cursed internally, alone amid protesters was the last place she wanted to be. A small group of rioters noticed that she was the only cop around and began to antagonize her. They swooped down on her, forming a menacing circle that grew tighter and tighter around her, not letting her advance beyond their taunting words.

She expertly pulled her nightstick from its sheath with one hand and grabbed the collar of one of the assailants with the other, stopping him cold in his tracks. She held onto him tightly with one hand and viciously swung her stick with the other, striking him repeatedly across the back, head, and anywhere else she could land the baton. She continued to swing her weapon with all her might as blow after blow landed on his quaking flesh. And even after the circle opened and gave her a way out, Emily did not take it. She was relentless, letting each thump release more of her pent-up aggression. When she finally came to her senses, she looked down at the bruised and bloody protester and felt a brief sense of empowerment overtake her.

Emily almost felt as if she had doled out justice for what happened to her son.

James came home from school earlier that afternoon sporting a black eye and quite a few bruises. Emily was distraught and enraged when she learned that a group of Black kids had jumped her son at school because he called a boy named Terell a "dirty, Black monkey."

Somewhat shamefully, Emily acknowledged to herself why her son said it. She knew he'd heard her refer to Black people as monkeys, and although she also acknowledged that it was offensive, she didn't think her son should have gotten beaten up for it.

Emily was a single mom, and she knew it was her duty to protect James from the ugly side of life. If it was her fault that he'd been beaten up, she couldn't forgive herself. She loved James more than life itself.

She wrenched her mind out of reminiscing and wondered, for the first time, what might happen to James if she was convicted and had to go to prison. It would destroy her to lose her son. She never wanted him to feel abandoned and alone the way she felt as a child. She tried to give James the childhood she never had: a happy home with two parents who love each other.

They seemed to have a perfect life until her husband, Jake, suddenly walked out on her and James. No notice, no reason he just left for work and never came home. He sent a text message a few weeks later, saying he was filing for divorce and that he would be back for the rest of his things.

Emily had never felt so alone as she did when her husband left. James and Emily had not seen or heard from her ex-husband since the divorce. He just disappeared out of their lives and left them to fend for themselves. Emily was so busy trying to put their lives back together that it made it easy for her to bury her feelings and focus solely on James. She couldn't cry in front of James; she had to be strong for both of them. Emily's team was surprised by how easily she seemed to be able to move past those awful first months of her separation, not realizing she'd had plenty of practice avoiding her feelings.

Emily's father had bounced in and out of her life when she was a child. He was a pleasant enough guy when he did show up, but his presence became rarer as she got older. Sometimes he remembered her birthday; sometimes, he didn't. She could count on one hand how many times he had shown up for Christmas or Thanksgiving.

He missed all her cheerleading competitions, school plays, and dance recitals. He caught the last part of her high school graduation, arriving just in time to see her walk across the stage as her name was called. He did show up at the after-party for that, strutting around like a proud parent, but he skipped the ceremony altogether when she graduated from the police academy, again only showing up for the celebration.

Her father had nothing to do with how Emily turned out, and he certainly could not take credit for any of her successes. She resented him for having the audacity even to show up when she graduated from the academy.

She most certainly had not invited him, and his presence made her feel uncomfortable. She felt that he was there pretending to care about her graduating from the police academy. Emily found herself sitting in a corner, maintaining a sour disposition and nursing tandem shots of tequila for the rest of the evening. She was in an unpleasant mood for a few more weeks beyond that moment, making her obnoxious and hard to work with. Unfortunately, her attitude earned her a reputation of being a bitter woman early in her career, and she could never reverse that perception throughout her career.

She was just a woman in pain. She felt alone and scared of having to face so many unknowns in her life, almost overnight. Her divorce papers had come in just days before graduation. Emily had made plans and done everything right, but her life was still unraveling. And the ones responsible for it were the two men who were supposed to love, protect, and support her.

As Emily sunk deeper into her thoughts, she began to wonder whether she'd made the right career choice. She would never have imagined she would find herself sitting outside of the courtroom waiting for a trial to begin that would determine her fate and potentially change her family forever. If she'd never joined the police force, none of this would be happening, she thought to herself.

Without warning, memories buried long ago came rushing back to her in vivid technicolor.

Emily saw the innocent beautiful face of her friend, Judy, in her mind's eye. Only now, one of her beautiful blue eyes was blackened, and her face and neck were covered with bruises and scratches. Emily swallowed hard, overcome with emotions, as vignettes of that unforgettable day's events involuntarily invaded her mind. She remembered begging Judy to tell her what happened, but Judy refused to talk about it and begged Emily to leave it alone. Emily, never one to back down, knew something was up, and she vowed that she wouldn't rest until she found out what it was.

Later that day, the pair sat outside on the back stairwell, enjoying the last of the afternoon sun's warmth. The wing of Wilson Barringford High School that housed the cafeteria was always deserted in the late afternoon. There was never any traffic on the back staircase after school since it only led to the closed doors that usually open out into the expansive dining hall. So, that's where the girls always met up at the end of the day. They met there to cut class and gossip about their young lives.

The day that changed Emily's life would have been like any other day the girls spent together, except for the bruises on Judy's body. Emily had balked when she saw them, immediately pressing Judy to tell her what happened.

As they sat on the staircase, Emily continued her interrogation; Mr. Stansfield, Judy's step-father approached them. Mr. Stansfield was tall and slender. He was rather nondescript beyond that, except that he had a bald patch in the middle of his head. He was just tall enough to say he was not short. His face was rather plain, and he always wore khaki pants, brown shoes, and either blue denim or white collared shirt. It was like a uniform, even though he wasn't required to follow a dress code.

Emily watched the blood drain from Judy's face the closer he got. They had been lounging, leaning up against the railings along the side of the staircase, but as he approached, Judy sat up ramrod straight. Her eyes widened exponentially. Emily looked over to where her friend's eyes were suddenly transfixed. He was descending the steps, and with every step he took, Judy's expression went from placid to panicked.

The girls were sitting in a staggered fashion, with Emily sitting just above Judy. Mr. Stansfield's facial expression was twisted into a strange, sinister smile as he bent down and caressed Judy's cheek softly.

"There you are," Mr. Stansfield said, his voice soft and breathy. "I was looking for you. You left in such a huff; I was just coming to make sure you're alright. I knew I would find you here, as usual, but I see you're busy. Don't worry, I'll see you later."

Emily watched Judy become visibly shaken, her blue eyes welling up with tears. It suddenly occurred to Emily that Mr. Stansfield must have been the one who hurt Judy.

Emily felt an emotion she had never felt before. Her rage swelled up in her, threatening to choke the air from her lungs. She vaulted to her feet. "Get away from her! Did you do this to her? I'm gonna tell. You're not going to get away with this!"

Emily would never forget the words she heard next. Mr. Stansfield said, "What happens in my house is none of your fucking business, you need to stay in a childs place, and if you don't know where that place is, well you know, I'm a helluva teacher." Mr. Stansfield said as he tugged at his belt buckle and casually walked away, with a slight grin on his face.

That was the moment in which Emily made a vow to protect kids from predators like him. She wanted to put monsters like him behind bars. That's why she joined the force, which was why it was so hard for her to believe that someone had charged her with aggravated assault.

"It wasn't supposed to turn out this way," Emily muttered under her breath.

"This hearing is ridiculous--only criminals are supposed to go to prison, and I'm no criminal," she continued.

Her trip down memory lane was interrupted as she heard her full name being called for the second time that day. It was time for her hearing. Emily stood, straightened her blazer, squared her shoulders, and sighed as she walked into the courtroom.

Almost immediately as she entered the courtroom, she was called to the stand. Her heels on the wooden floor echoed through the room as she approached. She raised her manicured hand to swear the oath. The pressure began to set in as she gazed across the courtroom. All eyes were on her. Emily knew she was a beautiful woman, so she wasn't unaccustomed to stares. But these looks were different; they were not looking at her admirably. These people, she felt, were judging, critiquing, and analyzing her.

Emily became aware of how nervous she was when the prosecutor approached and questioned her on the witness stand.

The blood rushed to her cheeks, and her heart was already racing. A million thoughts flashed through Emily's mind while she tried to focus on the prosecutor's questions. She tried to focus on the questions, but it was useless--her mind kept drifting back to James. She kept playing out all possible scenarios of this trial, imagining what would happen to him if she were convicted. She was afraid he would feel like she abandoned him too.

"Ms. Campbell, are you with us?" the prosecutor questioned. Emily shifted her attention back to the present moment.

"Yes, I am." She paused for a moment. "I'm sorry, what was the question?" Emily asked.

"I asked, what caused you to attack the protester in such an aggressive manner?" The prosecutor repeated, slightly annoyed by Emily's lack of focus.

"They were ganging up on me. They were menacingly surrounding me, taunting me. They had me pinned in, and I was afraid it was going to get dangerous. I looked around, and I realized that I was the only officer around. There was no backup in sight, so I had to defend myself."

Emily's lack of remorse in that moment was apparent to everyone, even to herself, and she could tell she hadn't begun on the best note. She was a trained observer and judging by the way the Judge leaned back in his chair and the jury member's expressions, she sensed she might be in trouble. Emily didn't understand any of this. *She was the victim.* She didn't seem to understand why everyone thought the person she defended herself from was the victim?

The prosecutor walked up to Emily and slammed a stack of photos onto the stand in front of her. Emily didn't flinch at the sound, just raised her eyebrows cooly before glancing down at them. The images were startling, and her stomach dropped.

Detailed pictures showed the discolored Black eye; several other pictures showed blood pouring from the broken nose and mouth of the victim of her beating. More photos showed giant purple and blue bruises over the man's abdomen.

Emily visibly shrugged as she glanced down at the horrid images, although she shuddered internally.

"Do you see what you did to this man?" the prosecutor began. "He sustained a broken nose and a fractured rib."

Emily shook her head, saying nothing.

"Do you think this man deserved to be beaten like this?" The prosecutor thundered accusatory and harsh.

Emily balked, "I don't know what to tell you. The rioters ganged up on me, and I defended myself. This is what we're trained to do as police."

The Judge, shocked by Emily's lack of remorse, sits up straight in his chair. Members of the jury shook their heads in disapproval as Emily threw her head back and sighed, knowing that her testimony didn't bode well.

Shortly after Emily's display of righteous indignation, both attorneys made their closing remarks to the jury. The judge then dismissed the jury to deliberate and decide

Emily's fate. She knew that it would be the fate of her career, and her son, and she felt the chances of continuing her life as it was the night before the riots, were bleak.

After a brief recess, the jury returned and read Emily her verdict. "We, the jury, find Emily Campbell guilty of aggravated assault," a juror delivered.

Emily wasn't surprised. She knew that she would be convicted as soon as the cross-examination had taken place. She could tell that neither the Judge nor the jury was on her side. Still, her skin went cool and clammy.

Emily felt herself going into shock. She recognized the symptoms: confusion, lightheadedness, irregular pulse.

She fought back tears as she buried her head in her hands, devastated by the verdict.

The only thing she could think about was James. She couldn't live without her son. Emily slowly made her way out of the courtroom as she became overwhelmed with emotions. Black mascara began to run down her face as she lost control and tears ran down her face. She had never felt so powerless and alone.

If she ever needed whatever calming effects cigarettes had provided her through the challenging and unforgivable moments in her life, she needed them now. Emily planted herself outside on the courthouse steps as the wind blew long, blonde strands of hair into her face.

Frustrated, she threw it back into a messy ponytail and lit a cigarette. Her hands shook as she took a long drag and blew smoke out slowly, watching the breeze carry it away. She stared out into space, contemplating what is going to happen to James. Even the reassuring buzz from nicotine wasn't enough to soothe her anxiety.

All Emily ever wanted to do was protect her son. She thought about how she wouldn't be able to cheer him on at his basketball games or see him walk across the stage at his graduation because she would be in prison. It was just the two of them against the world, but now she felt the world was delivering its blow and winning.

The thought of him being alone in the world devastated her, and she broke into tears on the courtroom stairs, not caring who saw her.

CHAPTER 5

OFFICER ROBERT WHITMORE

AUGUST 2020 CHARLOTTESVILLE, VA COURTHOUSE

A cool breeze carried a cloud of smoke across the courthouse stairs. A young man with short brown hair was on his way into the building when he noticed the source of the smoke was an attractive blonde woman who looked like she might be distraught.

He smirked to himself as he altered his path in an effort to get her attention.

"Could I bum a cigarette, darlin'?" he asked with a strong southern twang.

Emily rolled her eyes. "Leave me alone," she muttered.

Robert dismissed her response. He tugged on his belt and leaned down close to her and softly said, "Now, what could a beautiful woman like yourself be out here cryin' about?"

"Was I unclear? I don't want to talk about it," she sobbed.

Robert jumped back and attempted to gather his composure. "Well, I'm late for a date anyways," he said before continuing up the courthouse stairs and through the large double doors.

"Robert, where have you been?" Robert's attorney asked frantically, rushing towards the entrance. Robert rolled his eyes.

"You're late. We haven't even gone over the details of your case." the attorney exclaimed.

"Calm down, Caleb," Robert began, unbothered by the distressed man in front of him. "I'm here now, so I reckon we get started." He smiled, pocketing his hands.

"You need to take this seriously," Caleb begged. "This judge is notorious for convicting police brutality cases."

"Fine, then. Let's get to it," Robert said as he shrugged his shoulders in response. Maybe the judge was notorious, but Robert wasn't worried. Robert felt like the law, surely, would be on his side.

The pair sat down on a bench right outside of the courtroom. Caleb muddled through folders of paperwork as Robert leaned back in his seat and fixed his gaze on the ceiling.

"Alright, so you're being accused of using excessive force on a peaceful protester." Caleb began. "This incident occurred during the Black Lives Matter protest.

To win this case, we need to paint the picture of you being an upstanding guy and that this was just a misunderstanding."

Robert tugged on his tie. He looked very uncomfortable. "Man, I hate this monkey suit," Robert complained.

"Robert, are you even paying attention?" Caleb asked. "You realize if this doesn't pan out in your favor, you're facing prison time."

"Yeah, I'm listening," Robert mumbled. "It's hard to focus on anything right now. This thing is too damn tight," He grunted, violently yanking at his tie.

Robert wasn't used to dressing up. He spent most of his days in a t-shirt and jeans when he wasn't in uniform. He felt a man needed room to breathe in his clothing, and today he was suffocating.

"Look, we don't have time for this," Caleb snapped. "To be honest with you, I haven't had much time to prepare for your case, so we need to focus."

Robert nodded his head as he undid the first button of his shirt to make himself more comfortable.

Caleb glanced at Robert, resigned, noticing his well-dressed appearance unraveling before him.

Robert frowned petulantly at Caleb's sigh.

"Great. Let's go over the smaller details first. Tell me about your childhood?" Caleb inquired.

"Why do you want to know about my childhood," Robert protested.

"In most of my cases, I found that it is easier to defend the man today if I knew who he was yesterday," Caleb responded.

"Well, my dad died when I was young, and it was just Mama and me. So, I had to take control and be the man of the house early. We lived in Chariton County, in Missouri. It's a real small town; everybody knows everybody. Nothing really goes on. It's real quiet." Robert recalled.

"So it must not be very diverse there then, no Blacks, Hispanics?" Caleb questioned, trying to see if he can spin the incident in Robert's favor.

"No, almost all white folk. That's why it's so quiet. I never really saw Black people until I moved here," Robert explained.

Caleb paused for a moment. "What do you mean by, 'that's why it's so quiet?" Calebs eyes closed in frustration, fervently hoping that Robert misspoke.

"Where I grew up, there were almost no Black people. There was also almost no crime. You see what I'm sayin'?" Robert explained. "It wasn't until I moved here and joined the force that I actually had to deal with Black people, and most of 'em are criminals," he finished, clearly unashamed by his blatant prejudices.

Caleb's eyes widened, and he continued to rub the temples of his forehead as he processed what Robert just said. "Listen. You *cannot* say that on the stand." Caleb pleaded. "That's racist. Not even a miracle will stop them convicting you if you make statements like that."

"I am not a damn racist. Some of the cops I work with are Blacks. They're the good ones who aren't out there stealing and selling drugs for a living," Robert snapped back, quick to defend himself.

Caleb put his hand over his mouth in disbelief as he pondered how he could win Robert's case.

"Let's just... move on," he breathed, rubbing the back of his neck in a vain attempt to relieve some tension.

"Why did you join the force?" Caleb asked, hoping for somewhat of a normal answer.

"I've always respected the law. Laws keep people under control," Robert explained as Caleb took notes, pleasantly surprised by a decent answer.

"I wanted to help get all the blac- I mean bad people off the streets." Robert stuttered. "Look, I just want to protect the actual 'law abiding' citizens from these hoodlums on the streets."

"Oh goodness," Caleb scowled in response as he ruffled through more paperwork, desperately seeking something that would help Robert's case. "Okay, so you're rather young. How long have you been on the force?"

"I joined the force when I was 24 and have been a proud officer of the law for nine and a half years." Robert bragged with his head high. Robert had a stern but young face. He was almost 6'ft tall and had a slim, fit build. His straight brown hair was short on the sides and a little long on top. He prided himself on being a simple kind of guy.

Satisfied with his simple answer, Caleb took notes as he reviewed the rest of Robert's case. He clicked his pen nervously as he glanced up at the clock. They didn't have much time left before Robert went before the Judge.

"Alright, Let's just dive in," Caleb rushed. "What happened the night of the incident?"

"I remember being so tired that night. I had worked a double, and on top of that, I got called to those damn Black Lives Matter riots." Robert shook his head, as the memory threatened to drag him away from the present.

"It was crazy. They were setting businesses on fire and smashing car windows. It was absolute chaos."

"What happened with the protestor?" Caleb asked.

"Oh, I was holding the line with the other officers, trying to gain control, when someone cracked me over the head with a glass bottle. If people don't respect the law, then we could never get them under control. So, I had to make an example out of one of 'em and show 'em who was in charge," Robert recounted.

"It had been painful, getting smashed over the head with a glass bottle. No one should get away with assaulting a police officer." Robert continued.

"Well didn't you have on riot gear; Like a helmet or something?" Caleb asked.

"My chin strap was a bit uncomfortable, and I took my helmet off for a blazin second to adjust it, and that's when I felt something like an enormous bee sting at the back of my head, and when I looked down I saw a bottle fall, and smash into pieces. It stung me pretty good." Robert explained.

"That's when the incident happened?" Caleb asked.

"Yessir, I grabbed one of them protesters and put the fear of God into 'em," Robert asserted unapologetically.

"Yeah, I saw that. You went viral, Robert." Caleb pulled out his phone. "Look at how brutally you beat that protestor."

The small phone screen showed an officer dragging a citizen to the ground and striking him repeatedly with his nightstick. Other protesters were heard begging him to stop, but the video showed Robert continued to batter the protestor. He began kicking and stomping on the man, whose cries were so loud they were heard above all the chaos.

"You're gonna beat him to death," another officer yelled in the background of the video as he pulled Robert away from the bruised and bloodied protester.

"Do you really think that was necessary?" Caleb asked, pleading for Robert to show some kind of remorse.

Robert watched himself berating the protestor and scratched his head. He looked up at Caleb and shrugged his shoulders. "I don't know what you want to hear. They're disrespecting officers of the law. I needed to maintain order. That's my duty as a police officer."

"Robert, you need to show some kind of remorse, or you'll never get acquitted," Caleb cautioned.

"Why?" Robert snarled. "Those thugs were trying to make a fool out of me. All I did was put them back in their place. I'll bet they respect the badge now."

"You will definitely make my job of getting you off more difficult, acting like this," Caleb urged, his voice low and insistent.

"You're my attorney! It's your job to make sure that the jury understands my side of the story; Right?" Robert questioned.

"You're making that almost impossible," Caleb challenged. "You beat that man to a pulp, and need I remind you, I'm the only one who was willing to come near your case. They have witnesses, pictures, and a video. Any attorney worth his salt knows this case is a loser. Your best bet is to go into that courtroom and at least *act* like you're sorry."

"I'm a God-fearing man. I will not get on that stand and lie," Robert maintained. "Now, I will say that I had a long day, and it was just a one-time incident."

"No one's going to believe that, Robert, because it wasn't," Caleb sighed, pulling out Robert's file and handing it to him. "You have had ten other similar incidents."

"You can't use those!" Robert hollered out, heat rushing to his face.

"Even if I don't, the prosecutor sure as hell will. And if you aren't able to listen to me, that judge is going to throw the book at you." Caleb asserted.

"Caleb, the judge is a servant of the law, just like I am. I'm sure he'll understand my side of the story." Robert said, dismissing Caleb's warning.

"The Judge decides who is guilty of breaking the law, and if you don't change your tune, you'll make his decision very easy. You...Will...Get...Convicted." Caleb expressed with a sharp gaze in Robert's direction. Robert glanced at Caleb and looked away quickly, scorned.

Before Robert could respond, a clerk called his name from the courtroom. Robert walked down the center of the courtroom holding his tie, the first two buttons of his shirt undone.

When the prosecutor called him to the stand, he delivered his unashamed, remorseless account of the incident. The jury members listened with disdain to Robert's unapologetic attitude as he continued to spew his prejudice and racially biased views, seemingly unaware of anything except his thoughts and ideas.

"It's the same thing that happened two months ago. I stood up for what's right during those riots, too. I don't see how anything has changed since then. The chaos got out of hand, and I did what needed to be done, or else violence would run rampant." Robert exclaimed when questioned on the stand.

Caleb buried his head in his hands as the Judge's face turned to disgust.

"...and that is why I could not, as a law-abiding citizen and officer, allow those kinds of people to disrespect the badge. Without respect, there is no order, Your Honor." Robert finished and leaned back in the chair, cocking his head back and looking down his nose at the courtroom. *No one in their right mind would convict me,* he thought to himself.

The jury deliberated for a remarkably short time, filing back into the courtroom after a few minutes. Their faces didn't give much away as they filed back into the courtroom, to Robert's annoyance.

One glance in the direction of the judge, however, sent a chill through Robert. The judge, sat down with his hands interlaced over the girth of his abdomen. His small glasses dangled at the end of his hawkish nose, giving him a stern appearance, especially as he glared down at Robert.

A tense silence fell over the courtroom as the audience awaited the judge's statement following the jury's reading of the verdict.

The judge quietly cleared his throat before he began. "I have never in my years of being on this bench seen an officer so unmerciful, so shameless, and blatantly callous about the assault of a civilian you took an oath to protect and serve. You were not 'serving the law.' You've made a mockery of it," the judge announced.

Robert's eyebrows furrow at the judge's harsh words. He scoffed and crossed his arms as the judge called him to rise.

"Officer Robert Whitmore," the judge said in a stern tone. "You have been found guilty of aggravated assault."

He banged his gavel and peered down at Robert, whose dark eyes were heated and venomous. Without waiting for his dismissal, Robert snatched his tie from the table and stormed out of the courtroom.

"This is bullshit anyway," he muttered under his breath. His rage threatened to rise, but Robert knew this was neither the time nor the place. Instead, he stared bullets into the floor in front of him.

As Robert Whitmore left the courtroom, he noticed Commissioner Jameson on the back row rubbing his forehead vigorously. Jameson sulked, feeling this could tarnish the reputation of his entire department.

"Jameson," Robert said as he nodded politely, acknowledging his superior officer, before continuing the long walk out of the courtroom.

The commissioner sighed and nodded back after a moment, with far less goodwill. Jameson had far too many unpleasant surprises in the past few weeks. Now the judge is actually convicting officers for their offenses.

Jameson stepped outside of the courtroom to make a phone call.

"Rose, meet me in my office pronto," he ordered.

CHAPTER 6

OFFICER ROSE LIVINGSTON

AUGUST 2020 CHARLOTTESVILLE, VA POLICE HEADQUARTERS

Rose Livingston pushed through the door of police headquarters, twirling her keys around one slim finger. She was tempted momentarily to put off her meeting with Jameson to participate in the juicy police gossip she overheard. The office chatter was just one of the comforting familiarities of headquarters for Rose. She's practically lived there since childhood, and her fellow officers were considered family to her.

Commissioner Jamesom sounded worried on the phone, and he'd said it was urgent, so Rose made a beeline through the cubicles, and headed straight to the Commissioner's office in the back. She gave a perfunctory knock on the glass door. Jameson was seated behind his desk as he peered out the window, looking lost in thought.

"Hey Patrick," Rose greeted him, rushing into his office and shutting the door carefully behind her.

"What's going on? You sounded really worried on the phone," she said as she slid gracefully into the chair facing his desk and looked at Jameson expectantly.

"Rose," Jameson began, "Me and your dad have been friends for a long time, and you know you're like a daughter to me."

"Sure, Patrick. I know that," she said with a confused smile, furrowing her brow.

"Alright. Are you going to tell me what's going on?" Rose asked inquisitively.

"I just got back from Officer Robert Whitmore's trial, Rose," Jameson sighed, surveying her with sharp hazel eyes. "Our department might be in trouble. That judge isn't joking. After all that happened this year, you might be in some deep trouble."

Rose leaned back in her chair and bit her lip, frowning. The sky beyond the window began to fill with the colors of the day, swapping watch with the night.

"This was about that excessive force case, isn't it?" said Rose.

"Of course it's about that case!" Jameson snapped, standing abruptly.

Rose had never seen him so agitated, and she shrunk further into her chair as he continued.

"You falsified evidence that got an officer off, only for that same officer to assault the victim again. Rose."

"Jesus, Patrick. I know what I did."

"This is bad," Jameson leaned over his desk, frighteningly close.

She pushed her short brown hair away from her face and looked up at him with tight lips.

"If this goes before a judge, you'll get convicted!" And it's the rigid tone in the Commissioner's voice that terrified Rose the most.

Jameson kept lecturing her, but it might as well have been static. For all Rose heard, *"He is just like my father,"* she thought to herself, *"blaming me for everything. Nothing I ever do is good enough."*

Rose wasn't ever the girly girl like her father wanted her to be. She didn't wear dresses or heels. She felt much more comfortable in pants and sneakers. She didn't want to be seen as delicate or weak.

Even though Rose wasn't in touch with her feminine side, she knew she was an attractive woman. Her short hair was shiny and dark, and she had almond-shaped green eyes. She knew that part of her power was using her beauty to get what she wanted.

"Patrick," Rose interrupted, eyebrows raised, "This *won't* go to court. I was looking out for a fellow officer. It was just a one-time incident, and you know I acted for the greater good of the department."

"C'mon, Rose," he cajoled, and she frowned at his patronizing tone. "Where was he going with this?" She thought to herself.

"You're a good kid, a great kid. But your work is sloppy. You are one of my best detectives, but your paperwork is causing problems."

She winced internally, it hurt to hear this from a man she admired and respected.

"You're cutting corners, and you know it." Jameson asserted.

Rose swallowed hard. "I just want to be the best detective I can be," Rose insisted. "So, sometimes I twist words around or leave out a few details to get a conviction," she shrugged, hoping that she'll be able to play it off.

"Ahh, Rose," sighed Jameson.

His disappointment was like a stab in Rose's chest.

"You don't have to lie or manipulate evidence to be a good detective. You come from a line of great officers, kid. It's in your blood."

Rose smiled tightly. He seemed genuine, but he didn't understand. She couldn't just be a 'good detective.' She had to be the best there was.

Rose was the youngest in her family and the only girl out of five. Her father and brothers were well-decorated officers on the force. Her dad had recently retired after being Chief of Police for eleven years. Her family had never accepted that she made it on the force. Every day on the job was an effort to prove she belonged as much as any of them.

Rose cried out, "My dad always let me know how great my brothers are. But do you think he *ever* said he was proud of me?"

"And you think that lying and manipulating the law is gonna make your old man proud?" Jameson sighed before continuing in a more gentle voice.

"Think, Rose," he tapped the side of his head. "Trying to make your father proud has landed you in a world of trouble. What about making yourself proud?"

Rose didn't have a response. She lowered her gaze down to her feet and stared.

Jameson returned to his desk and sat heavily.

"Let's talk about your case," he pulled a manila file from the top drawer and spread the contents on the desk in front of Rose. "These are the details about your investigation into that excessive force claim."

Rose glanced over the immediately familiar files. The case hadn't happened long ago, but she'd thought it was some of her best work. "I know you think the officer was guilty. But, I felt like the victim who claimed that the officer used excessive force against him wasn't credible, I didn't believe his story it just didn't sound right." Rose explained.

"Why not?" questioned Jameson as he leaned back in his seat.

"Well, he didn't seem like he was telling the truth. From my perspective, it seemed like it was just another Black guy trying to victimize himself and demonize the police," Rose mentioned defensively.

"Dear God, Rose," Jameson groaned, shaking his head.

Rose quickly straightened, determined to explain herself.

"You're taking it the wrong way, Patrick. I did what I thought was best for the department. We didn't need another 'race' thing to stir up more controversy," she put air-quotes around the word 'race.' "I knew looking into it more would only stir up trouble, so I left out just a few details so that the officer wouldn't have to go to court."

"You *buried evidence,* Rose. The officer assaulted the victim a second time," Jameson emphasized.

"I didn't know that would happen!" exclaimed Rose, trying to defend herself.

"You obstructed justice," he countered, disappointment written plainly in his expression. "A family didn't get the justice they deserved because of you," he reiterated.

"I thought I made the right call," Rose muttered, letting her defense down. "Sorry, Patrick, but this is a bit hypocritical. You're acting like you'd do something different in my position when we both know damn well that you wouldn't."

"Rose, you can't be judge, jury, and executioner. Leave me out of this. The facts are the facts, and it's you on trial," he scolded. He pulled out the paperwork on his desk, tapping it against the desk to straighten the pile. "I've pulled some strings so we can handle this internally."

"Thank you so much, Patrick," Rose sighed, relief flooding through her. "It won't happen again." She rose quickly to leave, desperate to get away from Jameson's horrible, disappointed look.

"Hold on now," Jameson said harshly, stopping Rose in her tracks. "If you write another report like this, I promise you, daughter of Captain Livingston or not. You'll lose your job,"

"I understand, Sir," Rose grunted, feeling like she just had the wind knocked out of her. She never thought she'd hear those words from her mentor.

"I'm going to need you to sit back down. We're not finished here," Jameson said as he motioned for Rose to sit down once more.

Rose swallowed hard, praying that she'll make it through this conversation without crying. She slid back down into her seat and intertwined her fingers tightly, almost painfully.

"Rose, I said we could handle this internally, but that doesn't mean I'm going to sweep it under the rug," he looked hard at her. "You've advanced your career by lying. It's unethical."

"You don't understand what it's like, being the youngest girl with four brothers who are all amazing officers. They don't think I belong. Everyone compares me to them, and I need to be better than them," she knew that she sounded petulant, but she could barely keep it together.

"I've always had to prove myself, and that is something you'll *never* understand," Rose explained.

"And you think this is the way to make a name for yourself, Rose?" Jameson's snapped with his voice rising with each word, which made Rose feel tiny.

"As a detective, it's your job to seek justice. Instead, you've obstructed justice, and now someone is paying for that."

"I know, but-" Rose started.

"There are no 'buts,'" Jameson interjected.

Rose's mouth hung open for a moment before she regained control, schooling her features and glancing down at her feet.

"As a personal favor to me, I have arranged for a friend on the inside of Internal Affairs to deal with this case so it will not go to court. In order for you to keep your job, you need to cooperate fully with that department." He nodded slowly as if assessing her reaction.

"They have some new types of ideas and programs they are putting into place."

"What type of program--oh, like a 12-step or something," she grinned sideways, trying to regain her effortless charm.

Jameson wasn't buying it.

"It's an experimental program" he narrowed his eyes and scowled. I don't know all of the details yet, but my hands are tied, Rose. You have to go through with it, or you're fired," he said, folding his hand on his desk.

"Understood," Rose replied evenly. "Is that all?" "Or do you want to continue to tell me just how worthless I am, Patrick?"

Jameson nodded his head solemnly before turning around in his chair to face the window. Rose got up from her seat and scratched the back of her neck awkwardly before departing without another word.

Just as she was leaving, Captain Jenkins brushed past her as he hurriedly entered Jameson's office.

"Jameson, we need to talk about Ethan's case," bellowed Captain Jenkins in a huff.

"Rose, could you shut the door behind you?" Jameson ordered.

Rose was surprised by his frazzled demeanor. After all, Captain Jenkins and Jameson were really good golf buddies. Her ever-insistent curiosity tempted her to stay and listen, but she thought better of it. She didn't need any more trouble.

"Absolutely, sir," she said as she closed the door on her way out.

For just a moment, Rose's curiosity got the best of her, and she paused outside of the door. She tried to make sense of the muffled voices. "Ethan is being charged. He shot an undercover cop!" Rose overheard Captain Jenkins yell frantically at Jameson.

Rose gasped then quickly covered her mouth, hoping no one heard her.

"Jesus Christ, Jenkins. What is going on in this department? You do realize that eventually, it's all going to fall back on *me*," Jameson replied.

Rose hurried away, eyes wide. Ethan was a fellow police officer and Captain Jenkins' son. She couldn't believe what she just heard.

CHAPTER 7

OFFICER ETHAN JENKINS JR.

AUGUST 2020 CHARLOTTESVILLE, VA POLICE HEADQUARTERS

Captain Jenkins paced back and forth in Jameson's office. Captain Jenkins rubbed his balding head fervently, giving him the appearance of a madman. Jameson glared at his friend and colleague, unable to believe the news he just received.

Everything was falling apart in quick succession, and after his heated conversation with Rose, Jameson didn't know how much more he could stand. He rubbed his temples as he tried to process the fact that a fellow police officer charged Ethan with attempted murder.

After a moment, Jameson stood up and closed the blinds on his window, darkening the room in an attempt to alleviate his headache. It turned out to be useless. Captain Jenkins' voice was like a hammer banging inside of Jameson's head.

"What has that boy done!" Captain Jenkins yelled out as his face turned an angry shade of red. "My son is gonna go to prison," he boomed. "And over a Black man at that."

"We don't know that," said Jameson calmly.

"How did this happen? How did he end up shooting a cop?" Jameson asked.

"I don't know the exact details," growled Captain Jenkins. "I do know that the cop was Black, and they're gonna make this some kind of a racial thing," he complained as he continued pacing, becoming increasingly agitated.

"You have got to get these charges dropped." Captain Jenkins pleaded.

"Let's just get E.J. on the phone," Jameson reasoned. "Hear the story straight from the horse's mouth," Jameson continued as he smiled at Captain Jenkins who was obviously distressed. "I'll see what I can do once I have the details," Jameson asserted.

Captain Jenkins slumped back into the chair Rose had sat in moments before, and he closed his eyes as the phone rang loudly.

"Hello," Ethan's voice thundered over the receiver, terse and irritated.

"Boy, you better show some respect," Captain Jenkins ordered, leaning forward in his seat. "Patrick is the only person who can help you get off on these charges."

"Sorry," Ethan sighed. "Hey, Jameson," Ethan mumbled.

"Hi Ethan," Jameson began. "You want to tell me what the hell is going on here?"

"It was an accident. I swear to God," Ethan insisted, as his voice cracked a bit. "I didn't even know he was a cop. How could I have known? He wasn't in uniform or anything," Ethan stammered.

"I will admit, Ethan, it's going to be a lot harder to get these charges dismissed considering he was a fellow officer," Jameson pointed out.

"That's why we need to get ahead of this thing," Captain Jenkins offered mildly.

"E.J., I am just so disappointed in you!" Captain Jenkins chastised. "How could you be so careless to get caught? You've got to learn to cover your tracks."

"I get it, Dad," Ethan complained.

"How in the blazes did you end up shooting a cop? You should have said something. We could have made this disappear a long time ago," Captain Jenkins scolded.

"It's not just you at stake--it's the reputation of our entire goddamn department." Captain Jenkins ranted frantically.

Jameson looked at his friend and quickly added. "We might not be able to make it disappear, but we may be able to get the charges dismissed," Jameson proposed. "Now, tell me exactly what happened, don't leave anything out." Jameson enquired.

Ethan groaned over the phone, dreading having to go over the details again. He replayed that night over and over in his head for the last couple of months. The memory was still fresh. The humid air and the bitter taste of fear on his tongue once he realized what he'd done. All he wanted was to be able to put the whole incident behind him.

"Okay," Ethan sighed. "This is the last time I'm doing this."

"I don't think you're really in a position to negotiate terms here, E.J.," Jameson said dryly.

Ethan huffed and began to explain what happened that night. "I had been off duty that night, and I planned to have a night to just chill out. On my way home from the grocery store, I saw something that didn't look quite right. A Black guy was parked in the middle of the block sitting in his car, looking suspicious. I had a gut feeling that something wasn't right. It looked like he was waiting for someone like he was about to do a drug buy or somethig illegal." Ethan explained.

"I decided to investigate the situation a bit, so I sat and watched for a couple of minutes and after two or three people approached the car and left, I decided to confront the guy, you know find out what he was up to. I knocked on the window and the son of a bitch didn't want to lower the window until I knocked on the glass with my glock and he eventually lowered it."

"The guy started giving me attitude like they always do," Ethan continued. "And all of a sudden, he reached for his glove box, so I reacted," Ethan explained.

"How did you react, Ethan?" Jameson questioned sternly.

Jameson knew Ethan Jenkins Jr. his whole life and already felt like he knew the answer to the question the moment he asked it, but he wanted to ensure that he had all of the facts.

"I shot him," Ethan said quietly, "three times. I thought he was going for a weapon. I didn't know he was reaching for his damn badge," Ethan explained.

"He never said he was on the job. God, if I'd known I'd have to deal with all of this, I would have just killed the son of a bitch." Ethan blurted out.

Jameson raised his eyebrows and glanced at Captain Jenkins. He knew it was bad, but Ethan's harsh words still came as a shock. Worse, Captain Jenkins didn't interrupt or scold Ethan at all. Jameson always knew his old friend Captain Jenkins notoriously bailed Ethan out of every mess he had ever been in. However, this was different.

"Ethan," he pitched his voice low, cold as ice. "Never. Ever. Repeat that you should have killed him. You are going to put yourself in a mess that your father and I can't clean up." Jameson scoffed.

"Honestly, I'm tired of people telling me what to do. I don't need you or my dad to help me out. I can get myself out of this." Ethan fumed. "Court is a waste of time. Nothing is going to happen to me. I'm an officer; they can't charge me for doing my job."

"Junior, you are playing a dangerous game," warned Captain Jenkins.

"Yeah, well, I've gotta go. See you in court tomorrow." Ethan said, his voice completely monotone. A second later, the phone clicked off abruptly, and Jameson looked over at Captain Jenkins disparagingly.

"That boy has no idea the kind of trouble he's in," Jameson sighed.

"You better get him off," Captain Jenkins commanded. He pointed at Jameson, his jaw quivered, and eyes bulged, before storming out of the office.

Jameson put his head in his hands, finally alone to endure the headache Ethan and Rose had caused him.

CHARLOTTESVILLE COURTHOUSE STEPS THE NEXT DAY.

The blinding flash of news cameras and reporters surrounded Ethan as he pushed his way through a crowd to get up the courthouse stairs. Reporters tried stopping him to answer questions as their cameramen flashed a light in his face. Ethan began to lose his patience as he shoved through the mob of people to make his way into the courthouse.

Ethan sighed as he rubbed his forehead. He wasn't expecting to be met with so much commotion outside. It was just a court case. It was not like he killed anybody. He wore his nice blue suit that clung to his defined muscles.

Today, it felt like armor. Ethan straightened his tie and rolled his shoulders back as he prepared to enter the courtroom.

As Ethan sauntered into the courtroom, he held his head high. The pews looked unusually full. People were crammed in next to each other, seemingly eager to witness some type of cataclysm. A pit began to form in his stomach. Perhaps this was a bigger deal than he thought.

Nonetheless, Ethan was determined to get himself off of the charges without any help. The hushed whispers of the packed courtroom fell silent as the prosecutor approached Ethan on the stand.

"Officer Ethan Jenkins Jr.," the prosecutor began glaring deeply into Ethan's eyes. Her tall, well-dressed statuesque figure seemed foreboding. Ethan refused to be intimidated, staring right back at her.

"You shot an undercover cop three times while he was seated in his vehicle, striking him in his abdomen and lower body," she continued. "Why did you discharge your firearm on a fellow officer?"

"I didn't *know* he was an officer," Ethan snapped. "He didn't identify himself. He just reached for his glove box, and I thought he was reaching for a weapon, so I reacted," Ethan forced himself to keep his cool, to keep his voice steady.

"So you didn't think he could have been reaching for his wallet or perhaps his badge?" The prosecutor questioned.

Ethan scowled at her. He thought to himself, "Who did she think she was, using that tone with him?"

"You shot first and asked questions later!" the prosecutor boomed. Her voice echoed off the arched ceilings of the courtroom, and Ethan's heart began to race.

He paused and glanced at his defense attorney, unsure of how to respond. "I- I don't know," he stuttered, trying not to incriminate himself.

"Your honor, may I request a 5-minute recess to confer with my client?" Ethan's attorney asked the Judge.

"Counselor, do you object?" asked the judge.

The prosecutor, seeming confident that she had Ethan cornered, looked to the judge before replying."I have no objections, your honor."

Ethan's attorney quickly ushered Ethan into the hallway, "Look, Ethan, you aren't doing badly. You acted in self-defense. Just remember that," the attorney coached. "You have to hold it together up there. That prosecutor is a shark. If you mess up, she *will* eat you alive.

"Alright, alright. Let's just get this over with," Ethan complained, trying to shake off his nerves as he made his way back to the stand.

His heart beat rapidly, and his hands were sweating. He hadn't thought he would be this nervous. He cleared his throat before answering the prosecutor's next question.

"Let me restate my question for the record, your honor," the prosecutor quipped. "Officer Jenkins, why did you shoot first and ask questions later?"

"It was self-defense. I was in a potentially dangerous situation and was forced to protect myself," Ethan maintained in a cool, calm voice, looking to his attorney for approval. The defense attorney nodded encouragingly.

"Can you explain to the court why you approached the vehicle initially? You weren't even on duty or in uniform," the prosecutor questioned.

"Uhh-" Ethan stammered. "I umm. I was off duty, and yeah, I was in plain clothes, but I saw something suspicious. There was no one on duty around, so I checked it out," he rolled his shoulders and tilted his head back.

"And what did you see that was so suspicious?" The prosecutor asked.

"From the distance I could see a Black guy in a dark colored sedan with tinted windows parked in the middle of a vacant block. It looked like he was dealing," Ethan explained, beginning to get frustrated. "*No one is hearing me,*" he thought to himself.

Members of the crowd scoffed and whispered amongst themselves at his response. His defense attorney shook his head in disbelief as the prosecutor smirked.

"A Black man sitting in his car doesn't look right?" she questioned matter-of-factly. "What's suspicious about that?"

"Look, I'm not a racist, but he looked like he was up to something!" Ethan reiterated.

"Why did he look like he was up to something?" she quickly questioned, her voice forceful. She slammed a threatening hand down on the witness stand, and the noise reverberated in Ethan's head.

"Because Black people are always up to something!" Ethan screamed with desperation and anger.

The courtroom fell momentarily silent before erupting in an angry murmur. Ethan mentally berated himself for losing his self-control like that. The judge's brow furrowed with his expression, which was one of open disgust. He banged his gavel and called for order in the courtroom.

Ethan shrunk back in his chair and held his breath. The prosecutor smiled to herself as she shook her head at Ethan.

"Order! Order in the court," the judge demanded, silencing the courtroom.

"The prosecution rests its case, your honor," the prosecutor said as she glided back to her seat.

"We have no further questions. The defense rests, your honor," Ethan's attorney stated in a deflated tone.

The jurors got dismissed only to return two hours later with a verdict. The bailiff hands their verdict to the judge.

"Ethan Jenkins Jr., you have been found guilty of discharging your firearm on a fellow officer. You were off duty and failed to identify yourself as a police officer, further solidifying your guilt."

Ethan's jaw dropped in disbelief. Distantly, he noticed the cheering of the court and the prosecutor's smug smile. Ethan's vision turned red. He pounded his fist on the table, hard, before standing and storming out of the courtroom.

Where had his father been? Where was Jameson? Forgetting his own adamant assertions that he could handle this alone, all he thoughtg was, "they promised to help me." Neither had spoken a word in his defense. Ethan felt everyone in the courtroom had turned on him.

While Ethan walked out, Captain Jenkins stood up from his seat in the back of the courtroom.

"Damn It!" Captain Jenkins yelled as he directed his anger at Jameson, who was seated beside him. "Why in the hell couldn't you get him off? That Black son of a bitch didn't even die!" Captain Jenkins asserted.

Jameson scowled up at the larger man, refusing to be intimidated. "What did you expect, Jenkins? I can't control the words that come out of that boy's mouth. Ethan incriminated himself. This isn't on me." Jameson roared in return.

Captain Jenkins shook his head maniacally. "Dammit Jameson, you'd better hope he doesn't see the inside of a prison cell or so help me."

"Or what?" interjected Jameson, raising his eyebrows cooly. Captain Jenkins scoffed, glaring down at Jameson for a moment in shock still. Then he shook his head, brushed past Jameson, and stormed out of the busy courtroom as Ethan had just done minutes before.

CHAPTER 8

THE MEETING

Dr. Andre Langston, a renowned African-American neuropsychologist, was extremely proud of the team he assembled to work with him to create the Decennial Program. He was proud of the scientific breakthroughs they were able to accomplish and the fact that he and his team were able to complete their research with very little outside funding. They sought funding from various resources only to get turned down primarily because the entire team was African-American and the fact that the program they were developing had never been successfully accomplished by anyone, until now.

Dr. Langston and his team of doctors talked amongst

themselves as they sat at one end of a long conference table. Dr. Langston remembered the last time he was in that very room five years earlier. He attended a similar meeting alone. This time, Dr. Langston brought along Dr. Aaliyah Cooper, his Chief Behavioral Psychologist, Tyrese Brown, his IT Technician and Program Operator, and Dr. Sarah Hughes, one of the top Scientists and Molecular Engineers in the country. At the other end of the conference table, a harried-looking Jameson leaned back in his swivel chair as he glared at Dr. Langston as if they were back in the fifth grade having a staring contest. The disdain Dr. Langston and Jameson had for each other was palpable. Jameson's face was an open book. Dr. Langston felt that it was mainly because Jameson didn't know him and definitely didn't trust him professionally. Still, he suspected that Jameson also mistrusted him personally.

Dr. Langston frowned as thoughts of his last meeting with Jameson entered his mind. Jameson had been condescending and impolite. Dr. Langston realized that perhaps the feeling was mutual; he didn't trust Jameson either.

"Who called this meeting?" Dr. Langston asked, the timbre of his voice finally breaking the silence that hung heavily between himself and Jameson.

"I called the meeting," another man said, entering the conference room as if on cue. "The name is Pierce Ramsey. I have been newly appointed to head up Internal Affairs."

Jameson stood to shake Ramsey's hand and noticeably had his jaw dropped as he was expecting to see his old friend Teigan.

Dr. Langston stood to shake Ramsey's hand as well, along with the rest of the team. Ramsey's handshake was firm, his smile wide and friendly.

"You must be Dr. Langston. I've heard a lot about your program. I think it may be able to do us some good here." Ramsey said as he stared Dr. Langston squarely in the eyes with a welcoming smile on his face.

"You called us out here to make me relive our last meeting? I'm not going to explain my program again just to have you kick me out a second time. We're very busy people, come on, guys," Dr. Langston said as he rose from his seat and motioned his team to leave.

"Wait," Ramsey interrupted. "You never explained your program to me. I wouldn't call you out here to waste your time, Doctor."

Dr. Langston looked at his colleagues to decide whether to stay or go. "This could be our chance," Dr. Cooper said, hopeful.

"Maybe we should just cut our losses," Tyrese shrugged. "Don't let them throw you out twice. Let's just go."

"What's the harm in explaining it one more time?" Dr. Hughes offered in a measured voice. "We're already here."

Dr. Langston's team returned to their seats, Tyrese groaned reluctantly.

"It's called the Decennial Program," Dr. Langston began. "We would take a group of your officers who were convicted of racially motivated crimes and send them into a new world, a sort of an alternate reality, where they have to experience what it is like to be in the shoes of the citizens they are most likely to be prejudiced against. Usually, that means they would be experiencing the reality of a Black civilian," he continued as he pulled out his notes from his briefcase.

"Our research shows that in the most extreme cases of racial bias, one would undergo all ten sessions or ten years, and that is why we have named it the Decennial Program." Dr. Cooper chimed in.

"We would use the technology we've developed to send the officers into a dream-like state. Their bodies will be here, but their minds will be transported," Dr. Hughes added.

"And what do you suppose that will do?" Jameson interrupted.

Dr. Langston furrowed his brow. *"Isn't* it obvious?" Dr. Langston fired back at Jameson. "We have found that putting officers in the position of their victims will allow them to gain not only empathy but a better understanding of the communities they are policing, all of which will serve to challenge their prejudices and biases."

"I see the concept," Ramsey hedged, "but how could that work? Practically, I mean."

"The way it works is through an advanced time continuum algorithm that stimulates the neurons in the frontal lobe of the cerebral cortex transferring 16 billion bits of data from the prefrontal cortex to the hippocampus of the temporal lobe, which is then processed in the cerebellum..." In his excitement, Dr. Langston glanced at Ramsey and Jameson and noticed they were not able to follow his scientific explanation and quickly decided to try layman's terms.

"In other words, it's a computer program which we've developed in our labs that creates an alternate reality simulation. Once they're in the simulation, we tailor their experience to address their particular biases and are able to observe their responses," Dr. Langston explained.

Dr. Langston produced a few pages of the source code and passed them to Jameson and Ramsey. Ramsey glanced down at the code before sizing Dr. Langston up and being very impressed.

"The hope is that if they are on the receiving end of their own discriminatory actions, it will cause them to think more fairly when faced with the same scenarios in the future," Dr. Cooper offered.

"Ahh, I see," Ramsey said, nodding his head. "They'll learn how it feels to be treated the way they're treating the citizens they're charged with policing," he reiterated.

"Yes, exactly, Sir," Dr. Hughes agreed.

"We're going to need to review more of the research," Ramsey said hesitantly.

Dr. Langston, having expected this, produced several folders full of charts, tables, and reports that illustrated the extensive research his team had developed. Ramsey nodded his head in approval as he sifted through the information. Jameson scoffed and tossed the folder back down onto the table.

Ramsey leaned in to whisper to Jameson, but was audible across the table. "This could be an alternative to prison time," he muttered, "I know it seems far-fetched, but if the department approves it, I think we should give it a shot."

"I don't know, Ramsey," Jameson said. "We're just gonna hand our officers off to this team of mad scientists?" he questioned.

"Well, Jameson, our officers are going to prison unless we find a way to trust Dr. Langston," Ramsey countered.

Jameson sighed in surrender, and Dr. Langston knew at that moment he had them. "Dr. Langston," Jameson said reluctantly, "I think you may have the solution here. We'd like to move forward on a trial basis. Let's see how it goes for the first year, but we can't announce the results of the program to the public until we have more clinical trials and more proof of efficacy."

Dr. Langston and his team exchanged glances. This was far more than they expected from this meeting. Ramsey walked over to a filing cabinet tucked away in the corner of the conference room, and a moment later, he sat a small stack of manila folders in front of Dr. Langston and his team.

"In each of these files, you'll find the case of an officer who committed a racially motivated crime. They're decent officers, and the department has spent a lot of money on training them, but they've demonstrated strong racial biases. Those biases impede their ability to do their job, and I'd love to see them reformed. You can start there," Ramsey said.

Dr. Langston and his team were pleasantly surprised by Ramsey's enthusiasm. They hadn't been expecting any open-mindedness after the department had met the idea with such hostility. The team shook hands with Ramsey as they celebrated quietly amongst themselves.

Dr. Langston, in particular, was filled with cautious optimism. His team had committed so much time, attention, and financial resources to develop this program. For years, it had been a passion project, but now there was a shimmer of possibility. This could be a chance to get the Decennial Program off the ground at last.

Ramsey's friendly voice interrupted Dr. Langston's thoughts.

"We'd love to stop by and check in on the program periodically, just to get a better understanding of how it works," he said.

Meanwhile, Jameson stood and shook his head in bitter disapproval, "Speak for yourself," he grumbled, brushing past Dr. Langston as he headed for the exit.

"You, Officer Ramsey, will be welcomed in our lab anytime," Dr. Langston emphasized.

"Though I'm not sure I can say the same for your colleague," Dr. Langston said as he and his team gathered their things to leave.

"He'll come around eventually," Ramsey assured with a light chuckle. "I look forward to stopping by."

CHAPTER 9

THE DECENNIAL PROGRAM

OCTOBER 2020

Officer Ramsey, the head of internal affairs, walked down a dark corridor in the basement of police headquarters. He had never been down there before and was surprised by the dank smell and that the hall seemed to be as long as a football field. The sound of his department store dress shoes echoed off of the concrete walls with an eerie clickity-clack. As he reached his destination, he could hear several voices that were so loud they spilled into the hallway.

He braced himself for what was to come and took a deep breath before turning the handle and pushing through the door. A deafening hush fell over the room as he entered.

The smell in the room was equally bad. It was a small, windowless room that must have been an interrogation room in a past life. Ramsey wrinkled his nose as he entered. It smelled like stale urine and old coffee, he thought uncharitably.

One large table stood in the center, and several chairs leaned against the walls. In the chairs sat ten officers in various states of distress. None of them looked happy to be there, neither did Ramsey.

Ramsey prepared himself for a combative encounter. He doubted if these officers would take the news of the Decennial Program lightly. They would be the first ten participants in the Decennial Program just approved by the department. It was his job to inform them of their choices, prison or the Decennial Program.

"When I call your name, please raise your hand so I know you're here, and we won't have to send someone to pick you up," Ramsey said as he opened the first folder. "Sierra Brookes," he called.

An older, slightly overweight white woman rolled her eyes as she raised her hand. Ramsey glanced down at the file. "*Jesus, this is bad.* You were off duty in a drug store and took a robbery into your own hands," he dictated from the file, "pinning a teenager to the ground, dislocating his shoulder. Except there was no robbery at all, just children playing around in a store."

Ramsey glanced up at the woman, whose face had gone purple. "I didn't know they were playing; they looked like criminals to me. They were wearing those sagging pants and had that weird scarf around their head like gang bangers," Sierra explained as she heard a few chuckles around the room. Ramsey noted her voice was husky for a woman, almost like she had smoked a pack of cigarettes without the filter every day for the last 20 years.

"Moving on," Ramsey continued with a sigh. "Emily Campbell." Emily looked down at the sticky tile floor as she raised her hand, embarrassed. "Emily Campbell convicted of aggravated assault on a peaceful protester."

Ramsey surveyed the small blonde woman, who must be deceptively strong under her doll-like exterior based on the pictures of her victim's broken bones and bruises. He pushed down his disgust and moved to the next file.

"Paul Carter, convicted for aggravated assault as well." Ramsey said, "You defied orders to stand down and, instead, relentlessly beat a civilian at a protest."

A slender-built young man raised his hand discreetly before quickly putting it back down. He stayed silent. His eyes jumped around the room but never met Ramsey's.

"John Fletcher, it appears that you were on the task force during the Black Lives Matter protest, and you gave orders for your squad to use pepper spray and rubber bullets on a peaceful crowd, causing multiple injuries to civilians," Ramsey said in a monotone voice with a hint of disdain.

"That crowd wasn't peaceful; they were yelling and screaming at us," An older, very fit man huffed. John folded his arms and sank further down in his seat when he realized that he'd spoken out of turn.

The next file Ramsey opened was alarming. "Ethan Jenkins Jr., you shot a Black officer?"

Ethan groaned as he rubbed his head, annoyed with everything about the situation. "For the last time, I didn't know he was an officer."

Ramsey stared at Ethan for a moment, resisting the urge to scoff. Truly, Ethan Jenkins Jr. deserved prison, he thought to himself. Ramsey was willing to bet that the only reason he was in this program was that his daddy was the captain. Well, there was nothing he could do about that.

"Rose Livingston," Ramsey went on after a beat. "You did not go before a judge like everyone else here today. You're receiving disciplinary action for falsifying reports regarding complaints lodged by African-American victims," he read. Anxiety was written all over Rose's face as her fingers tapped a staccato on the arm of her chair.

"George McDuffie," Ramsey opened up George's file without more than a glance in his direction. "Wow, you paralyzed a young football player who you thought was reaching for a weapon when he was just reaching for his phone."

George raised his hand. "I didn't know-" he began.

"Yeah, yeah." Ramsey interrupted, waving his hand dismissively. "That's what all of you say. Moving on."

When Ramsey glanced at George again, George clenched his teeth and stared bullets at the stained tile floor.

"Roger Simms, you attacked a group of protesters because they were dismantling a statue of the Confederate officer you've gone on the record as saying you admire."

Roger raised his hand proudly. "I think it's bullshit that they're tearing down all the history of our great nation. People need to respect history."

"Simms, you used excessive force, and your actions incited a riot that resulted in several injuries and one casualty," Ramsey read aloud, talking over Simm's assertion.

"They committed a crime, so I did what an officer is supposed to do. I attempted to restore the scene to order. They have to obey the law. Sir"

"Well, look where your actions landed you," Ramsey declared, tossing Roger's folder down onto the table and opening another.

"Alex Stiles," Ramsey called. A handsomely tanned and muscular man with thick, brown hair nodded his head smugly at Ramsey. Ramsey immediately disliked him.

"You were called to a scene of an assault; you failed to intervene, resulting in the death of the victim."

"I reported to the call; when I got there, it was just a little fight between a few white guys and this Black dude. He looked tough, so I went on about my day. I didn't think they would kill him," Alex explained.

"I don't need to hear your excuses! Every one of you sorry motherfuckers has an excuse that didn't fly with the jury that convicted you of misconduct," Ramsey thundered at the group. A foreboding hush followed, and

Ramsey closed his eyes briefly, fighting to keep his temper in check.

"Allow me to continue." He waited for a beat as if he were waiting for an objection. Then he reluctantly flipped open the final manila folder. "And lastly, we have Robert Whitmore, convicted of aggravated assault on a peaceful protestor. Please, tell me how you justify that, officer," he continued. Robert cleared his throat, raising his hand but remaining silent. *At least someone got the message,* Ramsey thought.

"You are all here for the same reason," Ramsey said, tossing the last folder down onto the table.

"All of your crimes were against Black civilians. You are all aware that there has been a significant uptick in racially motivated crimes happening across this nation. And you know that racial bias amongst officers of the law is under closer scrutiny than ever before. But you didn't give a damn about that. You assholes have caused our entire department to be under investigation! It's clear that your personal biases are obstructing your ability to protect and serve everyone." Ramsey explained, his voice rose and fell with emotion.

He paced the length of the room. "Despite the fact that none of you deserve this, you're being presented with a unique opportunity. You can serve your sentence in prison, or you can participate in an experimental initiative called the Decennial Program."

Ramsey looked around the room at a sea of intrigued faces before continuing.

"It's an experimental program, but we can guarantee that it's safe-ish" Ramsey explained with a subtle chuckle in his voice. The way the Decennial Program works is that each of you will undergo a state of suspended animation in the real world, being transported into a virtual reality program where you would live as Black citizens of the same Virginia districts you patrol. This will allow you to experience the world created by some of your own biases. It will give you first-hand experiences with the trials and tribulations Black Americans go through on a daily basis," he continued to explain.

The room remained quiet.

"The program will tailor each officer's experience to challenge their racial biases. Essentially, you will find out how it feels to be on the receiving end of your very own prejudices."

"This is bullshit, Sir! I ain't no goddamn racist," George asserted.

"Then you should have nothing to worry about in the program. Once you've dealt with your biases to a satisfactory level, you'll graduate from the program."

Ramsey anticipated this meeting would be met with hesitation and resistance, as was prevalent from the angry and bewildered faces of the officers in the room.

"Alternatively, you could forego this opportunity and just serve your sentence. It's your call," Ramsey countered.

"I'm not doing this shit!" Robert huffed as he stood to leave.

"You can undergo this rehabilitative program, or you can go to prison. Think fast, though, because each of you only has until the end of the day to make your decision. You might want to sit your ass down and get all the facts before you blow outta here. This is the only briefing you will receive, and I will not repeat myself," Ramsey threw the words at Robert's back, but he was addressing the entire group.

Robert stopped dead in his tracks. He paused for a moment before he reluctantly returned to his seat. Ramsey waited for everyone to settle before he continued. "This program is ten sessions long. *If* you agree, you will receive half of your regular pay, you will ride the desk and handle the paperwork of your fellow officers who aren't shitheads like you seem to be, and you will report to Dr. Langston's lab once a month for your sessions."

"Each session is six hours in real-time, but in the program, it will seem like one year has passed," Ramsey explained. "Every sixty seconds in real-time that you are in the program represents an entire 24-hour day in the Decennial Program, so for you math geniuses, there are 60 seconds in a minute, and if you multiply 60 seconds times six hours; you get 360 days or just short of a year's experience worth of being a Black citizen in America. Congratulations! You will endure for six hours what they have to endure 24 hours a day seven days a week, no simulation," Ramsey cited.

"Let me put it another way. It works much like when you take a power nap for 30 minutes and have a dream in which you did way more than is possible in 30 minutes.

That's kinda how the Decennial Program works. You will go to your session once a month for 10 months or until you've satisfactorily completed the program by facing and overcoming your racial biases. Each of you will experience a year in the life of a different Black American. You'll continue in that same life from one session to the next session," Ramsey revealed.

"To further explain, the life and all that happens in that life during your first session will continue, and you will pick back up where you left off in that first session when you report for the second session. So the first session is year one, the second session is year two, and so on and so forth, you get the idea," Ramsey continued in a condescending tone.

After each session, your biases will be assessed by an algorithm, group discussions, and a multitude of simulated exercises, all of which will determine whether you will be able to return to your jobs. Any questions?" Ramsey concluded.

No one raised their hand, though Ramsey suspected that they had more than a few questions. Even after he spent hours reviewing the code and data that Dr. Langston had provided, Ramsey was still confused about some of the details. The officers couldn't possibly have a comprehensive idea of what they were getting into. Even so, they knew this program would allow them to avoid prison, to be available for their families, and to have an income, and that seemed good enough for them.

"If you've decided on door one, Rollins here is prepared to escort you to prison," Ramsey mentioned as he pointed to a guard in a uniform standing by a scuffed up door that looked like it was used to sled down a mountain removing most of its paint. After a brief silence, Ramsey nodded to the guard relieving him from his duty. He knew enthusiastic cooperation would be out of the question, and he was right.

"Great. Report to the Decennial Lab tomorrow at 8 a.m. The address is in your paperwork. Complete the waiver and put it on my desk by the end of the day," Ramsey said as he dismissed the officers. "Oh, and make sure you eat something first."

CHAPTER 10

SESSION I. YEAR ONE

Early in the morning at 7:45 a.m., all of the officers arrived at the Decennial Headquarters, as they were ordered. The receptionist escorted them to a spacious room. A large glass mirror at the far end of the space reflected their concerned looks back at them. They seemed to move in lockstep, entering the room further with greater reluctance. Black curtains adorned the room unsuccessfully concealing wires, circuit boards, electronic equipment, and what looked like a supercomputer from the 80's. A potted plant in the left corner of the room seemed to scream, "eh, we tried."

Heavy, dark drapes flanked both ends of the windows, but someone had flung them open, allowing the early morning sun to flood the space. In the middle of the room, ten identical stations were arranged in a circle. Within each area, there was a reclining seat, much like a dentist's chair.

Each chair had a small table next to it, with a mannequin head that was usually designated to display a woman's wig, which held a helmet with multicolored wires dangling from various areas of it. There was also a styrofoam cup on each table accompanied by a small water bottle, a paper vial containing a blue pill, and a red pill.

Shortly after the officers walked into the room, Dr. Langston and his team members entered the room. Dr. Langston entered last, slamming the door behind himself, startling the group of officers.

"Hello, I am Dr. Langston, lead researcher and the Director of The Decennial Program. This is Tyrese Brown. He developed an enormous portion of the hardware and software that we use to run the program. This is Dr. Aaliyah Cooper, our behavioral psychologist; she helps tailor your experiences to yield the desired result. Last but certainly not least, we have Dr. Sarah Hughes, chief scientist and molecular engineer. She created the sedative that allows us to send you into the program," he announced.

"Let's get started, shall we?" Dr. Langston said with enthusiasm.

The doctors helped the officers into their recliners and adjusted their helmets. Dr. Cooper made several notations on her clipboard and made sure she noted which officer was seated at each station. The team went around to each station to ensure each of the officers had been comfortably seated. Then they began to input the necessary configurations into the computer program.

Every action was precisely carried out. The team had gone over the initiation protocols hundreds of times and had eliminated even the slightest possibilities for error. After a few adjustments, the officers were instructed to take their pills. Within seconds, each officer fell into sedation, instantly thrusting their minds into the Decennial Program to live their lives as Black citizens.

DECENNIAL PROGRAM SESSION I

Sierra, Roger, John, Paul, and Alex suddenly found themselves outside of the Decennial Headquarters and on the city streets. The building that had been a polished laboratory was now an abandoned building with caution tape across the doors and windows preventing them from going back into the building.

Sierra Brooks, who was now Brandy Smith, looked at the abandoned building incredulously. Roger Simms, who was now Sean Robertson, saw himself in the reflection of the glass window and yelped.

"What the hell?" Sean yelled as he saw his now deep brown skin. "I'm Black!"

"Oh, my God, I can't believe this!" Alex Stiles, who was now Steven Andrews, uttered out loud.

Steven looked down at his caramel brown hands and began to shake.

Paul Carter and John Fletcher had become Carl Parker and Frank James, respectively. They all start to panic as they realize they're no longer themselves. Just as they attempted to calm down, they heard the siren of a police car pulling up behind them.

Two white officers stepped out of the vehicle and approached the group. "Can I get some I.D.?" one of the officers asked.

"Oh, we're fine, Sir. There's no problem. Thank you, though." Frank said as he reached his hand out for a handshake, only to be rebuffed.

"I said, I.D.," the officer repeated, evidently not taking no for an answer.

They were surprised by the officer's tone. Brandy especially didn't expect to be met with such malice. When they pulled out their I.D.s, they were made aware of their new names and addresses. They showed the officer their I.D.s and were permitted to go on about their day.

Although they had new information about themselves, they were still in a swirl of confusion. The first thing that confused them was why the police had approached them and demanded they present their identification when they were simply standing on the street talking.

ETHAN JENKINS JR. AS JAMAL EDWARDS

Ethan awakened abruptly in a twin-sized bed to the sound of a woman yelling. His mouth was suddenly dry, and his back ached. He was dressed in nothing but boxers and crew socks. *Where am I?* He groaned, rubbed his eyes, and sat up. The bedroom he was in was entirely unfamiliar. He realized that he forgot something important, what happened to put him there.

An older Black woman in a bathrobe burst into the bedroom and began to yell, "Jamal, you're going to be late!"

"Who the hell are you?" He yelled back in shock, as he covered himself with the blanket.

"Jamal, now you know I've changed your diapers, and I have seen everything you've got, so don't play. Get up! You're gonna be late."

"Who the hell is Jamal?" Ethan mumbled in confusion.

"Dear Lord, give me strength!" she looked up as if she was talking to the ceiling. "Jamal, please stop playing games and get up!" The woman shouted as she walked out of the room, muttering to herself.

Ethan threw the covers off of himself. That's what he'd forgotten. The Decennial Program. Sure enough, when he rushed to peer in the mirror hanging above the dresser, he realized he was no longer Ethan Jenkins Jr. Ethan marveled at his reflection, shocked when he saw his caramel brown skin. His hands shook as he touched the short, textured twists in his hair. He realized that he had been transformed into some guy named Jamal, who lived with this older woman he thought might be Jamal's mother.

The woman burst into the room again, startling him. "Hey, Jamal, run down to the coffee shop and get my regular, since you're gonna be late anyway," she said and shut the door immediately after the last word fell from her lips.

Jamal opened the closet door, and looked for something to wear, and saw a police uniform.

"Oh wow, I'm still a cop," he breathed to himself as he slipped into the slacks.

When he was fully dressed and groomed, he found his way down the stairs of the unfamiliar house. He then headed to the front door.

He turned the three locks, detached the chain-link lock, turned the doorknob, and stepped out onto a small porch at the top of three steps that led to the sidewalk. It was a chilly day. The wind cut right through his thin jacket. He stood on the stoop for a moment, taking in his surroundings. Jamal looked in both directions and finally saw a sign bearing the name 'Meechie's Café' at the street corner two blocks to the right of his house.

He decided to walk, especially since there was no way to know if he had a car, or how he was supposed to get to work, or much else at that moment. While he devised a plan to ask the woman who called him Jamal some questions, he figured he would comply with her demand and go to the coffee shop.

Jamal started thinking like a detective. He didn't know what her 'regular' was, but he imagined that the people at the coffee shop would know him if he was a regular at the store.

He thought he might be able to use context clues and find out more about this Black guy whose life he's supposed to learn something from. Ethan figured the quicker he played along, the faster this science expirement would be over. He entered the cafe, and the bell above the door jangled loudly, announcing his arrival.

"I'll be right with you," the barista yelled out.

Her back was turned to Jamal, but he instantly took an affinity to her voice. It was the first thing he noticed. A voice that's soft, like velveteen, yet strong as coffee. He felt mesmerized by the warmth in it and how she moved as she interacted with the couple at the other end of the counter.

He was astonished as he admired her figure. She was curvy and slender. Everything was proportioned well, like a stack of flapjacks made by a grandma who knew her way around a pancake.

Just as he was admiring how everything was stacked up, she turned around. She was so beautiful that it took his breath and all his senses away. He had never seen a Black woman as beautiful as she was in all his life. She had dark chocolate skin, deep brown eyes that shimmered with a hint of knowingness, and a head full of thick curls.

"Oh, hey Jamal," she began.

Jamal was afraid he wouldn't be able to speak ever again.

"Your mom called; I've got her coffee right here," she laughed.

He was stricken by the way the light in the room seemed to cascade around her shoulders, casting a hazy halo around her shiny hair. She looked angelic, and he couldn't take his eyes off of her face, though he knew he was staring. He struggled to collect his thoughts, he couldn't focus on anything else beyond the moment he was in, including why he was blessed to come into contact with this beautiful woman.

"Umm, Hello?" she giggled, waving her hand to get his attention. "Dude, are you okay?"

He suddenly realized that it was him she was talking to and cleared his throat.

"Oh umm, yeah, thanks," he said, quickly digging through his pocket to pay for the coffee. "Hey, let me ask you something. How do you know me?"

"Jamal, you come here almost every day. What are you talking about?" she smiled. Her smile was as bright and inviting as a summer day. Jamal had never seen a smile that pretty. He marveled to himself how straight her teeth were and how each one was perfectly placed to accentuate her beautiful full lips.

"Right, Right," he said, trying to recover smoothly. "Well, what I mean is how well do you know me, and how well do you want to know me, Miss...." he quickly glanced down at her nametag.

"Boy, you are still so corny," She chuckled good-naturedly as she handed him a large cup of coffee and a small bag containing a single glazed donut.

"See you tomorrow, Tasha," he said, turning to leave.

He moved so abruptly that he accidentally bumped shoulders with another woman walking away from the other register and almost dropped his coffee.

"Sorry," he said quickly. He glanced back at Tasha, the source of his distraction, and saw that she had already gotten back to work.

Embarrassed, he realized he just made a complete jerk out of himself, and Tasha wasn't even moved the least bit.

He helped the woman steady herself and asked if she was okay. When she assured him she was fine, he left and made his way back toward the unfamiliar, familiar house.

ROSE LIVINGSTON AS LINDA REED

Rose strolled down the street on her way to work. Her mind still tried to process the events of the last twenty-four hours. In that period, she had to accept becoming someone else, and, as if that wasn't off-putting enough, she also had to embrace being Black. Her nerves had been a wreck, so she decided to duck into a quaint corner café and pick up a coffee.

As she entered Meechie's Cafe, the sweet smell of coffee and pastries overwhelmed her, and she sighed happily. In the corner of her eye, she noticed a tall Black man in uniform standing motionless in the middle of the room. She assumed he was just looking at the menu or guarding the store, so she passed him and went to the register to make her order.

"Can I get a small coffee, Black?" she said to the barista as she grabbed her wallet from her purse. A search for her debit card revealed that all her cards said Linda Reed.

"What the hell?" She took out her I.D. and was momentarily taken aback by the photo of a dark-skinned Black woman with long, dark, straight hair.

Right, she thought, as everything rushed back to her.

Linda realized that the barista was staring at her, waiting for her to pay for the coffee. "Sorry," she muttered, handing the debit card over.

She sighed, trying to imagine how the rest of this experiment would go and wondering how being stripped of everything she knew about herself would help her become a better officer.

Already, she felt so lost in this world. She was annoyed and anxious about everything, and she couldn't put a finger on why.

She took deep breaths as she tried to relax. Finally, her coffee appeared on the counter. She picked it up and was on her way out when the guy in the uniform bumped into her. "Watch where you're going, huh?" She blurted, making her way back to the register to grab some napkins to wipe the spilled coffee from her hand and the bag containing her apple danish.

"Ugh, my morning is ruined now," Linda mumbled to herself. Linda's appetite vanished as irritation bubbled up in her chest. Linda abandoned her purchase altogether. She just wanted to punch someone or go for a run, and she didn't trust herself to exercise restraint. Everything was starting to wear on her nerves.

When she arrived at the Police Department, she pushed the call button for the elevator and muttered to herself, "this is just a dream."

The doors slowly swung open, and she stepped inside. When the elevator doors closed, she saw her reflection against the shiny, silver doors. She was a tall, slim, Black woman with deep dark brown skin and long dark wavy hair pulled up into a bun. She reached her hand out to touch the reflection, awestruck. She looked nothing like herself.

The elevator doors opened to her floor, and she stepped out cautiously. She peered around the precinct as she slowly moved through, trying to see if anything had Linda Reed on it.

"Linda!" The man she recognized as her supervisor Captain Jenkins called out to her.

"You alright?" Captain Jenkins said as he stood uncomfortably close to her and placed his hand on her lower back.

Still in shock, she nodded her head slowly.

"Okay, well, then get to work," he said as he patted her back and walked away. Linda took a deep breath to calm herself as she made her way to a desk that had her new name on it.

ROBERT WHITMORE AS WESLEY ROBERTS

Robert came into full consciousness as he drove down the street in an unfamiliar car and shortly noticed in his rear view mirror that a police car pulled directly behind him. He wasn't nervous in the slightest. He hadn't done anything wrong and continued steadily driving the speed limit. After being followed for a few blocks, the police car in his rear view flicked on the red and blue lights lighting up all the mirrors in the car. Robert immediately pulled over to see why he was being pulled over.

He looked for his badge and ID and couldn't find them. He glanced over and picked up the wallet that had been riding next to him in the console. He quickly dropped the wallet as he realized his hands were no longer white. He looked again at his hands and realized he had the hands of a Black man. He nearly had a panic attack as he quickly adjusted the rearview mirror to get a look at his face. His face was also the face of a Black man. He quickly recalled Ramsey's explanation about becoming a Black citizen and was now in full-on shock and panic mode.

Robert grabbed the wallet again and flipped it open to pull out the license. As he scanned the leather wallet, he saw a picture of a Black man.

"Who the hell is Wesley Roberts?" he muttered to himself as he stared at the smiling face of the man in the picture. He was so overwhelmed with the state of shock at his new identity that he hardly noticed the two officers approaching on both sides of his vehicle. One of them knocked impatiently on the driver's side window as the other shined a flashlight into the car.

Wesley rolled down his window cooperatively and handed the officer his license and the registration that was in the glove box.

"What seems to be the problem, officer?" Wesley asked as they continued to peer into the windows of his car.

"Step out of the vehicle, boy," The officer ordered, yanking the car door open forcefully.

"Whoa, what's goin' on?" Wesley asked, bewildered.

Still, he complied, stepping out of the car and onto the road.

"Is there a problem?" Wesley asked, and suddenly his face was being smashed against the hood of the car.

"What the hell!" Wesley yelled. "I haven't done anything wrong!"

"Why are you sweating so bad and your eyes red? What kind of drugs are you on, boy, and don't lie," the officer commanded.

"I'm not on any drugs," Wesley quickly replied.

"You look nervous and jittery like you're on something." the other officer said from the other side of the car.

"I am just having a heck of a day. It would be hard to explain," Wesley said.

"You're definitely not having a good day," the first officer said.

"I haven't done a thing wrong," Wesley said even more defensively.

"Yeah, right. We know you aren't innocent," the first officer said as he reached into a hidden pocket in his uniform and produced a small bag of white powder.

"Jesus," Wesley thought to himself, a pit forming in his stomach. *"That's crack cocaine."*

The police officer sneered at Wesley and tossed the packet into Wesley's car.

"Looks like you've got some drugs on your person," the cop taunted.

The other officer pulled Wesley's hands behind his back aggressively and Wesley suddenly felt the cold metal of the handcuffs bite into his wrists.

"I'm a goddamn police officer! I have never done any drugs," Wesley exclaimed as the bitter tang of fear was starting to rise in the back of his throat.

He was growing increasingly uncomfortable as he was again shoved on the hood of his car.

The police laughed off Wesley's claim and yanked him up from the car hood, and shoved him into the back of the squad car.

EMILY CAMPBELL AS CASSANDRA ELLIS

Emily had always turned to shopping for relief in stressful situations. Today, she decided to head to the mall—specifically, the shoe department. Freshly immersed in The Decennial Program, she was still unaware that she had become Cassandra Ellis, a brown-skinned Black woman with dark brown hair that came just past her shoulders.

She selected a few pairs of shoes, piling them on top of the stool until she could try them on all at once. She set her purse and jacket down on the stool next to the shoes. As she bent down to remove her boots, she got the eerie feeling that someone was watching her. She looked around and noticed an employee staring discreetly at her from the corner of her eye. When the woman immediately looked away without acknowledging her, Emily continued trying on the shoes.

"That was weird," she thought to herself. Deciding she didn't need shoes, she put them all back and strolled over to the blouses. She picked up a beautiful frilly floral button-down blouse that tied at the waist. It had happy-looking hydrangeas all over it, and it made her think of the ones her mother used to grow at nana's home in South Carolina. Only, her mother never grew anything; she also noted that she'd never lived in, or ever visited South Carolina, so she wondered where she got that idea from.

She made her way to the fitting room and began to undress, with her back facing the mirror. When she pulled the blouse over her head, she turned to see how it looked and came face to face with her new reflection. Her jaw dropped as she moved slowly towards the mirror, touching her fingertips to the glass, unsure if what she was seeing was real. She shook her hands and breathed out slowly to calm herself as she backed away from the mirror. She tore off the blouse and quickly changed back into her clothes before dashing out of the dressing room.

Before she could leave the store, the employee that had been watching her earlier approached her. "Ma'am, can we search your bag?" the employee said, stepping into Cassandra's path.

"What?" Cassandra asked as she stepped back. She had never been asked to submit to a search in all the years she had been shopping.

"Why do you need to search my bag?" She uttered defensively.

"Ma'am, I don't want any trouble. Could you please open your bag?" the employee repeated.

She looked incredulously at the store employee and was mortified. Not only was she being detained, but she was being questioned in front of everyone. The mall was supposed to be her sanctuary and now her only refuge had been defiled.

She felt her blood rising to her face as she reluctantly showed the employee the contents of her purse and was allowed to leave the store. She sat in her car and cried for about twenty minutes before she trusted herself to pull out of the parking lot and into traffic. She knew she would be returning to a home and life that was different from anything she had ever experienced. She wasn't sure she'd be able to last in this new environment if situations like that continued.

GEORGE MCDUFFIE AS MALIK GARDNER

George McDuffie awakened to a series of shrilling beeps that were getting progressively louder. He jumped up from the couch he was sleeping on and thought to himself how strange it was that the television was still on. He never ever slept with the television on. As he tried to gather his thoughts, he desperately searched for where the beeping was coming from so he could stop it and get back to sleep.

He appeared to make even more noise than the beeping sound as he tripped over all of the toys that were spread out on the floor near the couch. As he made his way to the door, he tripped on a remote-controlled police car that he didn't see in the doorway. Once he got up from the floor, he looked up and saw the digital clock on top of the television that read 4:05 a.m.

It was dark in the house, and nothing seemed familiar to him. He began to feel like he was just in a bad dream. The beeping sound was still going and seemingly getting louder. He just wanted to make it stop. It was giving him a headache. Once he got into the hallway, he realized that the sound was coming from a room in the back of the house. As he entered the room, he cut the light on and noticed a Black kid roughly six or seven years old laying on the bed lifeless with a machine hooked up to his chest. He panicked and immediately ran out of the room, and as he got halfway down the hall, he stopped himself and turned back.

He went back into the room and checked to see if the kid had a pulse as he was trained to do. As he reached for the kid's wrist, he pulled back with a jolt as he noticed his own hands were Black, just like the kid laying there. At this point, he started thinking to himself that this went from a bad dream to a horrible nightmare. The loud beeping from the machine snapped him out of his momentary trance and back into the moment.

He felt a light pulse and realized the kid was still alive, and at that moment, he searched for a phone to call 911. He panicked as he realized he didn't have a phone in any of his pockets, so he ran back to the living room and noticed there was a cell phone lying on a stack of bills on the coffee table. He quickly grabbed the phone and dialed 911.

"911, what is your emergency," a female voice said on the other end of the phone.

"I have a kid here who is unresponsive and needs help now," George said frantically.

"What's the address you're calling from, sir?" the operator calmly asked.

"I don't' know," George said as he looked around, still dazed and confused.

"Where are you calling from, sir?" The operator repeated.

"That's the thing. I don't know where I am right now," George specified.

"Can you look around and see if you can find the address on something," the operator said, remaining calm.

"I just woke up here and..." George started before being interrupted.

"Can you look around for anything that has the address on it, is there any mail laying around?" The operator asked.

George quickly remembered the phone was on a stack of bills, and bills would have the address on it, he thought to himself. He darted over to the coffee table and picked up a large stack of medical bills that had the name Malik Gardner and an address on it. After he quickly glanced at several pieces of mail that had the same name and address on them, he figured that must be the address and promptly gave it to the operator.

"It looks like the address is 1010 Chantilly Drive Charlottesville, Virginia," George told the operator.

"We are dispatching an ambulance to your address right now. They should be there in five minutes," the operator reported.

"Sir is the child breathing, foaming at the mouth, or have any other visible signs of distress?" the operator asked.

George sprinted back to the bedroom and noticed the kid was still lying there, unconscious.

"Can you wake him up by calling his name?" the operator inquired.

"I don't know this kid. I don't know his name," George replied.

"What is your relationship to the child, sir?" the operator asked dryly.

"I'm not sure I think I might be his father," George answered.

"Are you not sure whether your his father or not," the operator asked, slightly confused.

"Look, it's complicated. I just woke up and heard this machine beeping and called 911," George fired back.

George looked around the room and saw the name Samuel on the wall above the bed where the kid was lying.

"I think his name is Samuel," George told the operator.

Just as he told the operator the kid's name, George heard a knock on the door. He ran to the front door and quickly opened the door once he saw it was the paramedics. He proceeded to show the paramedics the room where Samuel was unconscious.

The female paramedic started checking Samuel's vitals while the male paramedic went to the machine that was attached to Samuel and stopped it from beeping. Both paramedics worked on Samuel for twenty minutes and were able to revive him. They carefully placed Samuel on a stretcher to take him to the hospital for a closer evaluation.

"Hey, is the kid going to be okay?" Georg asked with concern in his voice.

"Yes, it appears that your son has Cardiomyopathy," the male paramedic said.

"Cardio, what?" George asked.

"Cardiomyopathy it's a diseased heart muscle that becomes weak and enlarged, which makes it difficult to pump blood through the body. It's also referred to as an enlarged heart. It's a serious heart condition, and unfortunately, there is not a cure for cardiomyopathy in children, but it can be treated. In severe cases like this one, a heart transplant may be necessary. If the condition isn't treated, it can lead to a life-threatening arrhythmia or what's referred to as an irregular heartbeat, which can cause heart valve issues, risk for developing blood clots, and heart failure, and in some cases death" the female paramedic explained.

"Your son has a very rare type of Cardiomyopathy. It's pretty serious," the male paramedic mentioned as they wheeled Samuel out of the house and into the ambulance.

"Okay, make sure he gets what he needs to get better," George said to the paramedics while perfunctorily waving to Samuel.

"Um Sir, you probably should be coming with us. He is a minor and is going to need someone to sign off on his care," the female paramedic mentioned.

"Oh yeah; Right. I apparently am, umm, the kid's father, so uh, let me get my phone. I left it on the table inside," George said nervously as he ran inside the house.

As George grabbed the phone from the coffee table, he couldn't help but notice the large stack of medical bills that were on the table. He picked up a stack and looked at them.

"Malik Gardner, this one says Malik, this one too, hell all of these belong to Malik. I would hate to be this Malik guy. There's gotta be over a hundred thousand dollars in medical bills here," George said aloud as he flipped through the stack of bills.

George saw a credit card and a driver's license laying out on the table and picked them up.

"Dammit, I am Malik Gardner," he said aloud as he put them both in his wallet.

"How the hell does one person wrack up all this debt?" He continued as he walked out the door and got into the ambulance.

DECENNIAL HEADQUARTERS
END OF SESSION ONE

Six hours after the first session began and each officer slowly awakened from their unconscious state, Dr. Langston and his team emerged from behind their observation booth and began to check and record the officer's vital signs.

"How are you guys feeling?" Dr. Cooper asked as she took notes on her clipboard.

Emily groaned as she slowly peeled open her eyes.

"Groggy, huh? Dr. Cooper continued. "Yeah, it'll get better."

Dr. Langston and his team pulled up a stool on wheels and joined the circle of officers sitting up in their chairs. Dr. Langston's team was poised to scribble frantically as their subjects discuss the first session of the Decennial program.

"Congratulations," Dr. Langston began. Pride and excitement tinge his voice. "You've completed your first session. How does everyone feel so far?"

None of Dr. Langston's team were prepared for the room to be completely silent. Not one participant was interested in sharing how they felt about their experience. A few more moments of silence went by before Dr. Langston spoke again.

"Robert, anything to share?" he asked. Robert shook his head before folding his arms.

Realizing that he was not going to get anyone to speak today, he moved on. "Well, if you want to complete this program, you'll need to discuss what you just experienced. We'll continue this next session. We'll see you all next month," Dr. Langston said as he dismissed the group.

As the officers filed out of the building, they began to talk amongst each other. They tell one another bits and pieces of their experiences in the program. As the group stood outside of the building talking amongst themselves, Ethan slipped away to go to the coffee shop.

He had to see if Tasha was real. He needed to know if the way he experienced their meeting in the Decennial Program was just a fluke or if she really did stir something in him. After the session, he was so used to being Jamal that he felt a bit odd, almost uncomfortable navigating the world as Ethan again, he marveled at how realistic everything was in the program. Still, he made his way to the cafe and walked up to the window, peering around for Tasha.

Ethan's eyes scanned the room, carefully surveying the entire cafe. As he searched the entire cafe he was disappointed that he didn't see Tasha and began to wonder if she was only real in the Decennial Program. He glanced through the window one more time before walking away. Just as he was making his first steps to leave, Tasha strolled past him and walked into the shop for work, not giving him a second glance. He stared at her intently, realizing that Tasha was, in fact, a real person.

He wasn't sure if she was just a part of the program if she really did exist, and if she looked the same as he remembered her.

She was real. She looked the same, too, and his heart responded the same way as it had when he met her in the program as Jamal. He wanted desperately to go in, but he had no idea what he could say to her as Ethan. Instead, he sighed heavily and walked away, still in awe of her beauty and its effect on him as both Jamal and Ethan. The feeling was no fluke.

CHAPTER 11

SESSION II. YEAR TWO

One month later as the officers entered their second session of the Decennial Program, Dr. Langston's team assisted them in putting on their headgear and adjusting their recliners. The officers were still new to the process and had yet to become fully acclimated.

Paul pulled Dr. Langston to the side to talk to him.

"I don't think I need to participate in this program," Paul began. "I get it. racism is bad." Paul voiced.

"Paul, you get to exit the program when you change your mindset on race, and one session isn't gonna solve your shitty disposition." Dr. Langston explained.

"You can't talk your way out of this one. Everything is based on science, so we will be able to tell when you've reformed your views," Dr. Langston continued.

Paul went to his chair and prepared for session II. Just as everyone was strapped into their chairs, Ethan popped up and raised his hand like he was back in school.

"Yes, Ethan, you have a question?" Dr. Langston asked as he turned to face Ethan.

"How is it that while we are in this simulation that some of the people we come in contact with are actually real people," Ethan asked inquisitively.

Dr. Langston turned and glanced at Dr. Cooper and momentarily wondered if he should actually answer the question. He was astonished to receive some feedback about how the officers were feeling about the program.

Dr. Langston turned back towards Ethan.

"That's a great observation Ethan, did you encounter someone in the Decennial Program that you know in real life? Dr. Langston asked with a tinge of excitement in his voice as he stared at his team.

"Well, I might've, I'm not a hundred percent sure, but I was just curious as to whether that was even possible? Ethan asked expectedly.

"Listen up, everyone, the Decennial Program is a simulated environment that has partly been designed by our esteemed colleague Tyrese over there. However, a large part of the program's architecture and its inhabitants are created by the collective consciousness of everyone seated in these chairs. It's much like playing one of those online video games that you play with your friends, and all of them are visible to you, and everything they do also affects you while you are playing the game; it kinda works like that." Dr. Langston explained.

"The biggest difference is the architecture of the Decennial Program stores all of your experiences in and out of the program to build a world that is evolving and changing in real-time as much as each one of you. The Decennial Program seems so real because it is made up of all of the thoughts and interactions that each group brings into it, so no two groups experience the same simulation. All of your positive and negative interactions with people and places are stored in the depths of your mind, and the Decennial program opens the pathway to explore them," Dr. Langston continued.

"Everything that happens in the Decennial Program does not translate into the real world, but everything that happens in the real world can definitely enter into the Decennial Program," Dr. Cooper chimed in.

"All of your thoughts and experiences, Ethan, can indeed impact your fellow officers that enter these sessions with you. That goes for the rest of you as well. All of your collective biases make up the world you're experiencing while inside the Decennial Program. You may find that people and places that you dealt with, in the past, may interact with you or one of your fellow officers in these chairs. So, if things seem a bit extreme in the program, now you know why. If there is a concentration of racial hatred, it is a world of your making," Dr. Langston asserted.

"Ironically, the real world is very similar. The biases that you enact on people have lasting ripple effects in the real world; each and every one of you needs to keep that in mind. Showing you that very thing, is a major part of this whole experience," Dr. Langston declared.

"Alright, everyone, take your pills, and we will see you in about 6 hours." Dr. Lanston shouted with enthusiasm. Each of the officers does as they're told, more hesitantly this time, each of them quickly fading into unconsciousness one by one.

JAMAL EDWARDS

Ethan found himself awakening as Jamal amongst the hustle and bustle on the street. The first thing on his mind was Tasha. He found himself heading to the coffee shop to see her.

Before entering the coffee shop, Jamal rolled his shoulders back and forth like a fighter about to enter a heavyweight bout. He gave himself a pep talk before entering the coffee shop to make a move on Tasha. "Alright, you can do this," he muttered under his breath as he entered the shop.

The cafe was bustling, Jamal thoroughly scanned the shop, and he noticed that Tasha wasn't there. He slowly turned to walk out with his shoulders slumped over in utter disappointment. As Jamal walked toward the front door, he heard a distinct sound coming from the bell above the side entrance door. He felt the overwhelming urge to turn around, and as he did, Tasha rushed through the door. Her voice rung out as their eyes made brief contact as she brushed by him.

"Sorry I'm late," she yelled to her manager as she hurried to her register.

Jamal smiled to himself as he approached Tasha at the counter. "Hey Tasha, how are you today?" He asked, trying to make his voice sound smooth.

"Hi Jamal," she chuckled. "Are you getting your mother's regular?" she asked, as she rang up a purchase on her register.

"No, not this time. I came in because there is something I need your help with." Jamal said as he noticeably admired Tasha's beauty.

"What do you want this time?" Tasha asked, rolling her eyes playfully.

"To take you out to dinner," Jamal said confidently.

"Nice try. You've got jokes for days, I see," Tasha said with a slight giggle. "Now, are you gonna order something or what?" Tasha clamored.

Tasha seemed uninterested, but Jamal continued to pursue her despite it.

"Look, I know you're probably tired of coffee by the end of the day. So what do you say I take you out for a real drink tonight?" Jamal asked, leaning in over the counter, attempting to get closer to her.

"Better luck next time. Now go on, I have real customers," she grinned as she brushed him off.

Jamal smiled and chuckled to himself, fighting off disappointment as he turned to leave. "Hey, at least you know I'm persistent and that I'll be back," Jamal said as he walked out the door.

He wondered if he had been completely misreading Tasha. She was smiling, flirting a little; was she willing to consider the idea of them going out together? His thoughts were interrupted when two cops brushed past him on their way into the coffee shop, shoving him back a bit.

Jamal's first instinct was to respond, but instead, he paused and waited for the officers to apologize for bumping into him. When they didn't, he furrowed his brow in confusion. The officers don't even give him a second glance as they continue to order their coffee. Jamal couldn't understand why they would be so rude for no reason. Rather than cause a scene in front of Tasha, Jamal walked away, shaking his head ruefully.

CASSANDRA ELLIS

Cassandra tapped her heel as she and her Black son Terell sat across from the white principal in his office. She stared down at the chaotic piles of papers on his desk to distract herself. She had been preoccupied, worrying about the reason she and her son were there.

The office was strangely familiar to Cassandra. She faintly remembered being there in her real life, as Emily, with her white son James. As Emily, she entered the office, confident that the principal would be ammicable to her requests. Now, as a Black woman, the atmosphere in the office was somber. The principal pushed his glasses up on his nose and cleared his throat.

"Ms. Edwards, your son was involved in a bit of a "racial" incident." The principal used air quotes when he said the word 'racial,' and Cassandra fought the urge to roll her eyes. "It seemed that another boy here in school, James Campbell, was using "racial" slurs against Terell, and it got ugly."

Cassandra wondered again why he was using air quotes but decided to brush it off. She squeezed Terrel's shoulder reassuringly, dreading the answer to her next question.

"Um, so what did James say?" Cassandra curiously replied

"What's more important is Terell's involvement." the principal interjected.

"He ordered his friends to beat James up. Now, as you know, we have a zero-tolerance policy for bullying, so we're going to have to suspend Terell for three days for inciting violence against a fellow student."

"I didn't ask them to beat him up," Terell exclaimed, almost jumping out of his chair to defend himself.

"Son, you're not making this any easier by lying," said the principal as he sat back in his chair and laced his fingers together behind his head, stretching audibly.

"Now wait a minute, Mr. Jones. There must be some way to work this out besides suspension. Besides, it's probably just a misunderstanding between peers. And Terrell said he didn't do it," Cassandra countered. "And I want to know what James said to him."

"Ms. Edwards, I don't think-"

"I would like to know," She interrupted. Cassandra didn't understand precisely why Mr. Jones seemed so reluctant to repeat what was said, but she had a feeling there was a good reason. Besides, she had a right to know why her son was in trouble. She wanted the whole truth of what happened.

"After an altercation over a lost basketball game, it was 'alleged' that James called your son a series of racial slurs that I refuse to repeat. A student overheard him saying that 'Black guys are only good for dribbling balls and target practice,'" said the principal sarcastically.

The principal used those annoying air quotes again and avoided making eye contact with either of them as he recounted the scene.

"Oh, my God," the air whooshed out of Cassandra's lungs as she sunk back in her seat. She wished she could cover Terrel's ears. Someone said those things to him, and she felt like she's failed to protect him.

"Ms. Edwards, we would like to apologize…" The principal began.

His voice trailed off in Cassandra's mind as her thoughts overwhelmed her, and she struggled to fight off tears. Her heart fell into her stomach as it occurred to her that she hadn't just failed to protect Terrell—it was her fault in the first place.

When she was in the world as Emily, she taught James the horrible things he'd said. Now she was responsible for protecting Terrell, too—protecting him from people like her other self and James. She thought back to all of the times she had used that kind of language in front of James.

Cassandra suddenly felt her mind drift back in time to being Emily. She recalled sitting in the car with James and saying some of the same things he was accused of saying to Terrell. Whenever a Black person cut her off, Emily would become even more furious than necessary. She would yell, inapropriate racial slurs at her windshield. Emily hadn't thought it was a big deal since no one could hear her. She hadn't realized James was absorbing all of that hatefulness.

She remembered the time she taught James that exact phrase he used against Terell. She was with her friends, gossiping after her husband had left. James was around seven years old then. He was playing on the kitchen floor while Emily was sipping wine and chatting with her girlfriend.

"So why don't you try dating a Black guy?" her friend questioned, bringing her wine glass to her lips.

"Why would I do that? So my son can have a dad leave twice?" she chuckled. "Black men are only good for two things: dribbling basketballs and target practice," she giggled with her friend.

"Don't forget s-e-x," her friend spelled out so James wouldn't understand.

"I can spell," James said matter-of-factly from the corner where he was playing with his toy trains.

Emily and her friend had erupted in laughter as they poured another glass.

WESLEY ROBERTS

Wesley was seated in a blue button-down shirt and khaki pants on a bench outside of the courtroom. His public defender scrambled through paperwork, trying to find his notes for Wesley's case. Wesley was reminded of Caleb, who had been his attorney when he went on trial as Robert. Caleb had at least shown a little competence.

Several sheets of paper fluttered to the ground, and the attorney dove to pick them up like a bird going for a worm. "Sorry, I'm a little overwhelmed," he said, red-faced.

"It's alright," Wesley sighed, rubbing his face. "I just wish I could have gotten a real attorney," he mumbled.

The public defender paused. "Look, I'm up to my forehead in cases," he complained. "I'm only here because you have the right to an attorney. It's not my fault you can't afford one," he looked at Wesley frankly before opening his folder. "Drug charges, huh?"

"I didn't *have* any drugs," Wesley protested. "Those assholes put it in my car. They set me up!"

"Is there any way you could prove that?" said the public defender. When Wesley didn't respond, the public defender snapped back, "I didn't think so."

"That's not fair! Isn't *your* job to prove it?" Wesley exclaimed.

The public defender scoffed. "Regardless, I think the best chance you have here is a plea deal, you have to say you were guilty."

"Guilty?" Wesley shouted. "But I'm not guilty; I don't do drugs, and I've never done drugs. You can test me; I'm clean."

"Unfortunately, that doesn't matter," said the public defender.

He leaned into Wesley and looked him in the eye. Wesley caught a whiff of the public defender's cologne and wrinkled his nose.

"Here's the ugly truth: to that Judge, you are already guilty. If you plead not guilty and still get convicted, you're going away for a long time."

Wesley buried his head in his hands as he continued to listen to the public defender.

"But, If you plead guilty, you'll get a lesser sentence, and you'll be a free man sooner," the public defender explained.

Wesley picked his head up. "So, I have to say I committed a crime that I didn't do, to get less time in prison?" he asked. The public defender nodded his head, not seeming to grasp the irony.

"That's bullshit!" Wesley cursed. "I'm innocent."

The public defender shrugged his shoulders.

"And I wish I could help, but this is the only chance you've got. I have seen many cases just like this before. It's gonna be your word against the two arresting officers, and who do you think the jury is more likely to believe?" The public defender stated in a callous manner.

Wesley scowled at the defender as they called his name for his hearing. Wesley slowly approached his seat. The

Judge addressed the court and asked Wesley how he wanted to plead.

"Guilty, Your Honor," he said hesitantly, his voice strangled. "For the record, I am not guilty; I didn't commit this crime. I am doing this only for the plea deal." Wesley voiced.

"Your honor, my client has a clean record and has never been arrested. We would like to ask the court to consider a reduced sentence from the statutory twenty years to five years for a first-time felon," the public defender said, pleading to the judge.

"Thank you, counselor. The court will consider that and, having done so, hereby sentence Wesley Roberts to be remanded for no less than a period of ten years in a federal penitentiary. Court adjourned," the judge said casually like he was ordering lunch.

The arresting officers were seated on the front row behind the prosecutor and gave each other a congratulatory fist bump. Wesley resisted the urge to wipe the smug looks off of their faces.

Wesley's mind began to run wild. *"How is ten years a lesser sentence?" He thought to himself.* Even if he had been guilty, carrying drugs didn't hurt anyone, and ten years was a long time.

His thoughts were interrupted when the bailiff approached him to take him into custody.

"I'm innocent. I was framed!" Wesley yelled as he was being dragged away in handcuffs.

"Yeah, right, buddy," the bailiff snapped as he shoved him through the backdoor of the courtroom.

LINDA REED

Linda was seated at her desk with her legs crossed, typing up a report. She was staying late at the office to try to get ahead of her workload. The ordinarily busy office space was now dark and quiet, with just her desk lamp illuminating the area around her desk. She sighed, rolling her shoulders to stretch her body.

The silence was disturbed by the sound of a door creaking open as Captain Jenkins, her superior officer, emerged from his office. Linda frowned, a pit beginning to form in her stomach.

Captain Jenkins came up behind her and began rubbing her shoulders. Captain Jenkins was a tall and heavyset man with dusty blonde hair and glasses. Linda turned her focus to her computer, staring hard at it as if it might contain the secret to making him go away. He leaned down to whisper into Linda's ear. "Stressed?"

Linda could feel his hot breath on her neck along with the strong smell of whiskey. Her shoulder tensed up as she gently removed his hands.

"Just finishing a report," she said with an awkward laugh, trying to lighten the situation.

"Why don't we go for a drink tonight?" he asked; not taking the hint, he started rubbing her back in a slow circular motion.

Linda shifted uncomfortably, trying to lean away from Captain Jenkins.

"I don't drink," she replied, turning her chair around to get him to stop. She swallowed hard. The situation seemed worse now that she was facing him.

"Linda, I'm a hardworking man, and you're a hardworking woman. We're both stressed. Why don't we relieve each other?" he said in a hushed tone, leaning down to kiss Linda.

She jumped out of her chair and shoved him away.

"What the hell?!" Linda shouted.

"Linda, cmon baby," he said.

Linda continued to back away from Captain Jenkins to escape and was stopped when she felt the corner of her desk pierce the back of her thigh. Her heart began to pound rapidly as he stepped closer and closer to her. Not thinking twice, she slapped him, hard enough for it to leave a red mark on his cheek. The sound seemed to echo throughout the empty office.

"I'm done playing games with you," he growled as he yanked her by the arm.

Linda shrieked as he slammed her face down onto the wooden desk. His palms were sweaty, and she fought the urge to gag in disgust. Instead, she kicked out with her feet as hard as she could and twisted her arm behind her to claw at him. But Captain Jenkins overpowered her. He held her down with the weight of his body as he yanked up her skirt and ripped open her stockings, seemingly all in one motion.

She began to wail as he sexually assaulted her, stripping her of whatever dignity she had. Linda's cries soon stop as she realized no one was coming to save her. She tried her best to just lay there motionless in hopes that he would finish his business quickly. Linda's mind seemed to drift to someplace far away from the precinct. Her tears fell silently down to the carpet, where they slowly vanished.

After an intense inner battle Linda reported to work as usual the next day. The office was lively and bright, the hustle and bustle of daily life continued as per usual. Everything was the same, but nothing was the same. No one seemed to notice that she existed in a completely different world now. She stared down at her desk like it was a foreign object, unsure if she could muster the courage to sit down. Everything was a trigger forcing her to relive the nightmare that she experienced at the hands of Captain Jenkins.

"Goodmorning, Linda," Captain Jenkins said casually as he strolled past her desk. Linda gasped at him, completely in shock.

"How can he be so nonchalant after what he did to me?" she wondered.

Her vision instantly blurred red tones as she watched him walk into his office the same way he did every day. She shook her head furiously. There was no way she would let him do this. Resolute, she stormed after him, pushing into his office.

"You fucking bastard, you know what you did!" Her voice cracked from the pain.

"Did what?" he raised his eyebrows at her, closing the door to his office so no one could hear.

"You're a monster!" she growled through clenched teeth.

"And I'm going to Jameson. You're going to rot in prison," she exclaimed, fighting back the tears. She felt so powerless, despite having confronted her assailant in his office.

"No, I'm not," said Captain Jenkins confidently. He leaned back, putting his hands in his pockets.

"I *am* the police darlin'. Who's gonna believe you over me?" Captan Jenkins taunted, condescension plain in his voice.

"I mean, think about it, we've seen this movie before. You were wearing a tight little skirt; it was late at night, we had a few drinks..."

"I wasn't drinking," Linda fumed.

"That's not what I'll tell them," he countered, shrugging his shoulders as if to say, *better luck next time.*

Linda's breath became shaky as she slid down the wall and onto the floor, suddenly dizzy. She realized that unless she got proof, she didn't have a case. And he was right. She'd seen this movie before. All she had was her word against his. Linda knew she wouldn't win that battle. She began hyperventilating, and her hands started shaking.

How was she supposed to come back in here day after day and pretend as if nothing happened?

"Aww, Linda, it wasn't so bad, was it?" Captain Jenkins said as he went to help her up.

"Don't touch me!" Linda screamed, exploding to her feet and storming out of the office with tears streaming down her face.

MALIK GARDNER

Malik sighed as he entered yet another bank in an attempt to get another loan to take care of his son's growing medical expenses. He was holding out hope for a possible financial breather. He had exhausted all of his savings, retirement funds as well as loans from friends and family.

He was tapped out financially. He was under extreme pressure, racing against the clock to get the money needed for a heart transplant. Samuel was on the waiting list for the operation that could possibly save his life.

He couldn't understand why he kept getting turned down. He had good credit and made a decent income. Despite the mountain of medical bills he had for Samuel, he paid them at least something every month. He'd been perfectly polite to every banker he'd talked to. They could never give him a good reason as to why they were declining his applications. He just kept seeing DENIED!

Malik decided to go a different route and apply for a loan in person at the bank he had been a member of for years. He hoped if someone could just see him as a person, a person with a hardship, maybe the outcome would be different.

Malik glanced around the large, busy bank nervously as the banker typed his information into the computer. He needed this loan to come through--he'd tried almost every other alternative he knew.

The banker peered back at him from behind the screen.

"The loan was denied," the banker stated, his voice devoid of emotion.

"Sorry, Mr. Gardner, have a nice day," the banker concluded as he stood up, turned, and walked away.

"Wait. Wait," Malik said, stopping the banker from walking out.

"Can you tell me why I wasn't approved? I meet the qualifications for this loan." Malik asked calmly.

The banker returned to his seat begrudgingly, clearing his throat as he glanced at Malik with thinly concealed irritation. Malik looked around, hoping that no one else would be able to hear what the banker was going to say.

"Let's see here...it appears that you don't make enough income for this loan, Mr. Gardner, it appears you have quite a few loans already, and your income doesn't support any more loans," the banker disclosed in a tone loud enough that Malik was sure that everyone in the bank heard him. Malik was embarrassed and now had another bruise to add to his damaged pride.

"Have a nice day," the banker uttered before looking pointedly at the door and turning his back on Malik.

Malik remained seated at the banker's desk for a moment, feeling heated and not ready to stand. His ego was crushed. Not only did he get denied yet again, everyone in the bank overheard the conversation. Malik hurried out of the bank, careful to avoid eye contact with anyone in the bank. Frustration and shame surged in his chest, stealing the air from his lungs.

As a last resort, Malik decided to visit the human reosources department at his job to see if he could secure a raise, hardship loan, or something to help his family.

He had been on the police force for ten and half years and hoped that with his tenure on the job, he could receive some type of monetary assistance. Before walking into the office, he took a deep breath. He quickly glanced at the name plaque on the door. The nameplate read Martha Marshall. As he approached the lady working behind the desk, he noticed that she was preoccupied with her computer and seemed annoyed at being interrupted by him. Malik took a moment and gathered his thoughts, reminding himself that he was there for Samuel.

"Excuse me, Maam," Malik said respectfully.

"Yes, do you have an appointment," Martha grumbled.

"No, I don't have an appointment, but I do have an emergency," Malik responded quickly with a slight smile hoping to reduce the prevalent tension.

"What's your emergency umm, Mr, umm...," Martha questioned unenthusiastically.

"Malik, Malik Gardner, my apologies. Where are my manners," Malik stated?

"My name is Malik Gardner, and I've been over at the twenty-fifth for over ten and a half years. I have a bit of a financial situation that made me look at my finances, and I realized I have not had a raise in five years, and so I was hoping..." Malik was abruptly interrupted.

"Let me stop you right there, Mr. Gardner. You haven't gotten a raise because the city council has not given us any additional funds for raises, so that would explain that" Martha declared.

"So when will they fix that? Five years is a long time, prices goin' up on everything but my pay hasn't, that don't seem right," Malik squawked.

"Well, sir, you have to take that up at the next meeting with the city council. We have no control over that. Maybe next year, you can see about a raise," she reported.

Malik frowned. He wasn't expecting to get shut down so quickly. He couldn't afford to take "no" for an answer. His home depended on him getting money--his *son's life* depended on it.

"Well, what about a promotion? You can look me up on your computer. I have a great record," Malik countered.

"Well, it looks like you are eligible to take the sergeant's exam that will raise your salary. It's being offered next week," Martha suggested.

"That sounds great. Sign me up," Malik rejoiced.

"That's right on time. My son is in need of this special medical procedure that he is on the waitlist for. It's extremely expensive, and the insurance plan only covers sixty-five percent of the operation, and I have to pay the rest upfront," Malik rambled on enthusiastically as he finally felt like something might come through for him.

"Oh, wait a minute, it looks like the deadline to sign up was two months ago. They're not taking any more applications until next year. I'm really sorry, Mr. Gardner Martha expressed heartfeltly.

"Are you for real, is there any way they could make an exception?" Malik pleaded.

"No, I'm sorry these things are set in stone pretty much. There isn't anything I can do. I really am sorry for you and your son. There just isn't anything that I can do. I don't know what else to tell you. Maybe you can borrow against your 401k?" Martha asked.

Malik resisted the urge to pound his fist on the table. It felt like the entire world was conspiring against him, and there was nothing he could do to fight it.

"I already did that to help with the machine he's using to breathe," Malik concluded in a strained tone as if he was talking through his teeth.

Malik got up abruptly and stormed out of the office. He suddenly felt like the walls were closing in on him. He was desperate; he needed more money, and he needed it quickly. Time was running out for him and Samuel.

DECENNIAL OBSERVATION ROOM

Dr. Langston leaned back at his desk, watching distantly as Dr. Cooper and Dr. Hughes walked from station to station, removing the brain monitors from each participant. Dr. Langston stared proudly as he saw that his program was finally functioning the way he always envisioned it. The participants made groggy noises and stretched as they came out of sedation.

"Welcome back," Dr. Langston said dryly. "It's time for our second discussion."

The officers gathered themselves mentally and moved into an adjoining room. The room was large; it had low lighting and chairs evenly spaced in a circle. Everyone took a seat silently. Dr. Langston surveyed each participant. Rose looked ashen; her olive skin was pale, and her dark eyes rimmed with red. The other participants appeared similarly distressed, with the possible exception of Ethan, who simply looked distracted.

Dr. Langston exchanged a glance with his team--and thought to himself, "This should be interesting."

"Remember, this is what is keeping you all out of prison," Dr. Langston emphasized in an attempt to convince one of them to speak up.

Roger slowly raised his hand to speak.

"I guess sometimes Black people do have a harder time than other people, but there is still no excuse to do some of the things they do either. I mean, there's a right way and wrong way for doing everything."

"I see, Roger," Dr. Cooper said, taking notes on her clipboard.

"Let's tweak his experience just a bit; I don't think he's getting it," Dr. Cooper discretely whispered to Tyrese.

"Wait, you all control what happens in the program?" Emily asked.

"Well, it's more complicated than that, but the simple answer to your question is yes, we can also see your journey." Dr. Langston explained.

"There are monitors in our control center that display everything that you are seeing and hearing. So we can tweak the simulation to ensure your experience is tailored to each of you specifically," Dr. Langston continued.

"So don't lie, we're like Santa, we know who's being naughty and nice," Dr. Hughes joked.

"I think that's enough for tonight; I'll see you all for your next session," Dr. Langston declared as he dismissed the group.

LOCAL BAR NEAR DECENNIAL CHARLOTTESVILLE, VA

Emily sat next to Alex and Sierra at the bar near the Decennial Program Headquarters. She'd jumped at the opportunity to go out. A few drinks would help ease the stress of her day, and maybe they could commiserate about the program.

Emily leaned her back against the sticky wood of the bar, watching George and Ethan play pool in the corner. A single light hung from the ceiling, illuminating the rough surface of the pool table. George and Ethan appeared to be evenly matched, as far as Emily could tell.

She secretly enjoyed the occasional glances she received from both of them periodically.

"I can't believe they can see everything we see and know everything we think," Emily whined as she sipped on her Pina Colada.

"I don't like it. It's just so invasive," Emily continued as she played with her straw, glancing at Alex to see his response.

"Yeah, it's not cool, but that's kind of the whole point of the experiment. And, it's what we agreed to allow them to do," Alex said, bringing his beer to his lips.

"I don't see what the big deal is," Ethan complained, leaning over the pool table to take his shot. Emily found herself staring appreciatively at Ethan's muscular back and sculpted legs.

"This stupid program isn't gonna work anyway," Ethan mumbled.

"Hey, if all I've gotta do is be a Black guy for a while to avoid prison, I'm not complaining," Ethan conveyed.

Sierra chuckled quietly as she guzzled down her third gin and tonic.

"I can't stand it. There's a million other things I'd rather do than be Black, but going to prison isn't one of them," George complained, leaning on his pool stick.

"Well, is getting your ass beat at pool one of 'em?" Ethan taunted as he sunk the eight ball.

"I do believe the loser has to buy the next round. Whiskey for everyone!" Ethan raved.

"I don't drink whiskey," Emily said, sipping her fruity drink.

"George, get this pretty lady another Pina Colada," Ethan said as he sat next to Emily. Emily smiled and bit her straw flirtatiously.

"It would be nice to have some real-life interaction with a woman," Ethan thought to himself as he sensed Emily's attraction to him.

The officers chatted amongst themselves and shared complaints about the program. As the night continued, their inhibitions lowered. Eventually, the bartender announced the last call for alcohol, and the group headed out of the bar, stumbling and laughing together.

As they left the bar, they heard a tremendous amount of commotion coming from the alley behind the bar.

"I'm not going over there; I'm in too much trouble as it is," Ethan said as he got into his Uber.

"Emily, you coming home with me?" he asked, looking at her with bedroom eyes. Emily bit her lip and nodded yes as she climbed into the SUV.

Alex started walking towards the alley when George grabbed his arm.

"It's not worth it, Alex," George stammered, slurring his words a bit.

Alex pulled away, shaking his head, and continued down the alley where he saw a Black man surrounded by a small group of drunk white men. They were shoving him around and taunting him, calling him racial slurs and spitting at him.

"Hey! Break it up! That's enough," Alex yelled as he shoved his way into the circle of men. He stood as a barrier between the Black man and the group of drunken white men. The cool air and burst of adrenaline seemed to sober Alex up instantly.

"Move out of the way, boy," one of the men slurred. As Alex glanced in his direction, he noticed the man was short with a noticeably thick neck that was bright red even in the dim light of the alley.

"I'm Officer Stiles, and I don't want any trouble, so I suggest you leave now," Alex said sternly, standing his ground.

The group of men mumbled profanities to themselves as they slowly stumbled out of the alley.

"Thanks, for jumping in like you did. I was just trying to make my way home from working a double shift and out of nowhere I found myself surrounded," the Black man said as he brushed himself off.

"No thanks needed. I did what any decent human being would've done," Alex mentioned as he shook the Black man's hand.

For the first time in a long time, Alex felt proud of himself. But that moment only lasted briefly. Alex realized he had been one of those people who tormented others for no reason. He felt a bit nauseous as he thought about all of the messed up, racist things he had ever done. He went home, resolving to be a different man. Perhaps the Decennial Program was having an impact on his thinking.

CHAPTER 12

SESSION III. YEAR THREE

DECENNIAL HEADQUARTERS

The sun was noticeably absent from the sky, and the morning was a muggy, gloomy one. The officers sentenced to participate in The Decennial Program entered the building for session III. Several of the officers were doing their best to prepare for what they knew was coming.

"For a simulation program, this stuff sure seems real," Ethan leaned over and said to Emily.

Emily nervously smiled back as she leaned back in the recliner and adjusted the chin strap on her headgear.

"Okay, everyone, make sure you take the blue pill before taking the red pill," Dr. Cooper announced to the group.

"As we mentioned in the first session, you should eat something before coming here for your session," cautioned

Dr. Langston, as he observed from his usual post at his desk.

"We have set a five-minute timer to let you know when you should take the red pill," explained Dr. Hughes.

"Before you take the red pill, make sure you are lying back comfortably in your chair. The sedative works extremely quickly," Dr. Hughes's expressed in her usual soft and relaxing voice.

She glanced down at her stopwatch to record the speed of the sedative. Minutes later, the participants were in a deep, medically-induced sleep.

"Okay, everyone, it looks like all of our cohorts are accounted for in the program. Everyone's vitals are stable, and they are actively engaged in their alternate lives in The Decennial Program," Tyrese announced excitedly to the group of doctors. "I told yall my programming skills are on-point; this looks like we're watching pay-per-view," Tyrese said jokingly.

"Alright, young man, let's see whatcha got," said Dr. Langston as the Doctors turned their attention to the monitors showing the officers' interaction in the Decennial Program.

LINDA REED

Rose inhaled. She was Linda again, walking into the office. *"You can do this,"* she told herself, squaring her shoulders.

Linda tried to avoid the gazes of her fellow officers as she made her way to her desk. Eventually, though, she caved and looked around at their faces. Was it just her, or was everyone staring at her, disgust plain on their faces?

Other officers glanced at her quickly before looking away or walking in the other direction.

The news traveled quickly throughout the precinct that Linda filed a formal complaint with Internal Affairs against Captain Jenkins. The officers who used to smile in her direction have turned their backs on her. Not only had she been alienated from her fellow officers once she filed the complaint, apparently it had been for nothing because Captain Jenkins hadn't faced any repercussions. It left her feeling alienated, alone, persecuted, and violated all over again.

Linda tried to muscle through the humiliation and the hurt, but it was a haze, circling her and following her no matter how hard she fought. She sat at her desk, moving papers from one side of the desk to the other mechanically. Linda's head felt like it was full of cotton. She was nauseous and dizzy, not having eaten anything in what felt like weeks. She rested her head on the cold desk for a moment, trying to steady herself and work up enough energy to make it to the bathroom.

She forced herself to go to the bathroom, and she splashed water on her face to compose herself. For just a moment, Linda felt better, but then she realized she'd have to return to her desk.

While staring at herself in the mirror, Linda mumbled, "I can't believe this shit. He's the guilty one, and I'm the one who is paying. Why does everyone think I did something to his ass?" Linda muttered to herself.

A tear ran down her cheek and fell into the sink. She watched it leak into the drain.

"C'mon Linda, get it together. You can do this," she said, looking into her own determined brown eyes and taking a deep breath. She reminded herself that she was strong.

She dried her hands, left the bathroom, and returned to her desk. She sat alone at the back of the room during the daily briefing. Captain Jenkins carried on the meeting like nothing ever happened, never addressing the elephant in the room.

Captain Jenkins glanced at Linda with a smug confident smile. He was feeling invincible despite her complaint, and it was written all over his face. Linda stared back, swallowing hard. He looked like he was enjoying the feeling of getting what he wanted from her. Linda wondered if he was enjoying watching everyone turn their backs on her as well. *It probably made him feel powerful.*

Captain Jenkins strolled by Linda's desk and whispered discreetly,

"You should have just given it to me and enjoyed it, and none of this would be happening."

She felt him hovering over her shoulder, and at that moment, she felt numb, paralyzed even. She felt like there was an invisible force field strapping her to her chair.

"No one is going to believe *you* over me," he snarled as he strutted back to his office. Linda hurried to the bathroom once again and heaved out the contents of her stomach.

DECENNIAL OBSERVATION ROOM

As the Decennial Program staff observed what happened to Linda on their screen, one of them breaks the awkward silence.

"Wow, That's cold-blooded," Tyrese said to Dr. Cooper. "Doc, you're the psychologist. How does anyone handle that bullshit?" Tyrese continued.

Dr. Cooper replied, "We are going to continue to monitor her mental health, and we'll include some one-on-one counseling in her sessions. Let's move on to our next subject," Dr. Cooper said softly.

"Here is screen five, and surprise, surprise. Wesley is going to prison," Tyrese said sarcastically.

"Dr. Langston, why didn't you allow us to talk to them in their psyche or something when you were developing the way we patch into their brain waves?" Tyrese asked.

"We should be able to give them some kinda heads up or something," Tyrese exclaimed. "I'm mad as hell about that bullshit those cops did to him. He may as well have not joined our program if he was gonna wind up gettin' fucked, anyway."

"Alright, Tyrese, that's enough. You know very well that we don't create their fate here," Dr. Langston declared.

"Our job is to observe, report, and adjust the program to achieve the most realistic outcomes that could lead to a change in the way they police the citizens they're charged with protecting. We can't, or shouldn't, completely alter their journey, or this whole experiment would be a farce," Dr. Langston sighed. Watching their injuries take place wasn't easy for Dr. Langston, either.

"Wesley, like many of our Black men, is going to have to learn how to survive in prison," Dr. Langston maintained.

"Let's just do our job. Please put screen five on the main monitor, Tyrese," Dr. Langston uttered.

WESLEY ROBERTS

Wesley departed the prison bus and entered the prison's processing center. He looked around, trying to take it all in. Dr. Langston's team heard him reciting in his mind, "No weakness, show no weakness."

Wesley joined ten other men in a room where the correctional officers forced them to undress. Wesley's discomfort and hesitancy drew the attention of one of the guards. "Hey, that means you too, drop 'em now; we don't have all day, convict," The guard barked menacingly.

Wesley glanced around the room, scowling. He had never gone through anything like this before, and it was beyond humiliating. He stripped naked quickly and got back in a line where they were getting checked out, one by one. "Bend over like a shotgun," another guard yelled out, "Make sure you spread em and cough," the guard announced.

"The warden doesn't take too lightly to havin' y'all muthafuckas bringing contraband up in here, so if you get caught with it, that's your ass," the guard declared.

After getting a prison-issued uniform with shoes that seem hard to keep on his feet, one of the guards started to evaluate Wesley. Wesley answered what seemed like a million questions about his physical health, mental health, and any medications he was currently taking.

Another guard walked Wesley and a group of inmates down a long cell block. All Wesley could hear was a bunch of yelling, catcalling, and whistling from the other inmates who were already in their cells. Wesley could practically feel their eyes on his back as he was paraded down the hall. The guard eventually herded Wesley and the rest of the inmates into different cells. Wesley couldn't help but feel like he was a sheep being led to slaughter.

His heart was pounding out of his chest. He was sure the other inmates standing near him could hear it. He took a rattling breath, telling himself once again to keep it together. Wesley forced himself to keep looking straight ahead, silently talking to himself, "Don't make eye contact, whatever you do, just don't look at any of them. If you don't look at 'em, you'll be okay," Wesley said to convince himself.

As Wesley got to his cell, the guard yelled, "Open 13. Alright, let's go, convict."

As Wesley walked into the cell, his knees almost buckled, and he quickly caught himself. The reality of this tiny cold room being his home now was beginning to sink in. The gravity of his ten-year sentence suddenly hit him like a brick to the back of the head, hard.

"Close 13," the guard yelled.

Abruptly, Wesley heard the slamming of the door. His breath wooshed from his lungs as he looked frantically around the cell.

"This must be what a trapped mouse feels like." Wesley *thought to himself.*

Wesley leaned back and laid down on the meager cot. The cot was so thin he felt like he was lying on the concrete floor. He could still hear the cell door closing on him, a sound that continued to ring in his head again and again until he fell asleep.

JAMAL EDWARDS

Tyrese brought up screen one and said, "Let's see what's happening with Jamal," Tyrese stated as he dragged screen one up to the main monitor.

The team watched Jamal walk by a mirrored glass window. He seemed bothered by how different he looked.

"I can't believe Black people are comfortable wearing these shitty clothes," Jamal muttered under his breath as he pulled his sweat pants up.

"I wouldn't want to be caught dead in this stuff," Jamal muttered as he walked into the mall.

He made a beeline to a store where he saw a nice pair of cowboy boots on display in the window.

"That's what I'm talking about," he said to himself.

"I'll take a nice pair of cowboy boots over these tennis shoes any day," Jamal uttered to himself.

He stood there admiring the boots, wondering why he had never seen that pair as often as he remembered coming into that store on numerous occasions.

He walked into the store, found his size boot, and sat on the bench to remove his sneakers. While he was standing there trying on the boots, a group of white teenaged boys walked by, and they began to jeer him.

"Hey man, aren't you in the wrong store? The Foot Locker is down the hall," one of them yelled. The rest of them bent over, laughing as they walked by, shoving at each other playfully.

Jamal inhaled sharply. He had seemingly forgotten he's now showing up in the world as Jamal. He caught a glimpse of himself in the mirror across the room. He observed how he was dressed, his hair neatly pulled into cornrows, and his brown skin, and realized he was out of place.

Everyone in the store looked at him to see how he was going to react. That's when he noticed he was the only Black person in the store, and a feeling of embarrassment overcame him. He hastily stuffed his feet back into his tennis shoes, leaving the boots in a heap on the floor, and walked out of the store in an attempt to not cause an even bigger scene.

As he hurried out of the store, Jamal bumped into a woman who was on her phone. She was stressed about the phone call that she was on and lashed out at Jamal for not seeing her.

"Damn! You need to watch where the hell you're going," she screamed at him before returning her attention to whoever was on the other end of the receiver.

CASSANDRA ELLIS

"My son did what...that boy did what to him?" Her face tensed up, eyes wide.

"Oh no, I am not havin' this today." She yelled into the phone, pulling it away from her face momentarily in outrage. "I am on my way there right now," she continued.

Jamal went and sat on a bench in the courtyard. He couldn't handle all these new emotions today.

The woman who just cursed him out walked over and apologized.

"Sir, I'm sorry. I'm just having a bad day," she said.

"The principal at my son's school is getting on my last nerve. My son has every right to defend himself from these white-ass bullies, but he's the one getting suspended! That shit ain't right, and I'm not havin' it, not today! I'm gonna give this white motherfucker a piece of my motherfucking mind." Cassandra said as she turned and walked away from Jamal.

Cassandra walked toward the door, saying, "Ooooh. They don't know who they messin' wit."

When Cassandra arrived at the school, Terrel and James were in the principal's office, still going at each other. It was almost like being in the twilight zone, seeing both of her sons like this, while in the back of her mind, she wondered how the program had made this possible, then she quickly remembered Dr. Langston's "collective consciousness" speech. She snapped back to the present moment when the principal barked at her.

"Ms. Ellis, we need you to calm Terrel down right now. Otherwise, you'll be forcing us to involve the police," the principal shouted.

Cassandra blinked in shock and outrage. "how could the principal *possibly* be putting this on her?" She quickly thought to herself. The boys continued to push and shove one another, and James snarled,

"You better sit down, you little porch monkey," James yelled at Terrell.

Cassandra was in shock and amazement. She had never seen James act like that before.

"James had always been a respectful kid and a respecter of other people or maybe just white people," Cassandra thought to herself. She saw James in a new light. She felt bile rising in her throat when she realized that *she* was probably responsible for his use of racially charged language. She was responsible for the painful words her white son James was spewing at her Black son Terrel.

"Now, now James, we will not allow that kind of talk in here," the Principal scolded, in a voice that suggested he was talking to a very young child who doesn't know any better.

Cassandra was silently fuming. The principal hardly reacted to James' insults, but his tone was harsh and authoritative when he addressed Terrel. With James, his voice was gentle and cajoling, while he was practically berating Terrel.

Cassandra fought the sudden urge to cry. It was incredibly frustrating to feel so powerless when it came to protecting Terrel. She was desperate, but she was at a loss for anything other than a temporary solution. Meanwhile, the part of her that was still Emily was sickened with shame and disappointment. It hurt to know that James would speak this hatefully to another person.

She forgot herself for a moment and put a hand on James' shoulder, telling him to calm down. James pulled away violently; the look of disgust on his face was like a knife in her heart.

"What's your problem lady," James yelled, "get your filthy hands off of me."

"Right, I'm Cassandra," she remembered despondently.

At that moment, Terrell jumped up, and pushed at James' chest, and said, "Say another word to my momma and see what happens."

The principal pulled them apart and had them sit in separate corners of the room.

Cassandra grabbed Terrell and clutched him close as if she could protect him from the words he's already heard. She was still torn between the boys, but Terrel needed her more now.

The part of her brain that was still Emily, at that moment, was deeply ashamed; James used that word openly as she had only used it behind closed doors.

Thinking about everything that got her to this point dreadfully hurt, Cassandra thought back to her life as Emily. If she was honest with herself, she knew that she was the reason James acted this way. She was responsible for how he saw the world.

She remembered when she sat James down when he was ten years old, and she educated him about the difference between white and Black people. It was the first time he got into a brawl with a Black kid from his class.

Embarrassed when she remembered that she told him that people would believe what he told them because he was white, especially when dealing with someone Black. "Black people are constantly creating trouble, so if you tell them that you weren't the one to start a fight, even if you might've, you will still be believed. Make sure you look innocent, and anyone will believe that you were the victim. It's just how things work," she told him.

In Emily's mind, she was preparing him for the world and how to act in it. She felt like she was doing what any good parent who wanted to help and protect their son would do. It was how her parents raised her. She was just passing it on. She thought she was giving him tools to help him deal with trouble, but in reality, she was teaching him to discriminate and use his whiteness to his advantage, and even weaponize it.

She never thought that it would come back to bite her. And she never thought about how that venomous thinking could poison the Black person on the other side.

She now saw that what she was teaching her son was that right or wrong didn't matter, just whether you were Black or white. She would constantly tell James "white is right;" it's just how God made things.

As Cassandra, she had an entirely different perspective. She now saw that when you're Black it doesn't even matter whether you are doing the right thing or not, or whether you are right; people will always perceive your actions to be bad.

How does she teach Terrell to deal with that? She now asked herself.

MALIK GARDNER

Malik was seated at the kitchen table with a stack of bills, and his phone, trying to calculate how to make ends meet for the month.

Samuel cuddled an old stuffed dinosaur as he lay on the couch watching cartoons. He was hooked up to his heart monitoring machine, which continued to beep intermittently. Samuel had become so used to the device that he no longer seemed bothered by the sound or the wires attached to him.

For Malik, it was hard to tune out the beeps; for him, they were a constant reminder that the machine was helping Samuel stay alive.

Malik rubbed his forehead in frustration as he opened yet another medical bill for his son's treatment. He checked his credit score with an app on his phone, and his credit was still showing that it was in "good" standing. He couldn't understand what he was doing wrong. No one seemed to want to lend him any money.

Malik glanced back down at the table and noticed the brochure he got at the hospital for the heart transplant that Samuel needed. A mix of rage and helplessness immediately filled his thoughts.

"Goddamn it," he yelled, banging his fist on the table.

"That's a bad word, Daddy," Samuel said through his labored breathing as he looked up at his dad with his guileless brown eyes.

The sound of Samuel's voice softened Malik. Malik sighed and tossed his phone down onto the table. He acknowledged that he wouldn't be able to fix his financial problems that night. He walked over to sit next to Samuel on the couch. He gathered Samuel into his arms and gave him a tender embrace.

"I'm sorry, buddy, you're right. I shouldn't have said that. Dad is just a little upset right now. Don't worry. I will take care of it. Let's just watch some TV," Malik said as he kissed Samuel on the top of his head.

The hum of Samuel's breathing machine beeped in the background as they continued to watch cartoons together.

BREAKING NEWS ALERT

The breaking news alert blared from the television monitor on the wall of Dr. Langston's lab, and a ticker ran across the bottom of the screen.

Tyrese picked up the remote that was sitting on the desk next to the lunch he'd been eating. He turned the volume up, causing the rest of the team to stop and look at the monitor as well.

The distinguished news announcer reported, as protests are happening all over the country, most of which are peaceful, I might add, we're beginning to see progressive action, the likes of which we haven't seen since the sixties. As Black, Brown, and White people continue to hit the streets protesting police violence against Black citizens in America we may begin to see unprecedented changes across the country, starting with corporate America. Many CEOs of major corporations are taking a closer look at their organizations and vowing to create more opportunities for minorities at the executive level."

"Lawmakers must address this public outcry for police reform and the way we police our citizens of color," the reporter continued. "These policy changes come as a result of the efforts of the Black Lives Matter movement."

Dr. Langston looked at the rest of his team and silently smiled.

CHAPTER 13

SESSION IV. YEAR FOUR

GEORGE MCDUFFIE

As session four came to a close, the group woke up slowly, each returning to reality in their own time. George huffed and yanked off his helmet. "I hate this damn thing," he said as he dropped it onto his reclining seat.

Once again, they filed into the discussion room. The chairs were neatly set up circularly.

"Gather round, everyone." Dr. Hughes began. "Take a seat; let's discuss everything."

The officers sat in a circle, not nearly as tight-lipped as they'd been in the previous sessions.

They've grown slightly more comfortable sharing their thoughts than before. Everyone, that is, except George, who sat with his arms folded, unwilling to participate. The conversation still flowed with very few silent moments.

"I've got a question," George burst out, disrupting the group discussion.

Everyone's eyes turned to George in surprise.

"Why is it that nobody is thinking about helping my guy, Malik. I mean, this poor bastard is struggling to make ends meet. He's got a sick kid who needs surgery, and insurance won't cover it. He can't get a loan or a raise. I mean, who lives like that? It's just fuckin ridiculous," George snapped.

"A lot of people live lives just like that every day, George," Dr. Cooper said as gently as possible.

"Some people have it even worse," Dr. Cooper continued.

"Yeah, right," George scoffed.

"That's not how it is in real life. This whole program is completely unrealistic! The reason Black people can't get ahead is that they don't work for what they need. But in the program, that's not the case. Malik is working his ass off and still can't catch a break," George emphasized.

"Then why do you think it is that Malik can't get ahead?" Dr. Hughes chimed in.

"You're in his psyche now. You're working hard, right?" Dr. Hughes continued.

"Damn right, I am! I'm working the hardest I've ever worked, but everywhere I turn, there's another roadblock," George grumbled.

"How can I help myself if no one is willing to help me?" He tossed his arms up in frustration.

Dr. Cooper and Dr. Langston exchanged a knowing look.

The room was silent; everyone seemed to be lost in quiet contemplation.

Dr. Langston arose from his chair, saying, "Alright, that's it for this session. I will see you all next month."

ALEX STILES

As the officers begin to leave, Dr. Langston called Alex to stay behind. The others rushed out of the door, eager to get back to their regular lives.

Alex had a confused look on his face as he stood before the team of doctors.

"Is something wrong?" Alex asked, wondering why he had to stay behind.

"We observed what happened outside the bar in the last session." Dr. Cooper said as she smiled and gripped her clipboard.

"Oh, yeah, it was nothing. I just couldn't stand by and watch. I'm sorry, I know we're not supposed to be getting into any more trouble." Alex apologized.

The doctors shared a glance and laughed. Alex's already confused look became even more puzzled.

"Alex, you have achieved personal growth. You changed the way you look at the world. That is the point of the program." Dr. Hughes explained happily.

"Officer Stiles," Langston began as he walked over to Alex.

"You have completed The Decennial Program. You're done," he said, joyfully shaking Alex's hand.

Alex beamed as he shook the hands of the rest of Dr. Langston's team.

"Thank you guys so much; You have no idea how much this has changed me," Alex exclaimed.

"I bet we do," Tyrese joked as Alex stepped out of the office of The Decennial Program and into the world as a changed man.

As he burst through the doors, Alex allowed a smile to spread across his face. At that moment, he felt like he accomplished something huge. Alex felt good inside for finishing the program. It had been a challenge, yes, but he'd meant what he told the doctors. The program had changed him. Alex wondered about what would happen to the rest of his comrades in the program. Something new was happening in his life. He was actually starting to give a shit about people, about all people, not just people who looked like him.

He realized his outlook about why things happened to Black people had changed, too. Throughout the program, he'd been able to see how many ways the odds were stacked against their success. He felt empathy for their position, and he wanted to see change.

Today, the sun was so bright. He felt he had to squint against it, but the warm rays felt great on his skin. He felt invigorated. It was almost like he was experiencing sunshine for the first time. He had an entirely new outlook on the world.

The research team wiped down the stations in the lab, calibrating the equipment and running reports on the day's session. There seemed to be an unspoken air of celebration among them. Yet, they were still going about the business of running a laboratory that was conducting cutting-edge research that could likely change the course of policing across the country. It was a big ass deal, and they knew it.

"I knew that the program would work, but still, seeing it work is amazing," Dr. Langston shared with his team.

"One down, nine to go," he grinned.

Dr. Langston was more confident than ever that the Decennial Program would be a success.

"It's just a matter of time until the other officers come around," Dr. Cooper added.

ETHAN JENKINS JR.

Ethan leaned back in his police van, monitoring traffic speed. He laughed to himself as he watched vehicles brake suddenly when they spotted the sting operation.

"Sure, it's another bullshit job, but it beats paperwork," he thought to himself.

His father had pulled some strings in the precinct, so he could at least be outdoors instead of cooped up like a caged animal.

His relaxed day was interrupted when he received a call to report to the scene of a protest.

"Not this Black Lives Matter shit again," he mumbled as he reluctantly leaned his seat up and flipped his sirens on.

When he arrived, he saw that chaos had filled the streets again. He was blocks away when he discovered he couldn't get his vehicle even close to the scene. Traffic was standing still for miles. The crowd had made barricades of angry bodies moving in every direction across both sides of the highway.

Protesters and officers shoved each other back and forth in a war for control. Ethan could barely hear his thoughts over the chants, screams, and sirens. He noticed a scuffle between a few officers and a group of protestors.

Ethan pulled out his nightstick to help his fellow officers control the crowd. Out of the corner of his eye, he caught a glimpse of a face that looked familiar. He turned to face that direction, and there she was, just a few short yards away. It was *Tasha*—the realization of her presence made him momentarily stop cold in his tracks. He felt like he had one hundred-pound cement boots on.

For a moment, he felt paralyzed; the next moment, he felt himself springing into action, sprinting over to where she was. Her petite frame was being shoved backward with a police shield, and the officer on the other side wasn't letting up. The force knocked her and the man standing next to her to the ground. The officer holding the shield stood over them and raised his weapon to strike when Ethan intervened.

"Stop! Stop!" Ethan said as he grabbed the officer's baton. "Leave her alone. I've got this one," he yelled.

The officer glanced down at Tasha and her friend before turning his back and walking away.

Ethan bent down to help Tasha up. She was thankful but confused. "Tasha, are you okay? Did he hurt you?" Ethan asked, pulling Tasha up by her hands.

As Tasha climbed to her feet, a puzzled look crossed her face. She was wondering why a cop would defend her like that. It took a moment, and then she realized what he said.

"Wait, how do you know my name?" she asked, stepping back from him, concerned. Fear was evident in her eyes, and it hurt Ethan more than he cared to admit.

"I don't know you," Ethan murmured.

Quickly Ethan realized that Tasha only knew Jamal and that Ethan was a complete stranger to her. She had no idea who Ethan was. He stuttered, trying to find the words to explain. It didn't help that, as usual, her presence left him completely tongue-tied.

"I mean. Technically no, but yes. I know you," Ethan stammered.

"You're Tasha. You work at the coffee shop. You make my mom's- I mean Jamal's mom's coffee every morning." Ethan stammered almost inaudibly.

Ethan watched the confusion in Tasha's eyes become fear as he continued to explain himself. She grabbed her friend's arm and cautiously backed away before breaking into a jog, disappearing into the crowd.

Ethan hung his head and scolded himself internally.

"How did I completely lose it like that?" He sighed.

He felt like he might have just ruined any possible chance he ever had with Tasha in real life.

ROSE LIVINGSTON

Rose knocked lightly at Jameson's office door.

"You wanted to see me?" she asked, peeping her head through a crack in the door.

He motioned for her to take a seat.

"What can I do for you?" Rose said inquisitively.

"How is that Decennial Program going?" Jameson asked, organizing files on his desk.

"Ahh, it's umm...," she hesitated, not wanting to think about her experience in the program. `She found that as long as she kept pretending as if it had happened to someone else, it didn't hurt as much.

"It's very realistic," Rose stated as she laughed awkwardly, twiddling her thumbs.

"Hmm, I might stop by there later. I wanna see how things are going," Jameson said.

He tossed some files onto his desk, huffed, and laughed.

"As if I don't already have enough to deal with around here," Jameson said.

She smiled at his joke. Rose noticed a file on his desk with the name Linda Reed, and her stomach sank. Her smile faded, and her eyebrows furrow slightly. "Is that Linda Reed's case?" Rose inquired.

"Ahh yeah," Jameson picked up the file and frowned.

"Just another one of those girls who flirt with the boss and gets mad when they make a pass. It's nothing," he tossed the file back onto his desk without a second glance.

Rose felt anger bubbling up, and tears pricked the back of her eyes. She was determined not to cry.

"What do you mean, nothing?" Rose blurted out. She was surprised that her voice sounded steady, strong, and clear.

"It's a sexual assault report, isn't it?" Rose growled.

"These things hardly stick. I'm sure the woman played her part in it. Probably thought she could screw her way up the ladder," Jameson implied as he laughed.

Rose pushed out of her chair, practically leaping to her feet.

"That man *raped* her, Jameson. Raped!" She said as she stared down at Jameson.

"I can't believe you! It's because of monsters who think like you that rapists walk around freely every day," Rose continued.

Jameson stood, baffled by Rose's response. He never expected her to speak to him that way. She stared back, taking a deep breath before storming out, ignoring his call of, "*Rose, what's wrong,*" at her back.

Rose raced to her desk and grabbed her purse and her car keys. She fixed her face, trying not to let her expression show how upset she was. She was not going to give anyone the satisfaction of seeing her cry today. She'd already done that as Linda, and it had been enough humiliation for two lifetimes.

She started the car and put it in reverse. She drove around the corner from the precinct, knowing her state of mind would not allow her to get very far safely. A cluster of trees on the very far end of the building provided enough shelter from the prying, albeit concerned, eyes of her coworkers. She cut the engine off but not the radio. Her body jerked as she sobbed as quietly as she could.

She was a mixed bag of emotions. She wasn't sure whether she was crying tears of anger, frustration, betrayal, or pain? Maybe it was all of it.

EMILY CAMPBELL

After her previous experience in the principal's office as Cassandra, Emily took a minute to gather herself before heading to James' school. She just needed to see him so her world could feel right again. She parked on the far end, closest to the Blacktop. There was a pickup game of basketball happening, so she watched while she waited for him.

The last time she was at the school was when both of her sons were involved in a racist incident. She was conflicted because she knew that Terrel was completely justified in wanting to kick James' ass. Emily finally understood the pain that those words create and the pain that James' words had inflicted on Terrell and his family.

James hopped into the passenger seat, interrupting Emily's thoughts. He tossed his book bag in the backseat before he pulled out his phone. Seeing James allowed Emily to breathe a sigh of relief, though she was still angry at him for saying the things he said.

"How was school?" Emily asked as she pulled off. James, distracted by what he was watching on his phone, didn't answer.

"James!" she exclaimed, finally getting his attention.

"I said, how was school?" she repeated.

"It was cool, but check this out, mom," James began.

"My friends and I are gonna get that son of a bitch back who got me jumped," James announced.

"Language," Emily scolded.

"And what do you mean 'get him back ?'" Emily asked.

James explained his plan to Emily.

"Terell shoots free throws after school every day at the basketball court. So, once he's alone, we're gonna give that fuckin' monkey a taste of his own medicine," James explained.

"Aren't you all teammates?" Emily asked.

Emily was frozen in shock by her son's plan. She couldn't believe that she never noticed that James was like this. James was taking pleasure in his plot to hurt Terrell. Emily felt like she must have had a blindfold on for her entire life when it came to James.

A cold fear overtook her because anything James did would happen to Terel, and Cassandra would be devastated. Emily felt like she had to respond correctly to this crisis.

"James, you can't talk like that. Terell is a person, too. Besides, I thought it wasn't his idea to jump you anyway," she said in a measured voice, looking at James out of the corner of her eye.

"You're gonna believe him over me, Mom? You know all they do is lie," James retorted, huffing.

Emily pulled into her parking spot outside of their apartment.

"Terell didn't lie, James. And If you go through with this plan, so help me, God. I'll ground you for a month." Emily said sternly, putting her foot down.

"Why are you defending him? I'm your son! You're supposed to be on my side" James exclaimed, clearly frustrated.

"I never should've told you anything. I knew you wouldn't understand," James shouted.

James quickly jumped out of the car and pulled his book bag out after him before slamming the door and stomping up to their apartment.

Emily rested her forehead on the steering wheel as she realized that she had created a monster.

ROBERT WHITMORE

Robert sat eating a bacon cheeseburger alone at a local diner when his phone rang. It was his partner Jimmie, calling him in distress.

"Robbie, hey pal, how's it going with the desk duty stuff? Jimmie asked.

"It's cool, no big deal," Robert answered very calmly.

"I didn't call to bust your balls, just had a small favor to ask," Jimmie explained.

"What's the favor Jimmie, I'm kinda busy," Robert fired back, slightly annoyed.

"Look here. I'm sitting on a bust right now. I've been tailing this sack of shit all day and finally made a move," Jimmie explained nervously.

"I was positive I had the right guy. That tough Black bastard just wouldn't admit that he was the guy we were looking for, so I took him to our spot and worked him over a bit, nothing major, but still couldn't get him to tell me what I needed," Jimmie admitted.

"So, what do you need my help with?" Robert said as he washed his burger down with a few gulps of soda, knowing he would instantly regret asking.

"Turns out I had the wrong Black guy. Anyways, I need you to cover for me and help me with this report. You were always good with writing reports. I Just need you to help me word it so that the report says that this guy was the real perp. I know I can count on you, Robbie, right?" Jimmie's voice clambered through the phone.

Robert typically would help Jimmie out in instances like this. He knew Jimmie was a bit of a hothead. As a partner, Robert never minded that Jimmie was the kind of shoot first and ask questions later type of guy. Jimmie had surely got them both out of some major jams with his tactics.

The thought of putting an innocent man in prison after what Robert had gone through as Wesley was revolting. Robert had firsthand experience with what it's like to be set up for a crime that he didn't commit. He vividly remembered the horrible feeling of being powerless and the terrible feeling of knowing that the justice system doesn't work for Black people. It is strategically set up against them. No one stepped up to help Wesley. Robert recalled that even the lawyers that defend Black people have an uphill battle, and many acquiesce to the system by convincing Black people to take a deal even when they are innocent. He remembered that Wesley only had two choices, a bad situation or a worse situation.

Robert felt if there was something he could do to prevent the same thing from happening to another innocent man, he would do it. The thought of causing a good man to go to prison didn't sit right with him anymore.

"I can't help you, man," Robert said, focusing on how it felt to be innocent but treated like you're guilty.

"I'm not gonna tell anyone, but I can't put an innocent man away. I'm sorry," Robert explained.

Robert hung up the phone before Jimmie could respond. He didn't want to be chastised or guilt-tripped for his decision. He looked at his phone for a moment, then put it back into his pocket and finished his meal. At that moment, Robert realized that perhaps the Decennial Program really might be beginning to change him.

DECENNIAL HEADQUARTERS

Pierce Ramsey, the director of Internal Affairs, stared up at the Decennial office building before entering through the double doors. He stepped into the lobby, but there was nobody at the receptionist's desk when he walked in.

"Hello, anybody here?" Ramsey called out, only to have his voice echo back.

A beautiful young woman, wearing a red suit and a very colorful and festively tied headwrap, stepped around the corner. She smiled warmly and asked for Ramsey's name as she asked him to take a seat on the leather couch that was in the waiting room. She made a quick call then walked over to where Ramsey was sitting.

"Dr. Langston will be with you shortly; he's finishing up some work. Can I offer you some water or a cup of tea? We also have croissants in the break room if you haven't had breakfast. We got them delivered fresh," the receptionist asked with a very calming and soothing tone. Her manner immediately put Ramsey at ease. He accepted a glass of water from her, returning her smile with a slight smile on his face.

Before long, she walked around the desk and led Ramsey into the large observation room. Ramsey glanced at all of the officers who appeared to be sleeping in oversized reclining chairs that were arranged strategically in a circle.

"Officer Ramsey, we weren't expecting you," Dr. Hughes said as she greeted him. "What brings you in?" She continued.

"I just wanted to see how things are going around here," Ramsey explained as he took a good look around the observation room. Ramsey was impressed as he observed the myriad of computers and electronics that seemed to line all four walls like wallpaper.

Dr. Langston walked out of the control room with a clipboard in his hands. He looked as professional and intelligent as when they met, Ramsey noted.

"Ramsey, what a surprise!" Dr. Langston voiced.

"Yeah, right," Ramsey said with a chuckle.

"I know you expected me to come to see how my men are doing, Doc., so tell me, is this little virtual reality thing really working?" Ramsey questioned.

"I'd be happy to show you," Dr. Langston said, motioning Ramsey to follow him into the control center.

Dr. Hughes guided Ramsey into the control room of the Decennial Program. He was stunned when he saw all of the screens monitoring the officers' experience.

"Well, I'll be..." His voice trailed off as he looked around in awe. Ramsey never expected the program to be this in-depth. Secretly, he didn't think the program would be run with such intricacy since a team of African-American scientists was operating it. He was a bit ashamed of himself the moment he realized that was what he thought.

"Tyrese, pull up screen one on the main monitor," Dr. Langston asked.

Jamal Edwards' experience began playing as if they were watching a movie.

"You are watching footage of what's happening, real-time, in the mind of one of our participants. The man on this screen is Jamal Edwards, a.k.a Ethan Jenkins Jr. He's had some fair development in the program," Dr. Langston reported matter of factly.

"Everyone is progressing well." Dr. Hughes contended.

"Everyone seems to be doing well, except Officer Robert Whitmore," Tyrese chimed in as he brought screen five onto the main monitor.

"He was one tough nut to crack," Tyrese mentioned as they began, watching Wesley's most recent session on the screen.

"Woah, Woah," Ramsey interrupted.

"Is he in prison?" he asked, confused.

Dr. Langston explained to Ramsey that Wesley was framed and that he was innocent. He had Tyrese pull up the archived file of the arrest and put it onto the main screen for everyone to watch. The video clearly showed the two officers planted drugs in Wesley's car, arrested him, and then made sure he was convicted.

"Wesley is experiencing an unfortunate reality for many Black men," Dr. Langston asserted.

"No, No, this is unacceptable." Ramsey huffed.

"I'm gonna figure out what the hell is going on," Ramsey declared as he stormed out of the control room and into the lobby dialing his cell phone. Ramsey was disgusted by what he just saw and was determined to launch a full investigation against the officers who framed Wesley.

Frankly, Dr. Langston and his team were surprised that Ramsey didn't know this sort of thing happened all the time. Dr. Langston and his team hoped that Ramsey was sincere and that he would make the necessary changes he vowed to conduct, but they knew better than to hold their proverbial breath.

CHAPTER 14

SESSION V. YEAR FIVE

The officers reported, as usual, to the headquarters of the Decennial Program for their mandatory monthly session. They arrived one by one, escaping the summer heat in the Decennial building's air-conditioned lobby. While they waited for the receptionist to usher them back to the observation room, they made friendly small talk amongst themselves. Once everyone arrived, they were taken to the back, where they reported to their respective stations, almost robotically. They had grown accustomed to strapping on their headgear and reclining their seats back as they prepared their minds to enter another session of the Decennial Program.

"Greetings, everyone!" Dr. Langston said as he strolled into the middle of the room.

"As you can see, there are only eight of you left in the program," Dr. Langston announced, motioning to the empty stations that once belonged to Alex and Paul.

"Officer's Alex Stiles and Paul Cooper are no longer with us; they have completed The Decennial Program," Dr. Langston continued.

"What the hell?" Robert complained.

"Well, I wanna know what it's gonna take to get me out of this damn program," Robert blurted out loudly.

"To put it simply, Officer, you have to change," Dr. Langston explained, eyebrows raised and a slight smirk on his face.

"Now, everyone, please recline your seats and begin. You know the drill. Remember, blue then red. We'll see you in about 6 hours," Tyrese announced as he began heading off to the control room.

Dr. Langston's team took their stations in the control room.

"Hey, let's pull up screen five first," Dr. Langston said to Tyrese.

"I wanna see how our friend Wesley is doing."

WESLEY ROBERTS

The echo, of clamoring chatter, of hundreds of inmates, bounced off the concrete walls in the prison cafeteria. Wesley's face turned up in disgust as an older man working in the cafeteria slopped a spoonful of a brownish-gray substance onto Wesley's metallic lunch tray.

"What is this?" Wesley asked scornfully, not recognizing the pungent odor.

"Meatloaf," the server responded dryly.

"Next!" The server snapped, motioning for the next inmate in line and sending the message to Wesley to keep the line moving.

Wesley glanced around the packed cafeteria, searching for an empty table where he could sit.

Wesley purposely stayed to himself while he was in prison. He didn't have any friends and was not interested in making any. It was still a very uncomfortable place. Prison was a place you never allow yourself to get used to. Wesley knew that in prison, the moment you let your guard down will most likely be the instant you find a shiv in your back. Wesley noticed an open seat at the far end of the cafeteria and began to make his way to it.

As Wesley sat down, he gets shoved against the wall by a large, tattooed White guy, causing Wesley's dinner to splatter all over his clothes and the wall as the tray crashed to the floor.

"Look, man, I don't want no trouble," Wesley said as the man inched closer to him. *Shouldn't a guard be stopping this?* Wesley wondered distractedly.

"This is my section. You can't sit here unless I give you permission, and I don't recall doin' that," the man drawls.

Wesley couldn't help but notice the inmate's horrible breath. It was like he ate a fresh ass-sandwich right before coming over. At that moment, Wesley struggled with, which was worst, the inmate's ghastly breath or the sharpened toothbrush he felt being pressed into his abdomen.

"Any commissary you get goes to me," the inmate mumbled as he pressed the shiv deeper into Wesley's abdomen, almost breaking the skin.

"Aye, go on somewhere with all that, Tank," another inmate yelled as he and a large group of inmates approached Wesley and the inmate who had him pressed up against the wall.

Tank lowered his shiv and bucked at Wesley, making Wesley flinch before walking off. All the air whooshed from Wesley's lungs. He hadn't realized he'd been holding his breath in fear.

"I'm Tre. That's Tank. He's all talk. He won't do shit." Tre said.

"Imma put you on game real quick cuz if you don't find some people, you gon get killed in this muthafucka." Tre warned as he helped Wesley pick his tray up from the floor.

"You mean, like a gang?" Wesley questioned, cringing as he wiped the spattered food off of his jumpsuit.

Tre laughed. "Yeah, like a gang, you can ride with me and mines," Tre said, motioning to the group of men behind him.

As Wesley looked at the group of men, he observed that each man looked more intimidating than the one in front of them, with the meanest looking one standing at the back of the bunch, like a bouncer at a nightclub.

Wesley swallowed nervously. He didn't want to join a gang. The last thing he wanted to do was get himself into any more trouble, but the thought of what might happen to him if he didn't have protection was enough to change his mind.

"So what I owe you sumthin, 'cuz I aint down with that," Wesley expressed in his best authoritative voice.

"Naw some cats looked out for me when I did my first bid up north. I'm just payin' it forward on some serendipitous shit, ya feel me?" Tre fired back.

"Okay, cool. Call me Wes," he uttered, immediately unsure of his decision.

Wesley finished wiping himself off then joined Tre and his gang at their table.

"Oh my goodness," Dr. Cooper commented while watching the main monitor.

"Y'all are putting Robert through the wringer," she giggled.

"He needs it," Dr. Langston said as he took notes on his clipboard. "Otherwise, he won't learn," Dr. Langston continued.

"Tyrese, pull up Malik on screen three. I want to see how he's progressing," Dr. Langston commanded as the team continued to observe the monitors in the control room.

MALIK GARDNER

Tyrese put Malik's experience up on the main monitor, and Dr. Langston leaned back in his seat to observe.

Malik struggled up the stairs to his home. His legs and back were aching; Samuel was asleep in one arm while the other arm struggled to carry Samuel's breathing equipment. The porch light was out, leaving a street lamp as the only source of light. When Malik finally reached the door, he sat the breathing machine down and patted his pockets, searching for his keys.

"Aha," he whispered as he pulled them out of his back pocket to open the door.

"What the hell?" he muttered as he jiggled his key in the lock. He huffed as he tried another key.

"Come on," he grumbled in frustration as that one didn't even fit into the lock. He knew he was tired, but it didn't make sense that none of his keys worked.

That's when Malik noticed that there was a letter taped to his door. The letter was a drab yellow color, making it almost unnoticeable in the dark. Malik squinted his eyes to read the letter, murmuring the words as he read them.

"Eviction notice."

Malik's heart crashed to the floor, and a rush of emotions immediately flooded his mind.

"This can't be happening, not today, not right now," Malik scoffed.

He struggled to remain upright, staring at his home outside in the dark, holding his sleeping child. Rage and frustration rose in him like a volcano. And most of all, utter shame. He wondered how he would explain to Samuel that they don't have a home anymore. Malik sat on his steps for a moment and let out a silent tear as he rubbed Samuel's back.

Resigned, for now, he descended the steps, opened the back door of his 2005 Honda Civic, and placed Samuel back in his booster seat.

He tried his best to think of what to do next during the short drive to his ex-wife's house. They exchanged a few pleasantries as she scooped Samuel out of his arms, took him inside, and laid his sleeping body on the couch. When she returned moments later, she hugged Malik and told him that it would be okay. She attempted to console Malik, but the moment just felt awkward. She knew he was a good man and that he was doing the best he could.

They sat and talked on the steps for a few more minutes, then Malik stood, hugged her briefly, and got back in his car.

Malik swallowed his already damaged pride and called his best friend, Julian, and asked if he could sleep on his couch for the night. Malik spent the next few hours on a hardened and stained futon staring up at the ceiling fan. For so many reasons, it was going to be a sleepless night.

The following day, Malik was the first person in line when the welfare office opened.

His eyes were bloodshot, and he had slightly darkened circles around his eyes from exhaustion. Malik waited for over an hour before any caseworkers were able to meet with him. As he sat across from the caseworker's desk, Malik anxiously tapped his foot as he waited to hear about his medical assistance and emergency housing application.

"I'm sorry, Mr. Gardner," the caseworker began.

"Your application for assistance has been denied. I'm afraid you make too much money to qualify, even for emergency funds," she said, pushing her glasses up on her nose.

Malik let a sinister chuckle rise from deep within himself. He sat there, in disbelief, shaking his head. He pondered on how this woman could fail to see the irony of his situation.

"You're kidding me, right?" he asked, a slight smile pushing its way onto his face.

Apparently, his anger manifested itself as humor.

"I make too much for emergency relief? That's funny; because I don't make enough to get a loan to pay for the surgery my boy needs. I work and pay my taxes every day. How can I make too much money to qualify but not enough money to pay for anything else I need? Miss, do you know I was just evicted from my home? I don't even have a place to live anymore," Malik growled.

"I'm sorry," she said as she reached into her desk drawer and grabbed a worn pamphlet. The pamphlet displayed the sliding scale matrix they used to determine income eligibility for assistance. As Malik glanced at the pamphlet, he just felt himself getting angrier.

"It's pure bullshit!" he snapped, finally releasing his rage.

He stormed out of the welfare office, causing bystanders to stop and stare. When Malik reached his car, he got in and slammed the door. He punched the steering wheel, causing the horn to let out a loud beep in the middle of the parking garage.

LINDA REED

On the way from the garage to the precinct, Linda gripped her pepper spray tightly. She started carrying it in her hand, wherever she went, since the incident with Captain Jenkins. The small canister gave her a sense of feeling protected. Although the can was small, the sense of security it provided her had been invaluable.

She still found herself jumping at the sound of someone setting their car alarm in the garage. She had been on edge since the day Captain Jenkins assaulted her. She no longer felt safe anywhere. On top of feeling unsafe at work, she also felt like an outcast.

Ever since she filed a sexual harassment case against Captain Jenkins, her fellow officers had treated her with hostility and distrust. Worst of all, she had to bear witness to how he seemingly was unaffected by the allegations. He continued to waltz around the office like it never happend and was never held accountable for what he did. He lied about the entire incident, and his story was believed, and nobody believed her.

As the elevator doors opened on her floor, Linda reluctantly stepped out and walked to her desk. It was not easy to walk through a room full of people who think you are a liar.

As Linda sat her bag down at her desk and began to gather her thoughts, strategizing for the day's tasks, Captain Jenkins casually walked by her desk.

Linda felt a combination of rage and shame overwhelm her as he leaned in close.

"Hey, Linda. Looking good today," he smirked condescendingly and walked away.

Linda closed her eyes and let out a deep breath. All of a sudden, she got a boost of courage. She was done feeling like a powerless little girl. She felt someone should be feeling afraid and uncomfortable here, but it certainly shouldn't be her.

In that moment, she knew what she had to do. She got up from her desk abruptly and walked past the captain's office with her head held high. She rapped an urgent staccato against Jameson's door before stepping inside.

Jameson looked up at her and said, "What do you want, Reed?"

The feelings of confidence and surety that filled Linda a moment ago abandoned her. Her mind wanted to command her to leave, but her legs just wouldn't cooperate. As she realized that she was still there, and the captain deserved to pay for what he did, she blurted out.

"Commissioner, I can't sit here anymore and be harassed by that man. He rap..."

"Geez, Linda, do we have to go through this now? We've got Internal Affairs looking into your allegations, but it takes time," Jameson interrupted.

"Jenkins told me that you would be in here sooner or later to lodge another complaint. How long are you gonna sing this song, Linda? False allegations can ruin a man's career." Jameson scolded.

"Sir I-" she began.

"I like you, Linda. You're a good officer. Let me give you some advice. Don't flirt with the boss. It makes everything messy." Jameson interjected. His voice was condescending and dismissive.

Linda stood abruptly, shocked by his words. All the courage she had continued to melt away with every word Jameson said. She swallowed her frustration as Jameson continued to scold her. In her head, she kept repeating, "Don't cry. Just don't let him see you cry."

"You're making your fellow officers in the precinct uncomfortable, so I'm gonna put you on traffic duty until we can resolve your case. That way, you won't have to be uncomfortable around Captain Jenkins, and he won't be uncomfortable around you; it works for everyone concerned," he said as he tossed Linda a yellow and orange reflective vest.

Linda paused for a moment, processing what she had just heard.

"I'm getting demoted?" she stammered in disbelief.

"No, no, no, this is just temporary until things blow over. That way, you don't have to work with the captain. He doesn't have to work with you. everybody's happy." Jameson said as he ushered Linda to the door and out of his office, shutting the door in her face.

Linda stood staring at the door for a moment. She could feel the eyes of every one in the office glaring daggers into her back. She was in utter shock at the realization that this bad situation seemed to keep getting worse. She felt completely numb as she collected her things from her desk and headed towards the elevator, traffic vest in hand.

She now knew how it felt to be victimized further when no one believes you. It is far worst than the initial violation. She was even more convinced that when someone commits a wrongdoing, there is always hope that justice will prevail until it doesn't.

Linda began to realize just how damaging some of the reports she filed as Rose really were. She realized how she easily discredited the word of Black people frequently, so much so that it became habitual. As Rose, she was notorious for taking the word of a white person over that of a Black person. The perception was strong that when a white person, especially an officer, makes a claim against a Black person, it will always seem more credulous.

As Linda passed Captain Jenkins on her way out, he whispered, in a barely audible voice, "I like orange on you. Very sexy."

As the elevator doors closed, she let a tear fall from her eyes as she covered her face with her hands.

"That's one sick, twisted son of a bitch!" Dr. Hughes said, watching Linda's monitor in disgust.

"I can't watch this anymore; change the main monitor, please, Tyrese," Dr. Hughes pleaded as she looked down at the charts in her hand.

"You got it. Screen four coming up," Tyrese uttered as he brought the image of Cassandra Ellis onto the main monitor.

"Look, Sarah, it's just a basketball game," Tyrese said gently, nudging Dr. Hughes. She rolled her eyes and observed the monitor, still unsettled from Linda's experience.

CASSANDRA ELLIS

The gymnasium was packed full of screaming fans from the floor to the top of the bleachers. Terrell and James' team had made it to the State Championship game. If they won this game, it would be the first championship victory for their school in over ten years. The crowd roared as the score of the game got closer and closer. The opposing team had a commanding lead almost the entire game, but as the time was winding down, the lead was cut down to four points. Cassandra cheered Terrell on from the stands as he scored the three-point shot that edged them closer to victory.

The game came down to the fourth quarter with only fifteen seconds on the clock, and Terrell and James' team was down by one point. The coach called a timeout, and the boys huddled in a circle. They were out of breath and dripping with sweat. It had been a tough game for both teams. Cassandra was happy to see the boys playing together. One of the starters got injured at the beginning of the fourth quarter, and this was the first time James had been off the bench the entire season, and he had been playing well. The coach told all of the players to get the ball to Terrell. Terrell was the team captain, and he was the best shooter on the team.

The players went back to the court, and the clock started running. The ball got passed around before finally making it to Terrell. Terrell was getting double-teamed with only eight seconds left on the clock, and he didn't have a clear shot.

His eyes darted around the court, looking for an open player. The only player open was James, mainly because it was well known that he wasn't a good shooter. Terrell struggled internally with what to do. Should he pass the ball to the white kid who wasn't very good and who tormented him for being Black, or should he just take the shot and possibly have it blocked? With three seconds left on the clock, Terrell threw the ball to James, who was so surprised that he almost didn't catch it. James took a jump shot and launched the ball towards the hoop just as the buzzer rang.

Everyone in the gym held their breath as the ball flew through the air, seemingly in slow motion. It rolled around the rim of the hoop twice before falling in, securing the championship title for the team. The crowd erupted in celebration as the players ran towards each other to celebrate. James and Terrell shared a high five as they celebrated their victory. Cassandra jumped up and down on the bleachers as the players lifted James into the air, praising him for making the winning shot.

After all of the game's excitement settled, James walked behind the bleachers to call his mom. James waited for her to answer, excited to tell her about his game-winning shot. His excitement faded as the call inevitably went to voicemail.

"Hey, mom," he began leaving a voicemail, sounding slightly disappointed.

"Good news, we won the championship. And you'll never believe it: I made the game-winning shot!" he said.

"Anyways, I can't wait to tell you about it. Call me back. Bye."

Terrell had overheard the conversation from where he sat on the bleachers. He peered around the corner to see James looking down at his phone.

"Hey," Terrell called to James hesitantly.

"You wanna come over to my house? We can play 2K. My mom's making dinner." Terrell offered kindly.

Cassandra's heart warmed with pride. Terrell was seeing the James she recognized.

"Uhh yeah, sure," James replied. His tone made it evident he felt sorry for the way that he treated Terrell before.

When they arrived at Terrell's house, they both headed straight to the couch to play video games on the TV.

Cassandra watched them from the kitchen while she cooked dinner on the stove. It warmed her heart to see them getting along. Once dinner was ready, she called them both to the table.

"For my state championship winners," she said happily as she served them each a big plate of spaghetti and meatballs.

"Thanks, Mom," Terrell chimed as he dug into his food.

"Yeah, thank you, Ms. Ellis," James added, twirling his spaghetti onto his fork.

"Aww, you're welcome," Cassandra said happily.

The three of them sat together and ate, chatting idly.

Cassandra couldn't help but smile as James and Terell talked excitedly about the highlights of the game. After a while, Terrell excused himself to go to the restroom, leaving Cassandra and James in awkward silence.

James looked down at his plate and pushed his meatball around his plate with his fork. Cassandra cleared her throat and took a sip of water, not knowing what to say to James.

"Ms. Ellis, I'm sorry," James blurted out, breaking the silence.

"I never meant to hurt Terrell or anything. I just-" he paused, trying to find the right words.

"My mom always taught me that people like him- Black people- I mean," James stuttered as he tried to talk.

"She always said that they were lazy and violent and just bad people."

Cassandra hung her head, knowing that it was her, as Emily, who taught him these things.

"It's okay, sweetie," she began, thinking long and hard about what James had just said. She wondered if maybe this was a chance to make up for some of the wrongs she taught James.

"Sometimes, we make mistakes, and we judge people without knowing who they are." Cassandra expressed.

"Well, my mom was wrong," James said apologetically. A moment later, Terrell returned from the bathroom. Cassandra discretely wiped a tear from her eyes.

"How about we celebrate you boys' win with some ice cream!" she exclaimed and allowed a smile to cover her true emotions.

"Cmon, grab your jackets!" Cassandra announced as she got up from the table.

JAMAL EDWARDS

Jamal strolled down the street, passing an ice cream shop on his way to the cafe. He saw Tasha sitting at a table near the window and smiled before entering.

"Hi, pretty lady," he said flirtatiously as he walked up to the table to greet Tasha.

"Hi, Jamal," she chuckled softly, and then quickly, her smile faded from her face.

"What's wrong?" Jamal asked, sliding down into the seat across from her.

"It's nothing, just something weird happened, and I can't stop thinking about it," Tasha confessed.

"You can talk to me if you want, Tasha. I promise, no flirting, just listening," he said, putting his elbows onto the table.

"I'm all ears," Jamal continued anxiously, waiting for what she was about to say. He was extremely content just being in her presence and was totally happy that she wanted to talk to him at all.

She glanced up at him and smiled a bit before opening up.

"I was at a rally, and these cops started harassing my friend and me. I got pushed to the ground, and one of them raised his nightstick to hit me, and out of nowhere, this other cop jumped in and stopped him," Tasha explained.

"Well, that doesn't seem so weird," Jamal commented.

"It was a white cop, and he knew me by name," she stressed.

"Then he started babbling about how I make coffee and how I make your mom coffee," she continued.

"It was the creepiest thing ever. He's probably some wacko stalker serial killer or something. You know most serial killers are white men," she joked.

"Maybe he just knew you from the coffee shop," Jamal suggested, maintaining a calm demeanor though he was freaking out internally. He couldn't possibly tell her that it was really him.

"Or maybe he knew me. The man did save you. It sounds like he might have a crush on you. You probably made him nervous," Jamal mentioned trying to ease her anxiety about the situation.

"Oh yeah, right," she laughed. Jamal thought her laugh was maybe the most beautiful sound he had ever heard.

"I'm just saying he'd be crazy not to have a crush on you. I mean, look at you. You're beautiful. You're kind, your eyes are just--wow, And you're obviously smart— because you're gonna let me take you out," he said, looking deep into Tasha's eyes.

"Hey, you said no flirting!" Tasha said with a burst of girlish laughter.

"But, thank you, Jamal," she reached across the table and grasped Jamal's hands, her small hands seemed to be completely enveloped in his larger hands.

"I've gotta go; my break is over," she said abruptly, once she realized what she had done. Nonetheless, she let her hand linger in Jamal's for a moment. Jamal couldn't wipe the smile off of his face. He felt like he had just won the lottery.

His eyes stayed glued to her tiny frame as she walked away. Jamal couldn't help but admire how curvacious her body was as she glided across the floor. Tasha turned back and smiled at Jamal before exiting the ice cream shop. Her smile ignited sparks of hope in Jamal's heart. Albeit, a small gesture, he felt like they just shared a genuine moment and couldn't help but feeling like he was getting closer and closer to Tasha.

CHAPTER 15

SESSION VI. YEAR SIX

DECENNIAL HEADQUARTERS

A strange sound interrupted the team as they entered the lab and prepared each station for session six of the Decennial Program. It was a ringing sound coming from the lobby area.

"What's that ringing sound?" Dr. Langston asked Tyrese.

"Doc, I believe that's the front door buzzer," replied Tyrese. The Decennial Lab was off the beaten path, hidden from the street, and was not prone to guests.

"Well, no one else knows we're here. Everyone on the schedule is already here," Dr. Langston replied, his voice tinged with suspicious concern.

"Did you order carryout again, Tyrese?" Dr. Cooper chided.

Before Tyrese could answer, the bell rang again.

"Tyrese, find out who that is, and it better not be food! We've got work to do here." Dr. Langston growled.

"Well, now, let me pull up our security cam and take a look, but I didn't order--" Tyrese shot back.

He interrupted himself when he saw who was standing outside their lab,

"Uh Doc. you're not gonna believe this, you need to check this out. I didn't know we had a site visit today," Tyrese exclaimed.

Dr. Langston walked over to the screen and saw Jameson, Pierce Ramsey, and three other decorated officers standing at the front door.

"I don't believe this, not again," Dr. Langston sighed.

"Buzz them in, Tyrese. Let's make this quick; we're on a tight schedule," Dr. Langston huffed.

The receptionist let Jameson, Ramsey, and the rest of the officers into the building. Dr. Langston's team kept the doors locked after the first unscheduled visit so that their work didn't get interrupted.

As Jameson entered the observation room with the rest of the officers, he looked around and then looked directly at Dr. Langston and said, "Fancy digs you have here, Doc How are you guys paying for all of this?"

"We have several funding sources for our research," Dr. Langston snapped.

"I'm sorry, Jameson, we don't have a lot of time for this. We have a tight schedule. In fact, we kinda need to know when you boys are planning to stop in from now on, so we can plan our time more efficiently," Dr. Langston expressed.

"Yeah, we have to initiate our session promptly within the next ten minutes. If we're off by even a minute, catastrophic things could happen to our subjects, and we don't want to fry the brains of a couple of abusive cops, do we, Commissioner?" Tyrese said sarcastically.

Ramsey interrupted, frowning. "Whoa. Come on, everyone, this is a friendly visit. We just want to see how your research is going."

Ramsey casually walked over to Dr. Cooper, the behavioral psychologist, hoping to get more cooperative information.

"Can you tell me if the program is working? I'm intrigued, don't get me wrong, but is your research changing the way these officers really think?"

Dr. Cooper responded, "Why don't you take a look for yourself?"

Ramsey peered into the observation room. The officers were being strapped into the chairs, but two seats were conspicuously empty.

"Wait a minute. Didn't you start with ten officers?" Ramsey asked with concern in his voice.

Dr. Cooper responded in her usual calm demeanor, "Yes, Alex Stiles and Paul Carter both have completed the program. Some people respond quicker than others; in fact, unconscious bias is one of those things that affect everyone differently. You never know what situations will trigger a true and lasting change in the way someone processes bias. The Decennial Program creates a simulation that forces our subjects to face their biases up close and personal. It appears the best way to change someone's perspective is to allow them to experience situations they have only viewed one way, from the other side. It gives them an opportunity to see that same situation as if they're looking in a mirror. It's really not scientific at all. In fact, it's just good ol' fashioned empathy, and that's something any one of us can choose to employ without all of the fancy gadgets here in our lab. Once given a different perspective, people tend to change; or as the saying goes, unless you walk a mile in someone's shoes, you will never really know what their journey is really like," Dr. Cooper expressed.

A ringtone blared from Ethan's phone and interrupted the preparation protocol.

Dr. Langston quickly hit the intercom, which projected his voice into the observation room.

"I know we told you guys to turn off your phones when you enter the observation room. Do it. Now! We can't afford any more delays whatsoever today," Dr. Langston said, his voice an angry rasp.

Ethan got up from his chair to answer his phone, "I have to take this. It's my father, you know, the police Captain?" Ethan said sarcastically.

Dr. Langston walked into the observation room, furious. He thought to himself, "This idiot was not only putting his own safety at risk but the efficacy of the whole program."

"Listen, you asshole. I don't care if it's the Pope himself; if you're not in your chair when the system engagement starts, we're not sure what will happen. This is the last thing we need, especially with this goon squad showing up unannounced," Dr. Langston bellowed, referencing Jameson and his team.

Ethan had already answered his phone, as Captain Jenkins' voice emanated through the receiver, loud enough to be heard by everyone in the observation room.

"Are you done with that bullshit program? I need you to get back to doing some real police work," Captain Jenkins bellowed.

"Dad. Th-This is not a good time," Ethan responded; glancing around the room, he noticed everyone's eyes were on him.

"I gotta go," Ethan muttered.

"I told you that program would be a bunch of bullshit; it has no chance of changing anyone," Captain Jenkins barked.

"Surprisingly, the program has been a bit helpful," Ethan replied sheepishly, surprising himself. He glanced at Dr. Langston's face, which was still drawn with anger.

"Don't let those Nigg-- I mean, Black's brainwash you into being weak like them," Captain Jenkins hissed.

Ethan felt the blood rush to his face, and he knew he probably looked like a tomato. Instead of arguing, Ethan mumbled, "I'll see what I can do to get out of here. I really gotta go," Ethan thundered as he hung up the phone abruptly.

Dr. Langston broke the awkward silence by saying, "Well, that was an interesting call, to say the least," in a sharp, sarcastic tone.

"I'm sorry, my dad just gets worked up sometimes," Ethan said, feeling obligated to defend his father, though he wasn't happy about it.

Tyrese blurted out, "Is anyone gonna address the elephant in the room? I could've sworn he used the N-word."

"Man, I'm about to turn his headgear on air-fry and see how he feels about us then," Tyrese mumbled to himself.

Dr. Langston yelled out, "Alright, alright, everyone. We have a schedule to keep. Tyrese, let's get this sequence initiated."

Dr. Cooper walked over to Ethan and quietly asked, "How are you going to handle that situation? Because you do know what happens to you if you don't complete this program, right?" She asked in a genuinely concerned manner.

"Yeah, I know. Look, I've got it under control. Let's just get this session over with," Ethan responded, anxious to be anywhere except where he was right then.

Tyrese started the sequence and counted down out loud, "threeeee, twooooo, oneeeeee, rock-a-bye baby. Elvis has left the building."

The officers all fell into a deep sleep, and session six began.

Ramsey motioned to Jameson to come into the control room. "Jameson, this is the case I brought you down here to see, Ramsey urged.

"Dr. Langston, can you show us the guy that ended up in prison? What was his name?" Ramsey made hand gestures as he struggled to remember the officer's name.

Dr. Langston interjected, "The young man's name is Wesley, Wesley Roberts."

"Jameson, what do you plan to do with cops on the force who are planting evidence on civilians? They're out here 'hookin and bookin' Black men for no reason other than being Black?" Ramsey asked, putting Jameson on the spot.

Ramsey was revolted that Jameson would tolerate such behavior on the force, but he wouldn't put it past the man to be willfully ignorant.

"Whoa, now, I don't buy that. I find it hard to believe that my men would do something as despicable as planting evidence, and frankly, I don't take too kindly to accusations like that, Ramsey," Jameson growled.

Dr. Langston chimed in, "It's sad but true, Sir."

"We captured the entire incident. Tyrese, please pull up that footage from screen five for these fine folks." Dr. Langston continued.

Jameson and his team began reviewing the footage on Wesley and his arrest. Ramsey was relieved to see outrage on Jameson's face.

"Who are those cops?" Jameson asked angrily.

One of the Lieutenants with them said, "That's Roswell and Norberg sir, I believe they are from the 57th precinct."

Ramsey jumped in, "We have several complaints in our office from that precinct." He turned to Jameson, "We need to handle this right away. Cops like those two give good cops a bad name. I'm gonna have my office launch a full investigation on those two."

Jameson was speechless as he watched the footage.

"Well, if you think that was something, you might want to check this out," Tyrese uttered to the group. Ramsey asked Tyrese to put the live feed from screen five onto the main display for everyone.

WESLEY ROBERTS

Welsey was being pushed and shoved between two members of the Aryan nation like he was a ragdoll.

"Look, monkey, next time you decide to take a stroll in our part of the yard without payin' your toll, ya gonna end up in the infirmary. Keep your Black ass where it belongs," one of them yelled as he delivered a devastating blow to Wesley's stomach.

All of the air in Wesley's lungs quickly disappeared as Wesley fell on one knee, gasping for breath.

The shorter inmate reached in his back pocket for his shank, but before he could grab it, he noticed a large group of Black guys approaching them from across the yard. Before they reached the scene, the taller inmate punched Wesley in the jaw, dropping him to the ground and the two of them took off in the other direction.

Tre reached Wesley first. He extended his hand to Wesley, helping him up from the ground. "Hey man, you cool? It looked like they was about to whup that ass," Tre mentioned.

"You lucky you one of us now. Man, I told your silly ass about watching where you go around here. There's rules to this shit; you better get hip to the game, or it ain't gonna be good partna," warned Tre.

Wesley dusted himself off. "I can handle myself," Wesley said indignantly, temporarily forgetting that he's not Officer Robert Whitmore anymore. As he walked away, he began to realize that even outside of being an officer, he never had to fear white guys. And he never would've imagined in a million years being rescued by a group of Black guys, and some of whom he might have been responsible for putting in prison in the first place. That realization made it feel like the world was tilting on its axis, and everything was upside down.

As Welsey returned to his cell, he had flashbacks of his life as Robert.

He began to feel the weight of the tug of war that had been happening inside of his head.

He found himself struggling to feel comfortable. It was beginning to become apparent that everything he's been taught and believed about Black people was inaccurate. Something about being in a Black body felt awkward and inauthentic to him, but he had no way of knowing why he felt that way as Wesley. It felt as if he was living as a Black man while thinking and feeling like a white guy on the inside—and he struggled to reconcile the two identities in his mind.

He began to realize that he never really even tried to get to know a Black person before. Before now, the thought had never even crossed his mind.

As Robert, he never felt the need to even consider the humanity of Black people, much less to hang out with them; and now he had found himself depending on a group of Black guys for his very survival in prison.

The whole situation was so hard to grasp. For Robert, it was like living in the "twilight zone."

Jameson plopped down in one of the swivel office chairs in the control room.

"That was hard to watch," he gasped. After seeing Robert's trial, Jameson knew the man had it coming to him, but still. It would be hard to watch anyone in that position.

Dr. Cooper aimed a measured look at Jameson. "Well, today is your lucky day. You're getting a full view of the Black experience," she said, making air quotes.

"Tyrese, bring screen three up to the main screen, please," she asked.

Tyrese mumbled to himself, "This scenario is just a little too realistic for me."

Dr. Cooper asked, "Tyrese, did you say something?"

"Nope, I'm just gonna bring this screen up right here and drag it up just so, and bam! Here we go," Tyrese quickly responded.

MALIK GARDNER

Malik was seen walking to his mother's house. His body language made it clear that he was feeling down on himself after losing his home and learning that he was not able to get a loan or any other financial help. He just felt stuck and imagined that life couldn't get any worse than sleeping in your old twin bed at your momma's house.

Malik's cell phone rung in his pocket.

He glanced down at his phone and noticed it was the human resource department at his job. *"What now?"* He wondered. He quickly thought maybe they reconsidered giving him that promotion after all.

"Hello?" He said dryly as he answered his phone.

"Hi Malik, this is Jill. I feel like I have had to make a million calls today, so I'm going to just get to it. I have some good news, and I have some bad news," She went on to say.

"Well, it's been kinda a rough day for me. I could use some good news right now," Malik said.

Jill replied, "well, the good news is that we have had to change your shift from day shift to night shift."

Malik stopped in his tracks. "Whoa, wait a minute. Isn't the night shift fewer hours than the day shift?"

"Yes, about ten to fifteen hours less," said Jill.

"How is that good news? And, if that's the good news, what the hell is the bad news?" Malik said in both a sarcastic but fearful tone.

"The good news is you still have a job," Jill said flippantly. "We are laying off a ton of people, so this is not a fun day for me either."

Malik resisted the urge to fire something back at her.

Jill must have realized how insensitive she sounded because she softened her tone a bit when she added, "Look, Malik, I'm sorry, but I need to give the supervisor an answer right now. Are you able to start the night shift tomorrow, or what?"

Malik paused for a moment; everything in him wanted to say, 'take that job and shove it where the sun doesn't shine.'

Jill chimed in and said, "Look, Mr. Gardner, if I were you, I would be happy to have a job at all. I am looking at your timesheets for the last ninety days. Are you aware that you have no more vacation days, sick days, or any leave left at all? You've used it all, and you still missed two days last week alone."

"Y'all know my son is sick. I'm trying to get help for an expensive procedure that he needs, and my son comes first. I missed a few days because I had to go to social services for housing assistance. They're closed by the time I leave work, and right now, I'm trying to figure out how to keep my home and cover my son's medical expenses," Malik desperately tried to explain.

"I understand, and we feel bad for you. Right now, the whole economy is bad, and as I said, you are one of the lucky ones who still has a job." She paused briefly before asking, "What's it gonna be? I'm sure the next person I have to call would prefer to have a change in shifts than not to have a job at all."

"Dammit!" he muttered to himself while holding his hand over the phone. He waited for a moment before he unenthusiastically said, "Yeah, I guess I'll be there tomorrow night."

Malik knew he was barely making it with a full-time check coming in, and now he'd been reduced to part-time hours. *What's next?* He thought.

Just then, a voice in the distance called out his name. "Hey, Malik! Is that you, bro?"

"Yo Breezy, what up, dawg?" Malik said, acknowledging his childhood friend from the neighborhood. Everyone in the neighborhood knew Breezy. In the 'hood, he was the man.

Breezy and Malik grew up together and went to the same schools from elementary to high school until Breezy dropped out when they were sixteen. Breezy never went back to get his diploma because he got caught up in the drug game. The hard life that came with that choice was etched all over his face, aging him prematurely.

"Let me holla at you," Breezy said as he threw his arm around the neck of Malik. I see you back in the hood, and I could use a soldier like you in my crew. We go way back, bro, and I always admired the fact that you ain't never back down from nobody, nah mean? So, check this out, I got some serious stuff about to pop off, and I can put you down with ten G's, just like that," he said as he snapped his fingers to signify how easy it would be.

"Naw, man, I'm good," Malik responded quickly.

Breezy looked him up and down and said, "Man, Stevie Wonder could see you ain't livin, large. From the looks of it, you look like you need some paper, patna."

"I'm chill, just workin' on a couple things is all," Malik said defensively, trying to keep his thoughts from straying to all the things he could do with ten thousand dollars. Not the least of which was getting Samuel the surgery he needed. The offer was very tempting, considering his string of recent financial luck.

Breezy removed his arm and said, "Well, you know where to find me if you need a lil' sumthin, I got you."

Malik dapped Breezy up and said, "Bet, that's good to know man. Good looking out. I'll hit you up if I need anything, but you do know I've been on the police force for ten years now, right?"

Breezy gave Malik a look that made Malik feel a mixture of stupidity and naivety.

"You know how that sounds, right?" Breezy questioned Malik with a puzzled look on his face. "Do you know how many officers I have to pay off to do what I do? Just think about it," Breezy continued.

As Malik walked toward his car, he noticed a female cop walking away from his car after placing a parking ticket on it. He looked at it in disbelief. He had only been parked there for a few minutes.

"This day just keeps getting better and better," he said to himself.

He looked at the parking ticket and saw the name of the officer on it and decided to yell out to her, "Hey, Linda Reed, why don't you at least let me take you to dinner!"

He was trying to look suave in front of Breezy and his boys, who were all watching but knowing he'd be in trouble if she said yes. He knew he couldn't afford to feed himself, let alone dinner for two.

Linda kept walking. She never looked back to see who was yelling her name.

LINDA REED

As Linda walked back to her squad car, she saw a friendly face coming towards her. It was her coworker, Sarah.

"Hey girl, I see you are out here writing tickets, too," Sarah said to Linda with a disparaging grin.

Linda replied, "Yeah, ever since I reported that incident with the Captain, he's done everything he can to make my life a living hell. I hate this shit, but at least I don't have to be in the office and have to look at him." She sighed heavily, happy to finally confide in a friend.

"I swear, I wanna beat the shit out of him every time he even opens his mouth to say hello. He struts around as if he's fuckin' innocent!" Linda continued.

"Girl, I'm sorry. That really sucks, but you know that kinda stuff has been happening, and it will probably continue to happen. All the shit you're going through right now is why nobody speaks out about it." Sarah insisted. Linda frowned. It wasn't what she wanted to hear.

"Why do you think I'm on this shitty detail? I refused to give one of them what they wanted, then all of a sudden, I got reassigned," Sarah explained.

"I didn't know that," Linda said quietly.

"Hell, It's a man's world. What did you expect to happen, Linda?" Sarah asked rhetorically.

"I was expecting some decency and respect," Linda said in a clear, forceful, and sure tone.

"Listen, Linda. I'm a cop too, you know? I lay my life on the line just like you, so I get it. I'm a woman who has to deal with some of that, also—so. I get it. What can we do about it, though?" Sarah shook her head, resigned.

"Nah, fuck that, Sis! How am I gonna act like I can protect and serve the people in these streets when I can't even do that for myself? If I just accept that protection and justice don't exist for me, how can I expect it to exist for anyone else? Honestly, this shit pisses me off," Linda said, "I was at least expecting people to believe me. I thought they'd give it a serious look, at least. I wouldn't make up some shit like that."

"Linda, you gotta know that Jameson plays golf with most of those guys, especially Captain Jenkins. They hang out together every weekend, smoking cigars and trading stories. You think they're gonna turn on each other for you? Girl, you were sadly mistaken. Look, I gotta get back, but it was nice to see you, though. Try and keep your head up. It'll get better, baby girl." Sarah said, leaving Linda standing there.

CASSANDRA ELLIS

James and Terell became closer after winning the state championships together. It seemed that their playing together helped them develop a rhythm that allowed them to overlook the things they didn't like about one another for the sake of the team's success. Terrel and James spent a lot of time outside of practice working on their game together.

The two of them developed an amazing chemistry on the court. They seemed to know exactly where the other one was at all times. James' shot became more consistent, and he made it into the starting line-up. They drove their team to yet another victory, and Cassandra was excited to hear all of the highlights they would undoubtedly be talking about for the next few days. She smiled to herself as she waited for them in the car. She was going to take them out for pizza after the game.

As the boys piled into the car with all of their basketball gear, the principal approached Cassandra's car. He leaned in to speak with Cassandra through the slightly lowered window.

"You must be proud of these guys, especially with the rocky start they got off to. There are a lot of adults who can learn from those two," the principal said as he pointed to the boys on the back seat. They work so well together out there. You wouldn't ever guess they were enemies not so long ago." He said, directing his conversation to the guys, "Excellent teamwork, fellas. I'm looking forward to seeing how you all do at the regional level."

Cassandra felt a bit of embarrassment when he said, "I wish adults would learn from these two," because she knew that she, as Emily, was one of the adults he was referencing. She would never have thought that James would be the one teaching her the benefit of not judging people strictly because of the color of their skin.

As Cassandra drove the boys home, she glanced in the rearview periodically, watching James. Images from the past flashed in her mind. Instances of her expressing racist ideas in his presence or of him expressing his own bias that was surely reflective of what she taught him.

She knew that she was the reason he used to behave that way; she had biased his thoughts and ideas about race at a very young age. The more she thought about it, the more she realized that she had never even given James a chance to have a different, unbiased perspective.

Perhaps it hadn't been her intent to make her son hateful, but it had happened. She had repeated the same ideologies that her parents had taught her. She never thought for a moment that what she had taught James was wrong in any way. She simply didn't have the benefit of seeing life any other way; she never had a reason to.

As a parent, she should have made sure he knew that he would have to live in a world that was made up of more than White people. It was her responsibility to give James a worldview, not a Whiteview. She didn't give him that, and for that, she had failed James. Cassandra was happy that James was beginning to see people of other races in a whole new light. It was not too late for him.

Now, she could see how the ideology she exposed James to was an impediment, not preparation. She recognized this moment in her life for what it was—a second chance, an opportunity to make things right. She thought to herself how sometimes trying to do the right thing can be the wrong thing. Driving down the road with the two boys chatting in the backseat, she thought about how different her views were now due to the Decennial Program.

JAMAL EDWARDS

Jamal was exuberant as he headed to his favorite place, Meechie's Cafe. He was elated that it was part of his morning routine. As Jamal entered the coffee shop where Tasha worked, he walked into what appeared to be a Valentine's Day wonderland. There were heart-shaped balloons and red and pink roses everywhere. Streamers dangled from the ceiling, and heart-shaped glitter was sprinkled all over the tables.

"It looked like Cupid threw up in here," Jamal joked as he approached Tasha at the counter. She wiped down the surface of the counter with a rag, and Jamal was amazed by how she could make such a simple task look enchanting.

"Yeah, the owner is a little nuts about Valentine's day," she laughed.

"What about you?" Jamal asked playfully. "Do you have a Valentine? Don't tell me, you're not a romantic, right?" Jamal inquired.

"Nah, I used to be," she giggled. "I've been hurt a few too many times, I'm afraid."

"What... so, you're not willing to open your heart ever again?" Jamal asked as he leaned over the counter.

Tasha seemed hesitant to open up. She bit her lip and focused on wiping the counter. Jamal stayed quiet, giving her the space to decide if she trusted him enough to open up a bit more.

"You know," Tasha finally said, voice soft but strong. "People lie, or they cheat; they break your trust. So, you close that part of yourself off to keep from feeling that kind of pain, but it kinda takes the fun out of Valentine's Day."

"You can't let the actions of a few idiots ruin all of your Valentine's Day fun for eternity," Jamal replied gently, reassuring her. Tasha looked down to the counter to hide her sad eyes, but Jamal had already seen them.

"You mind if we sit for a little while?" Jamal asked as he moved to an empty table in the cafe. Tasha shrugged her shoulders slightly in agreement and came from behind the counter. The two sat at a table right by the window. The light shined through the window and was only interrupted by the heart, and kiss decals stuck on the glass. The glare made Tasha's eyes appear to glow.

"I... just have this ex," Tasha began. "He was my first love. I'd had other boyfriends before him, but he was something else. I saw my future with him; like, I wanted to marry him. He lied to me, and I found out about it in the worst way because he wasn't the one who told me. He'd been seeing another woman for about six months, and I didn't even know until he finally admitted to me that he had a fiance —the day before Valentine's Day," she said. The words came in a rush as she fidgeted with the limp rag in her hands.

"That's horrible, Tasha. I'm sorry," Jamal said, laying a comforting hand on her hands that were resting on the table.

"It is what it is," she sighed. "So, now I don't trust very easily. And, now you also know why I'll be spending Valentine's Day alone."

As they sat talking, Tasha realized this was the first time she'd opened up to a guy about the impact that experience had on her dating life. It was her very first time having more than just a passing conversation with Jamal.

As for Jamal, he hoped her confession meant they were getting even closer. They continued to have many meaningful talks at the coffee shop in the coming weeks. Jamal had slowly chipped away at the wall Tasha had built around her heart. He would stop in after his shift, and they'd sit and talk for hours about almost everything. He felt she was finally getting comfortable enough to show him a different side of her.

As time went on, Jamal worked up the courage to ask her out on a date outside of the coffee shop, and she finally obliged.

DECENNIAL HEADQUARTERS WRAP-UP SESSION

Dr. Langston fought to suppress a satisfied smile as the officers chatted, sitting around for the post-session discussion. The Decennial Program seemed to be getting through to the officers finally, and it was so gratifying for Dr. Langston to see his life's work coming together.

Dr. Langston's team mirrored Dr. Langston's sunny disposition regarding the program; they were equally surprised and ecstatic by the participants' willingness to put effort into the discussion for a change.

George bitterly vented about Malik's financial situation. He was clearly frustrated. His blue eyes glistened with an unshed tear. George gruffly mentioned that a cop named

Linda gave him a ticket just when he thought he had hit rock bottom. "No one is even giving Malik a chance," George mentioned as he shook his head.

Rose had an epiphany. A look of realization was prevalent on her face as she heard Linda's name. That was one aspect of the Decennial Program that Dr. Langston took particular pride in. The participant's lives were intertwined, within and outside of the program. As Rose shared some of her experiences in the Decennial Program, she referenced her time frame and experience of being a meter maid.

Her petite frame seemed to shrink even further as the eyes of the other participants turned to her. "No one feels like they deserve a ticket, even when they're wrong," she muttered. We still have a job to do. We have no control over what other hardships are happening in someone's life when we do our job," she mentioned defensively.

Dr. Langston directed the discussion to Ethan, who tentatively began to talk about his unfolding relationship with Tasha.

"You know, I met a Black woman in the Decennial Program that I really like. I just never thought I would be interested in anyone outside of my race," he confided. He seemed eager to open up, but at the same time, embarrassed to share even the small amount that he already had. Despite his embarrassment, Ethan continued to talk, as Emily glared at him with a tinge of jealousy, which Ethan tactfully ignored.

"I know she is interacting with Jamal, the Black guy that I have become, in the Decennial Program, but it is actually my consciousness, my thoughts, and my actual feelings that are involved. I ...umm, even ventured to the same coffee shop just to see if what I had been experiencing was even real. I was shocked to find out that she actually does exist in real life."

Ethan continued, "As a White cop, I just don't know if I could ever approach her. I want to, but ..I kinda don't know-how. Mostly I am worried about getting rejected, and I don't want to end what I have been feeling the last couple of months." Ethan was looking down at the floor the entire time he was talking and decided to look up as he was wrapping up and found everyone's eyes focused on him. He suddenly bcame even more embarrassed. He slumped in his chair and returned his eyes to the floor.

The conversation took a darker turn as Rose decided to talk about her experience. How she processed what Linda was going through as a victim of sexual assault. She nudged one booted foot against the ground, staring hard at her own feet as she talked.

"I get how covering up a crime like that...it hurts people," Rose mentioned. Dr. Langston suddenly recalled her file and the instances in which she was entered into the program for covering up a fellow officer's racially motivated violence, burying evidence.

Rose looked around the group, her green eyes blazed. "I've always felt like I was unheard and dismissed. But being Linda..." She trailed off, shaking her head.

"No one believes a word Linda says! It fuckin' sucks to see how many people--especially my fellow officers— have turned on me, I mean her. They're supposed to be family. They're supposed to support me, but now that I'm wearing this 'Linda' costume, they've abandoned me. It's not fuckin' right that she doesn't get any kind of justice simply because she's Black. She's still a woman who was violated, for fuck's sake!"Linda clamored.

"I didn't realize how horrible Black people get treated until I saw it for myself," Emily added, breaking the momentary silence.

"I always felt like 'White privilege' was a buzzword people threw around to avoid taking responsibility for their part in matters. I now see that there is a deep-seated unconscious bias that can only be uncovered when you're willing to look deep within yourself."

Emily began to tell them that she never fully understood that the ideas she had about Black people were wrong and that by sharing them with her son, she had unwittingly been programming him to be a racist.

"I never, ever believed that my views were wrong. I felt like I was preparing my son to navigate the world of different races but didn't realize I was taking away his chance to see people for who they are. I taught him to judge them based on their race and how they look."

"I think if you don't correct it when you see it and acknowledge that you have racist ideas that you're trying to correct, you'll fall back into those same racist tendencies, and you're still a part of the problem," Sierra chimed in.

"Like, just because you don't say and do racist things anymore doesn't mean that you're not contributing to racism," she continued.

"Yeah! It's like a 'see something, say something' kinda thing," Rose added in agreement.

Dr. Hughes and Dr. Cooper looked at each other and then looked at Emily. Emily looked down at her feet in shame and embarrassment, her blond hair falling around her face.

Dr. Langston looked over to Robert, who had been conspicuously quiet. He listened as he leaned back in his chair with his muscled arms folded across his chest. His dark eyes were staring bullets into the floor.

"Robert?" Dr. Langston asked, wondering if he would have anything to say about Wesely, about experiencing prison life, and the violence he dealt with first hand.

Everyone's eyes turned to him. He cleared his throat and paused for a moment as if trying to gather his thoughts. He was still dealing with the trauma he had been going through in the program. Dr. Langston realized he was clearly shaken.

Robert's sadness was apparent even to Dr. Langston, who sat at the opposite end of the circle. He didn't seem ready to open up, so the discussion moved on to John Fletcher.

John fidgeted, his sturdy frame uncomfortably squeezed between the armrests of his chair. He admitted to seeing a lot as an officer, including the creative bending of some laws when it suited the force's needs.

"I'm just not sure how I feel about law enforcement anymore," John said, rubbing the back of his neck feverishly.

"Wrong is wrong, and right is right--no matter who you are," he goes on. "I thought I was making a difference, but if I'm being honest, I can admit that I probably screwed over a lot of Black people that probably didn't deserve it. I never took a moment to think about how I might be impacting the rest of someone's life. I think my biggest takeaway is that racially inflicted bruises have lasting ripple effects that are not always visible. They don't usually heal. They just fester, breeding further mistrust that Black people have towards White people. I think I get it now," John concluded.

John immediately felt like a hundred-pound weight had been lifted from his chest. He didn't realize he had been drowning in what he was feeling. He had to tell someone, and he felt the small crew of officers in the program would understand.

Robert was in a daze for most of the session, but he finally started to return to his usual surly disposition. He had been very contemplative since his experience as Wesley began.

Coming out of a session as Wesley always made him feel like he'd just woke up from a horrible nightmare. It dawned on him that Black people never get to wake up from their experience, and it made him feel somewhat troubled. He felt a tightness in his chest and tears welling up inside his eyes.

Though he was still hesitant about sharing, he finally decided to talk about it. He thought to himself that if talking about his experience as Wesley was all it would take to put an end to reliving that nightmare every month, he could sing all day.

"Wesley had his freedom stolen from him, his life, his family. This shit is just nuts!" Robert blurted out as he stood abruptly, adrenaline coursing through his entire body.

Feeling the sudden urge to hit something, he lashed out, kicking one of the flimsy desks. It went careening across the room, where it eventually crashed into the wall, sending papers fluttering in every direction. He instantly felt a release of pent-up tension and slowly began to calm down as he surveyed the shocked looks of everyone in the room.

"Everything's fucked, man," he shook his head, not returning to his seat. "I mean, this Wesley motherfucker ain't even living, I'm, I mean, he's just trying to survive. It's hard, man! It's just...too fuckin' hard. I don't know how Black people deal with that type of shit every day."

Dr. Langston's team was shocked to see that the toughest nut might be beginning to crack. Their silent glance to one another acknowledged that Robert just might be understanding why the Decennial Program was created in the first place.

Eventually, Robert sat down, and as soon as he was back in his chair, the door opened. Dr. Langston turned to see Ramsey and Jameson standing on the other side of the glass door. He let the group know that he would be back momentarily and stepped out of the meeting room.

"Officer Ramsey, always a pleasure," Dr. Langston said, shaking the wiry officer's hand. He turned to Jameson, who was looking on, as usual, with poorly concealed disapproval. "Commissioner," Dr. Langston greeted him dryly.

The three men stepped into the conference room to talk.

"We just wanted to come by to let you know that we've opened a case against the officers that set Wesley up," Ramsey revealed. Dr. Langston raised his eyebrows in awe of the news Ramsey shared.

"Your program's already doing some good," Ramsey admitted.

"Thanks for the update," Dr. Langston said quietly before walking them out. "And to update you, I believe 'some' of your officers are making some real breakthroughs," Dr. Langston continued.

Dr. Langston escorted Jameson and Ramsey out of the building and returned to the group discussion as the officers continued to share their thoughts and experiences.

"I don't think it's realistic to think folks are gonna say something every time they see something racist. Not all of us want to be social justice warriors. I like to mind my business, keep my head down. I can't control what other folks do," Roger complained.

"You're an officer, Roger. It's *literally* your job to intervene when you see something wrong," Ethan countered.

"Oh, so now, we're the morality police, too?! It's not enough that I get my balls handed to me for fighting real crime. Now I gotta pretend to be a nigger lover, too? Get the fuck outta here!" Roger exploded.

"Well, we're definitely turning the heat up on that asshole," Tyrese whispered as he leaned towards Dr. Cooper.

"This may not be our real lives, but millions of people are impacted by racism in their real lives every day," Ethan continued.

"As Jamal, I can't tell you how many White women cross the street when they see me heading in their direction, even in broad daylight. That never happened to me before, but I'm the same guy," he said. Do you know how that makes me feel? You gotta take this seriously. There is a huge difference between how people respond to me and deal with me when I'm White and how they respond to me and deal with me when I'm Black."

"Black people treat white people differently too," Roger argued.

"Yeah, and that's not cool either, but who started the fight? Was it Black people? Probably not. I mean, who has the power? Can Black people truly be racist when they don't have the power to affect your ability to survive if they disapprove of you or just straight up don't like your ass? I can see why it's so hard for Black people to trust us." Ethan admitted.

The room went silent, and the session came to an end. As the participants filed out of the room, the doctors gathered to review their notes.

"Some of them have come a long way since beginning the program," Dr. Hughes mentioned to the team after the officers were dismissed.

"Some of them still have a long way to go," Tyrese said as he began the long process of cataloging their experiences on their respective monitors.

I know we heard from everybody for the first time, but did anyone else hear John Fletcher today?" Dr. Cooper asked.

"I think we all did, loud and clear, prepare his release papers along with Sierra Brooks. I believe they have successfully completed the program," Dr. Langston ordered.

CHAPTER 16

SESSION VII. YEAR SEVEN

JAMAL EDWARDS

Ethan was full of nerves at the start of the Decennial Program's seventh session, but not for the usual reasons. He was preoccupied because he was finally getting a date with Tasha. He met Tasha by happenstance in the first session of the program, and he felt like he had spent years of work lowering her defenses. He never had to work this hard for a first date. Tasha finally agreed to go out with him in the last session, and as he was finalizing all of the plans for the perfect date, the session was over, and he was waking up in the reclining chair of the Decennial Program. The very reclining chair that he despised initially was now his highway to happiness. As he was getting situated for the upcoming session, his date with Tasha was all he had been able to think about.

As Jamal's consciousness awakened in the Decennial Program, he immediately picked up where he left off. He had painstakingly laid out every detail of the date with Tasha, even down to what he was going to wear. Jamal knew the perfect place to take her to dinner. It was a restaurant his father. Captain Jenkins would take the family to, for all special occasions.

Jamal remembered going there as Ethan so many times that he knew all of the staff, and they knew him. He always felt special when he went there because the entire staff and even the owner would always come to their table and make small talk. The owner himself would open a bottle of their best wine and pour it for the table. The ambience was very fancy. The lighting always seemed perfect there, not too bright and not so dark that you couldn't read the menu. Every table had linen tablecloths on them, and the waiter would put your linen napkin on your lap for you. It was the perfect place to make a great impression on Tasha.

As they arrived at Ethan's favorite restaurant, Jamal jumped out of his car and ran around to open Tasha's door for her.

"What a gentleman," she said, smiling.

"Yeah, that's me," he replied laughingly.

Jamal very smoothly tossed the keys to the valet as Tasha took his hand, and the pair walked through the upscale Italian bistro's glass doors and made their way to the host station.

"Reservation for two," Jamal said confidently to the hostess. "Last name Jenkins- I mean- Edwards," he stuttered.

The hostess stared at Jamal, his hair, his clothes, and almost instantly determined he must be at the wrong place. Then she casually looked down at her tablet where all the reservations were stored. "Oh, what a shame, I don't see it here," she said dryly.

"Could you check again? the reservation was made some time ago," Jamal said, straightening the collar on his shirt. He knew that he had made that reservation well in advance. He planned this date meticulously; he wanted everything to be perfect for Tasha.

"Ohh, I see it here. It looks like someone canceled that reservation earlier today. Must be a computer error," the hostess said. "There's an hour and a half wait for a table right now, and I'm sure you probably don't want to wait that long. There is a diner in the next block you might enjoy," she offered.

"We can go somewhere else," Tasha suggested, gently pulling Jamal to the side. She could tell by the hostess's attitude that they weren't welcomed there.

"Hold on, Tasha," he said, going back up to the hostess. "I've been coming here for years, is there any way we could get a table sooner?"

"I don't recall anyone like you. I mean, that looks like, you know what I mean, I don't recognize you at all, and I have been working here for over a year now," the hostess explained.

Jamal instantly realized that he wasn't Ethan, as Jamal no one knew him there. He was just an ordinary guy. He was still hopeful that perhaps everything will be fine. A good restaurant is a good restaurant, he thought to himself.

Jamal slightly leaned over the stand and whispered to the hostess as he slid a twenty-dollar bill across the stand."How about now, can you get us a good table, you know one of the tables near the piano player, today is a special occasion."

"I highly doubt that," she said, stuffing the $20 into her pocket. Jamal stared at her incredulously. "The wait is still an hour and a half."

"What's the holdup?" A voice boomed from behind them. "Some of us are hungry and actually have reservations."

Jamal recognized the voice instantly, and his jaw dropped open when he realized it was his father, Captain Jenkins. It was surreal for Ethan to encounter his father while being in Jamal's body. His father didn't recognize him at all; it was eerie.

"My apologies, sir," the hostess smiled. "You can wait over there," she said to Jamal and Tasha as she pointed to the empty waiting area.

Tasha rolled her eyes and grabbed Jamal by the arm, "Let's just go," she pleaded.

"Why is the wait so long if we're the only ones waiting?" Jamal asked, trying to remain calm.

"For God's sake, can't you people hear? The lady said, go wait, so I suggest you...Go... wait," Captain Jenkins huffed as he pushed past Jamal to speak to the hostess.

"Could I get a table, darlin'? These folks are holding up the line," he said, glaring at Jamal and Tasha.

"Of course, sir, right this way," she replied, showing Captain Jenkins to his table.

Jamal was in shock. "Does my dad just go around treating everyday people like shit or just Black people?" he wondered to himself.

He had always known that his father wasn't perfect. Jamal recalled many times that, as Ethan, he ended up on the wrong side of his dad's temperament, and it was never a good place to be. Internally, Ethan knew that his dad had a lot of hostility towards Black people inside of him as well, but he never expected to be on the receiving end of that hate.

Tasha tugged lightly on Jamal's arm, begging him to leave. He barely noticed.

Instead, Jamal stood there frozen in that spot. Disbelief, along with a million other thoughts, rushed through his mind. The room seemed to be spinning out of control as his perfect date was getting ruined. For a moment, he considered revealing his true identity to Captain Jenkins, but he wasn't ready to tell Tasha the truth yet.

His mind snapped back to reality when Tasha released his arm from her vice-like grip.

He turned slowly to see Tasha shaking her head in disbelief before rushing out of the restaurant. Jamal quickly gathered himself and followed her, hoping that he hadn't ruined any chance he had with her. He yelled out her name as he chased her down the sidewalk.

LINDA REED

Linda was dying to get home so she could relax and feel marginally safe after a long day of walking the streets and handing out tickets. She looked at her watch and remembered she had to report to Jameson's office. She removed her reflective vest and wiped her brow as she sat in the driver's seat of her squad car.

As she arrived at the precinct, Jameson met her at the door.

"Linda, we need to talk," Jameson said in a low tone when she walked in. He motioned for her to meet him in his office.

"Shit!" she muttered under her breath. This was supposed to be a quick report, and she had no desire to spend any more time in the precinct than she had to.

She briefly sat down in the chair at her desk and put her things in the drawer. She put her head in her hands and took a big gulp of air before walking toward Jameson's office.

"Close the door," Jameson said as Linda walked into his office.

Linda quietly took a seat across from Jameson's desk.

"In regards to your case," he began, holding up her file. "I have found that there are absolutely no merits to your allegations."

Linda opened her mouth to speak, but he quickly shut her down.

"Let me finish!" he warned sternly.

"I'm throwing this case out. Your complaints have created a toxic work environment for everyone else. No one wants to work with you after this, so I don't know what's gonna happen to your career in law enforcement," Jameson bellowed.

Frustration crept up in the back of Linda's throat, cutting off her air and blurring her vision with unshed tears.

"As I see it, you have two choices," Jameson said. "You can stay on traffic duty, permanently, or you always have the option of seeking employment elsewhere," he suggested.

The reality of the situation settled in her mind. Jameson was forcing her to take a demotion or lose her job.

"You want me just to roll over and take it or quit?" Linda hissed, fighting her tears.

She sprang to her feet. "I had my soul ripped out of my body by that man, and you wanna punish me?! He took everything! My happiness, my security, my sanity, and you wanna give him my job too? "

"Like. I. Said." He thundered, standing up from his seat to match her height. "You have two choices. Now, get out of my office before I choose for you."

Linda stared hard at Jameson for a moment, eye to eye. Then she whirled and stormed out of the office without another word. The part of her that was Rose was fueled with disappointment. This man—her mentor—was ruining the life of an innocent woman to save the reputation of his friend and the department.

Linda drew a shaky breath as she made her way out of the headquarters. She wanted to quit, to never see those men again, but that would only hurt her more than it would hurt them. There would be no justice, and she didn't think she had the emotional bandwidth to let Captain Jenkins go on without punishment. Fury and pain swirled around in her head as she left the building once again, without justice.

MALIK GARDNER

Malik awakened from a rough night's sleep with a stabbing pain in his lower back from sleeping on the rock-like futon at his friend's house.

He rubbed the sleep from his eyes and stretched his arms above his head, and realized he had a bit of body odor from sleeping in yesterday's clothes. Scratching his head, he stumbled down the hall to the restroom and splashed water on his unshaven face. When he caught his reflection in the mirror, he was startled at not recognizing himself again. He muttered to himself, "I don't think I'm ever gonna get used to this." Referring to waking up in a Black person's body.

Malik had to face the fact that he was officially homeless. Not only was he evicted from his home, but he was also at work when the landlord put all of his belongings on the street. By the time his shift was over, and he made it home, what was left was the useless stuff that seemed to accumulate in his house that he didn't want or use, but for some reason, he just never threw it away.

He was appreciative of one of his friends allowing him to stay on his couch so that he wasn't on the streets. Malik was careful not to wear out his welcome, so he spent as little time there as possible. Mainly slept, showered, and left.

Malik was mostly distraught because now that he was homeless and did not have access to electricity to power Samuel's breathing machine, it limited the amount of time he could spend with him. Samuel now resided with Malik's ex-wife and her new family while Malik worked on getting himself together.

Malik struggled to not take Breezy up on his offer to get some fast cash looking the other way while Breezy's crew sold drugs on the street, especially after losing his job shortly after the eviction. He was fired for missing too many days trying to secure a home and medical assistance. He found out the hard way that there just aren't as many resources for men struggling to take care of their families as there are for women in the same situation. He tried every avenue he knew to be a responsible dad, only to lose everything.

Turning the faucet of the shower on hot, Malik quickly disrobed and stepped into the shower. A cloud of steam filled the air as he stood motionless, letting the water run down his face. All the stress and frustration of the trials he had faced came boiling up to the surface. The realization of his inability to provide basic care for his son, Samuel's needs made him feel inadequate as a father and as a man.

All the embarrassment and resentment from being denied and turned away he'd managed to push down for a long time overwhelmed him, making his body writhe from the weight of holding it for so long. And still, he refused to let any sounds escape, only tears and the sound of water falling on flesh.

Dr. Cooper leaned away from the monitor as she wiped a single tear from her face, hoping her colleagues wouldn't notice.

"Are you crying?" Tyrese asked. "These barbarians don't deserve your pity, Doc. Remember, these officers are here because they abused their powers. And that's just the shit we *know* about. They committed acts of violence, all of which were perpetrated against Black people," he crossed his arms. "Every last one of these motherfuckers would kill your mama without a second thought and then go have breakfast at IHOP. How can you cry for them? How about crying for all the mamas who lost children at the hands of these hateful assholes," Tyrese ranted.

"It's never easy to watch people hit rock bottom. Even though this is a simulation for them, this happens to people every day." Dr. Cooper said, "life's not fair, especially when you're Black in America."

"Hopefully, they'll see it too," Langston said as he requested Cassandra's experience be pulled up on the main monitor.

CASSANDRA ELLIS

Cassandra hummed to herself as she pulled clothes out of the washing machine and tossed them into the dryer. As she's putting another load in the washer, she heard a knock at her door.

"Oh, hi James, what a surprise," she said as she answered the door. "Terrell isn't here. I sent him to the store for a few things.

"Oh, alright, I'll come back later," he said, turning to leave.

"You're welcome to wait," she offered kindly. "Terrell should be back any minute," she said, stepping to the side, inviting James in.

"Thanks," he said as he walked into the living room and sat on the couch.

James had been to Terells home a few times but never really looked around, mainly because they would just dive right into playing video games. He noticed a painting of

The Last Supper above the dining room table. The picture illustrated Jesus and his apostles as Black people.

"Oh, my mom has that painting too," he said, pointing at the large painting on the wall "Ours has Jesus as a White guy, though," he noted jokingly.

Cassandra smiled as she folded the laundry. "You never really talk about your mom," she noted. "What's she like?" She asked nonchalantly, trying to get some insight on how James felt about Emily.

"Ehh, she's whatever," he said, leaning back into the couch. "You seem like a better mom than her."

Cassandra doesn't know whether to feel insulted or complimented. She had always thought that she was a pretty good mom to him as Emily. Maybe she hadn't been perfect, but she'd done her best. "Why is that?" She asked, her voice small.

"You spend time with Terrell; my mom is never home. And I bet you didn't teach Terrell to hate White people," he complained. "I'll never forgive my mom for the things she tried to teach me. What kind of monster teaches their kid to hate people? You and Terrell have been so nice to me, even after all the bad things I said." he contended

Cassandra could sense that James must have had that on his mind for a long time. She felt disappointed in herself. James was the one person in the world Emily loved, and here he was, with hatred, confusion and disappointment toward her and the way she had raised him.

Terrell came through the door with bags of groceries. "What's up, James?" he said, tossing the bags onto the counter. "You wanna get beat at Fifa?" he challenged playfully.

Cassandra casually went back to laundry as the pair began gaming, masking her pain. She never expected James to open up to her about his feelings that easily. He never shared with her as Emily. Most of all, she felt a hole in her heart. How could the person she loved the most harbor that much resentment for her?

WESLEY ROBERTS

Wesley stood in the shower stall, rubbing a bar of cheap soap all over his body as the cold water from the prion shower dribbled down his skin. He didn't think he would ever get used to showering in front of other men. As he made his way back to his cell, a bald man with a swastika tattooed across the back of his head stepped into his path.

"I heard you run with Tre and his gang," the man said, inching closer to Wesley's face. The man's voice was deep and rough like gravel.

Instead of speaking, Wesley simply nodded his head. He surveyed his surroundings, desperately hoping for a glimpse of Tre or one of the other guys. No one was there. The man smiled down at him menacingly.

"I got a message for Tre and his bitches," he sneered. "You tell them that the Aryan Nation is watching his ass," the man growled, shoulder checking Wesley as he left. Wesley was relieved there was no violence.

Despite being in prison for what had been years in the program, he hadn't needed to defend himself since joining Tre and his crew.

When Wesley returned to his cell, his bed was tossed. All of his belongings were in a pile on the floor. Wesley took the rest of the day to put things back in the right place, he was grateful and slightly bewildered to find that all of his things were still there.

At the end of the day, he lay awake, listening out for anyone who might try to attack him in his sleep. He hardly slept at all that night. Instead, he sat straight up, staring at the concrete wall. He could never get enough sleep on that stone-hard bed and nothing but a thin blanket to keep him warm.

He thought about the time when he, as Robert, almost joined the Aryan Nation. He had been a young adult and just beginning to think about the things he did and their long-term consequences, so the only reason he didn't officially join was that he didn't think it would look good on his record if he decided to become an officer.

He contemplated getting a small swastika tattooed on his ankle as a teen, and now more than ever, he was glad he didn't. It wasn't until he came into the Decennial Program that he could recognize the humanity of Black people and that they hurt and have the same feelings and challenges as he had as Robert.

His thoughts were interrupted when the doors of his cell slid open. The sound was so loud it caused Wesley's ears to ring. "Wakey, Wakey, princess," an officer snarled, pulling him out of his bed.

"Up against the wall," another officer ordered, shoving Wesley's face against the concrete blocks.

Two officers tore through Wesley's belongings, dumping everything into a pile on the floor again. They flipped his mattress over onto the ground and ripped off his sheets.

"What's going on?" Wesley questioned. He wondered if they were *the ones who had tossed his bed earlier?* His voice was muffled because the guard was still pressing his face against the wall.

He tried looking back, but the officer was holding his neck in a grip so tight he thought he would lose consciousness for a moment.

"Word on the yard is you got some paraphernalia." The officer restraining Wesley said.

"I don't have anything!" Wesley yelled as they continued to ransack his cell. He struggled, trying to get the guard to loosen his painful grip.

"Then what's this?" the other officer removed a shiv from behind Wesley's toilet.

Wesley looked at the weapon in horror, but he knew better than to try to convince them it wasn't his. It wouldn't do him any good, and he knew it. The officers cuffed Wesley with the zip ties and walked him down the cell block. The man with the swastika tattoo smirked and blew a kiss to Wesley as he was dragged away to solitary confinement.

With his arms cuffed behind his back, Wesley was tossed onto the floor of a gray padded room, face first. An officer knelt down and pinned him in place with his knee while undoing the handcuffs, and the two quickly exited, slamming the door behind them.

After a time, Wesley pulled himself to his feet and examined his new surroundings. There was no handle on the door, and the room was entirely padded; there was a small slot cut into the door so they could pass him a tray of food. The room was small, with only a tiny dust smudged window at the top of the wall allowing the slightest ray of light to creep in. Wesley banged his head against the cushioned wall in frustration.

"They're treating him like an animal," Tyrese said as he moved Wesley's experience from the main monitor.

"That's the prison system for you," Dr. Cooper replied evenly, taking notes down on her clipboard. The alarm on her phone beeped. "Time to wrap up. Their sedation will be wearing off soon," she said as she exited the control room.

"Did you see what happened on the news?" Dr. Hughes asked Dr. Langston as the officers began to awaken from their sedation.

"What happened this time?" Dr. Langston said as he looked up from his notepad, seeming mildly curious.

"Another Black man was killed by the police. He was only 21." Dr. Hughes revealed. "No one has been charged yet. They're saying it was an accidental shooting. The officer went for their gun instead of their taser and killed the guy."

"There'll definitely be riots tonight," Dr. Cooper said as she recorded the officer's stats on her clipboard.

"They already started," Tyrese said as he showed the video footage on his phone to the team. The streets of downtown Charlottesville were engulfed in flames, and rioters smashed glass against brick walls. Windows were shattering, people were panicking, and turmoil flooded the streets once again.

ETHAN JENKINS JR.

Ethan watched the chaos unfold from his living room couch as he flipped through the news stations on the television. His phone dinged from across the room on the kitchen island. He hurried over, not taking his eyes off of the television. When he did, he saw that it was his father calling. Ethan had not spoken to his dad since he ran into him as Jamal in the restaurant.

"Hello," Ethan finally answered, distracted by the mayhem unfolding on screen.

"Son, I'm headed down to the bistro for lunch. Why don't you join me?" Captain Jenkins asked.

Ethan had no desire to talk to his father, Captain Jenkins, and he certainly didn't want to return to the place where his father ruined Jamal's date with Tasha.

He had been trying to put words to the feeling since it had happened. The word he kept coming back to was 'disappointed.' Ethan knew that his father was a piece of work, but he never thought he could be so horrible, rude, and dismissive.

"I don't know, Dad. Are you gonna act like an ass again?" Ethan snapped.

"You better watch yourself with me, son," his father ordered. "Anyway, what are you talking about? When have I been an ass?"

"Last time you were there, you pushed past a Black couple and cut them in line," Ethan revealed, reprimanding his father.

What in God's name are you talking about?" Captain Jenkins fired back, "I surely don't remeber that."

Ethan quickly remebered that Captain Jenkins wasnt actually there it just felt like he was. Ethan recalled that he was part of the collective consciousness that populates the world in the Decennial Program, and he must have brought his father into Decennial. Ethan also realized that Captain Jenkins' response to Jamal in the program was created by his own subconscious ideas of how he felt his father would have acted in that situation.

"What do you care, anyway about how I treat some Black guy?" Captain Jenkins asked, slightly annoyed. "What are you, some kind of goddamn social justice warrior now?"

"I care because it was me!" Ethan barked.

"The Decennial Program! The guy you shoved was me! I was on a date with a Black woman that I really liked, and you ruined it. You pushed me out of the way like I was nothing!" he revealed, his voice thick with emotion.

Captain Jenkins went silent for a few moments as he thought about what Ethan had said. "Oh, so you're dating Black girls now, huh? Damn, that program's got your head all fucked up. Well, just make sure you use protection because I don't want any mulatto grandchildren calling me 'granddaddy,'" Captain Jenkins belted out with a chuckle.

"Dad, just stop," Ethan warned. "I really care about this woman. If you ever cared about me, you'd respect that."

"Son, did they erase your whole goddamned mind in that fuckin program? Listen, it's okay to have a little fun with a Black girl, E.J., but you better not ever bring any Black girls home to meet me. You hear me?" His father retorted.

"There's something really wrong with you," Ethan replied as he hung up the phone, irritated. He tossed his cellphone down on the table and ran his hands over his face in angst. He slumped down onto the couch, watching his fellow officers attempt to control the chaos in the city.

ROSE LIVINGSTON

Rose was on duty alongside other officers attempting to protect the city from further damage. The protestors' ferocious cries for justice filled the air around them. She was surprised to find that the rage she would usually feel as protestors screamed in her face was gone. In its place, she felt only apathy and numbness.

She was far too emotionally drained from her own experiences with racism since being in the program; she was not to be upended by these protestors. Besides, Rose could now understand how it felt to be the one crying for justice and having nobody listen.

Rose was snapped back to reality when she heard a familiar voice call her name. It was one of her brothers, Ryan. "What are you doing here? They must've called everyone to the scene," he yelled over the chaos.

Just as she responded, a protestor was shoved into Ryan, causing him to stumble. He immediately pushed the protester to the ground and placed his foot on their chest. "No, Ryan! It was an accident," Rose screamed to her brother just as he raised his fist to strike them.

"These. People. Never. Learn." he yelled, beating the protestor with every word. Rose leaped into action, pulling Ryan off the guy by his safety vest as best she could. "What are you doing, Rose?" He hissed. The victim laid motionless on the ground. A pool of blood was pouring from his mouth.

"Look at him!" she yelled, going to aid the protestor. "You could have killed him!"

"They only respond to violence. You know that!" Ryan stressed, picking himself up off the ground. Rose looked up at him from where she was crouched over the victim shielding him from another one of Ryan's blows and shook her head.

Rose quickly turned her attention back to the man on the ground as she called for an ambulance on her walkie-talkie. Ryan scoffed as he walked off, annoyed that his sister reprimanded his actions.

The following morning, the riots had finally settled a bit, and the precinct was buzzing with the kind of activity that usually followed an incident of unrest. Every bench and chair seemed to be occupied, full of people waiting to be processed for one crime or another related to the riots.

When Rose exited the elevator, her colleagues' icy-hot stares fell on her back as she walked to her desk, and their murmurings followed her. She was just too exhausted to worry about it. She had been up late last night wrestling with herself, deciding whether or not to file a report on her brother's behavior during the riots.

She wrestled with the idea of going against the unspoken rule that allowed officers to protect one another when their actions come under scrutiny. And this was not just another officer; it was her brother--her flesh and blood. But whenever she thought back to her traumatic experience as Linda, she was convinced it's the right thing to do. Maybe if one person had been brave enough to stand up for her, she would've gotten the justice she deserved.

As Rose prepared her report, her mind drifted back to all the times she left out facts that may have helped or facilitated justice for another person. She decided justice could not afford to be blind any longer.

The following day when Rose arrived at the precinct, Jameson was standing at her desk, asking to see her in his office before she could even put her things away and get settled. Rose glanced around the precinct as she followed him, and everyone seemed to be peering sheepishly from behind computers and around piles of papers and files on their desks.

When they arrived at Jameson's office, Rose took a seat. Jameson shut the doors and closed the blinds at the big plate glass window before sitting down and staring at her.

"You women officers are a real piece of work, you know. First Linda, and now you. Rose, I can't believe you filed a report on your brother Ryan!" He shook his head, sounding absolutely and completely astonished. "What are you thinking, Rose? That's your family."

"Yes, I did," she said, nodding her head and standing her ground. "He beat a protester so badly that the man started choking on his own blood. He might have died out there if I didn't intervene. How would that look like for the force, huh? I want Ryan to stop and think next time he attacks someone."

"Rosie," Jameson cajoled, taking a rather condescending tone, "sometimes you've gotta look the other way. I've looked the other way for you."

"Well, maybe you shouldn't have because now there are dozens of people out there who will not get the justice they deserve! We're the law, Patrick. Have you forgotten that?" She met his dark eyes with her own, steadily. "Facts are facts," Rose continued.

"Rose, you're taking what I said out of context," he grumbled. "We've always got to protect our own," he said, motioning between the two of them.

"*We protect our own?*" Rose exploded, her voice scathing. "Like you protected Linda? You let the Captain rape her and walk away scot-free! Linda is one of our own, and you completely alienated her. So don't you dare talk to me about *protecting our own.*"

Jameson's face drained of color as he stared, wide-eyed, at her.

Captain Jenkins walked in on Rose going into a complete irate fit.

"What's going on here?" Captain Jenkins yelled as he swung the door open. "I can hear you all the way in my office."

"Good! I hope the entire precinct hears!" Rose snapped.

"Rose, you need to calm down," Captain Jenkins said. He put his meaty hands on her shoulders, and nausea suddenly overcame her. Rose tried not to think about how he did the same thing to Linda moments before assaulting her.

"Don't touch me!" Rose yelled.

"Rose, you've got to relax," Jameson said, trying to hush her.

"What's going on with her?" Captain Jenkins asked. Rose scowled; they began talking about Rose like she was no longer in the room.

"She wrote Ryan up for police brutality and came in here like a firecracker. I'm trying to convince her to recant," Jameson replied.

"Why would you turn on your family?" Captain Jenkins asked, screwing up his face in judgment. Rose stood, full of energy and frustration. She wasn't sure what she was going to do, but she might explode if she didn't do something. Suddenly, there was a knock at the office door.

"Internal Affairs," an officer announced from the other side of the door before turning the knob and entering. It was Pierce Ramsey.

"Is everything alright in here?" Ramsey asked.

Rose knew she must look crazy. "No, everything is not alright," she said.

Ramsey turned his attention to Captain Jenkins and Jameson, who seemed far too unbothered by the scene.

"What's her deal?" Ramsey asked.

"Are you serious?" Rose demanded, shaking her head. Blood rushed to her face, and tears sprang to her eyes.

"It's nothing really, a misunderstanding that we are handling amongst ourselves, nothing you need to be concerned with," Captain Jenkins told Ramsey. Ramsey took a cursory look at Rose and seemed hesitant to leave.

Jameson stood dumbfounded, not knowing how to explain the situation playing out without incriminating himself or Captain Jenkins. He looked to Captain Jenkins to speak up.

"Uhh," Captain Jenkins stammered. "We're just having a little discussion, nothing major, just departmental stuff," he said unconvincingly.

Rose closed her eyes and worked up the courage to speak. She was done being silenced.

"Jameson wanted me to recant the report I filed against my brother Ryan yesterday for the use of excessive force," Rose recounted.

Any part of her that felt guilty about turning on her mentor was silenced when she remembered that he covered for Captain Jenkins in Linda's case.

Ramsey glanced over at Jameson. "Is that true, Jameson?" He asked.

Jameson stood silently, trying to come up with an answer.

"He wanted me to make it, 'go away,'" Rose continued, using air quotes. "Just like he made Linda Reed's sexual assault case against the captain go away," she fumed.

"Woah, woah, woah, sexual assault case?" Ramsey questioned. "All sexual assault allegations are to be reported to Internal Affairs immediately."

"I was just about to send it over," Jameson replied. Rose knew he was lying through his teeth.

"We'll see about that," Ramsey replied skeptically, pulling out his notepad. "We're gonna have to ask you two a few questions," He motioned to Jameson and the Captain. "If you'll excuse us, Officer Livingston."

Rose left Jameson's office feeling a bit of the weight lifted from her shoulders. She was proud of herself for standing up to Jameson and the captain and sighed a breath of relief. The feeling was short-lived as her phone began to buzz with calls and texts from her family and other officers about the report she filed against her brother.

She read her messages as she slumped into her car. She couldn't tear her eyes away from the vile, awful texts and venomous voicemails calling her a sell-out and an ingrate. Tears welled up in her eyes as she read her family's disapproving messages. One voicemail message from her father stung her heart in particular.

"How could you, Rose?" her father asked angrily over the phone. "That's your brother! You're definitely no child of mine because I didn't raise a snake." Her heart sank as she listened to it again.

Rose's breath became shaky as she listened to one hurtful message after another. Not only did she have to deal with the backlash from work, but her family too. She was conflicted with emotion. She knew she did what was right, but the consequences were still devastating. She threw her phone on the backseat in frustration before letting out a heart-breaking wail, releasing the whirlpool of emotions that were building for so long.

Although she didn't sleep well that night, Rose arrived at work ahead of schedule the next morning. She had been trying to get out of the car for twenty minutes, but her feet wouldn't move. Her heart pounded, and sweat seemed to pour down her back, forming a pool at the waistband of her slacks. All the havoc in her life had drained Rose's usually boundless energy. Still, she knew she must face the day.

Rose gathered her resolve, said a silent prayer, and ejected herself from the car. She whispered a quiet pep talk to herself as she walked toward the building and climbed into the elevator. As she prepared herself to face more scrutiny, she was surprised when all eyes were not on her as she walked to her desk. All eyes were focused across the room. She was shocked to see Captain Jenkins being read his Miranda rights as an officer cuffed his hands behind his back.

"What's going on?" Rose whispered to one of her coworkers.

"Captain Jenkins is being brought up on sexual assault charges," her coworker whispered back.

Rose watched in disbelief as he was escorted out of the building.

It seemed that since Rose complained to Internal Affairs about the incident with Linda, several other female officers in the precinct--Black and White alike--came forward with similar experiences. Rose slumped into her chair, put her head on the desk, and cried tears of joy. Linda and so many others were finally being heard and getting the justice they deserved.

CHAPTER 17

SESSION VIII. YEAR EIGHT

ROSE LIVINGSTON

The remaining officers prepared for yet another session within the Decennial Program. They arrived at their stations and strapped on their equipment effortlessly. They grew accustomed to the process, and it had become second nature to them at this point.

As Rose secured the chin strap on her helmet, Dr. Langston approached her chair.

"Rose, We heard about what you did at the precinct... reporting your brother. Standing up for what's right isn't always easy, but it's always worth it," Dr. Langston said. I think you've made significant progress toward reforming your ideas. I think your time here with us is finished."

Rose looked up at Dr. Langston with a confused look on her face.

"Yes, you heard me correctly, you've successfully completed the Decennial Program. Congratulations, Rose. You're done," Dr. Langston repeated.

Rose sat up, grinning from ear to ear. This was great news, but it was tinged with regret. Rose realized that this meant she had to say goodbye to being Linda, just as she would finally be getting justice for what happened to her. Rose would've never imagined that being a Black woman would've taught her what it meant to be fearless, honest, and strong? She knew in her heart that the Decennial Program forever changed her and that she would take the lessons she learned with her throughout the rest of her life.

"Thank you for everything," Rose said as she shook hands with each member of Dr. Langston's team and turned to leave. "I will never forget this experience."

When Rose exited the building this time, she walked into a familiar and somewhat new world. She felt better than she had in a very long time. She took long, confident strides as she crossed the street, but her euphoria was short-lived. Just as she got into her car, her phone beeped with a text message alert telling her to report to the Internal Affairs office ASAP. Her heart felt like it was in her throat and pounding as if it were trying to escape her body.

Suddenly, her mood shifted from utter joy to pure anxiety as she made her way to the precinct. Her mind started racing, wondering what they could possibly want.

She already gave her statement, and she knew they hadn't completed their investigation yet, so she couldn't imagine what more they needed.

When Rose arrived at the precinct, she parked her car, took a deep breath, and made her way towards the building. She sat in the waiting area outside of Ramsey's office, perusing American Cop, Crime Magazine, and Correctional News as she waited. After forty minutes of nervously consuming two cups of coffee and three donuts and looking through five publications, the office assistant escorted her into Ramsey's office.

He looked up from his phone call as she entered, and he motioned for her to take a seat across the desk from him. After a few moments, he placed the phone back on the cradle and turned his attention to her.

After a bit of small talk, he got right to the point:

"Rose, I called you here to share something very important with you." Ramsey began. Rose gulped, her mind racing with the anticipation of what he would say next. "Your dedication to integrity and the bravery that you exhibited during this trying time in our community is admirable. So admirable, in fact, that I would like to offer you a position on a new task force we have recently formed. It's our new Special Operations Unit. This unit will be responsible for looking into all matters of injustice inflicted by officers, with a focus on racial injustices. This department is committed to making sure that every member of our community gets treated equally in the eyes of the law. No one race better, or other race worse. We want to know if you are up for the challenge of making sure equal justice is upheld no matter what it takes, even if it takes arresting fellow officers and removing the bad cops that give the good ones a bad name?"

Rose jumped up from her seat, heart pounding.

"Are you serious?" she asked excitedly, "You want me to head up a task force?" Rose asked, unsure if she heard Ramsey correctly the first time. "Yes, of course, I would love to head up the Special Operations Unit. This is the absolute best day I've had in a very long time. I wasn't really sure what I was walking into today. A task force was the last thing I would've imagined!" she exclaimed.

The anxiety, Rose had before arriving melted away and was replaced with the type of joy a kid feels at Christmas time, when they receive a gift they have been waiting for all year.

Ramsey briefed Rose on the nature of the task force and the duties she would be assigned. She happily accepted the position–which came with a considerable pay increase and a team that she was told would consist of some of the best officers on the force that have proven to have a great deal of integrity. When the meeting was over, Ramsey ushered Rose to her new, plush corner office. Along the way, they stopped at Jameson's office.

"Jameson, I'd like you to meet the new head of our Special Operations Unit, Officer Rose Livingston. She'll be overseeing the team and this entire department," he revealed.

Jameson congratulated her on her new position.

"I know you'll make us proud. You've earned this job, and you deserve it, Rose. We all know how difficult the challenges you've faced have been and how hard you've worked these last few months. Some of the choices you had to make couldn't have been easy, either, but all of it led you to this moment in your career. I know your father is gonna be very proud when you give him the news. We wanted you to be the one to tell him," Jameson said with a kind smile.

"Thank you," she said, letting a faint smile spread across her face. Rose wasn't sure if she was ready to forgive him yet, but today was too good to ruin it with a fight.

As she walked away, Jameson said, "Before you go, Rose..."

She stopped and turned back to where he stood. He extended his hand to shake hers, looking into her eyes, and with sincerity, said, "I want to apologize. For....well, for everything. You're a real tough kid and a fine officer, Rose."

Knowing apologies were not Jameson's strong suit, it meant a lot that he was attempting to correct his wrongs. Instead of taking his hand, she smiled and embraced him in a hug before continuing to her office.

CASSANDRA ELLIS

Cassandra, Terrell, and James talked and laughed together at the dining room table over another dinner.

James had become a frequent guest at their home since Emily was rarely home at the dinner hour. Cassandra didn't mind his presence, and it was rarely a problem to add a few more ingredients to make whatever she was cooking stretch enough to feed two growing basketball stars.

Besides, Terrell enjoyed his company, and over time, they've become as close as brothers. They even thought about which colleges they would attend and whether they would play for the same team in the NBA.

As they finished their meals, Terrell excused himself from the dinner table.

"You're not slick, Terrell." Cassandra playfully threw the words at his, retreating back as she stacked the used dinner plates. "He never wants to help clear the table, " she said jokingly to James.

"I'll help, Ms. Ellis," James said as he collected a few items from the table and followed her into the kitchen. An awkward silence filled the room as they worked to put the kitchen back in order.

"James, I wanna talk to you about something for a second," Cassandra said, breaking the silence.

Something heavy had been weighing on her mind for quite some time. She thought about the hateful things she'd taught James as Emily and the impact they had on him. Emily had taught him to hate and degrade people for no other reason than the color of their skin. Through Cassandra's eyes, Emily had seen how racist she was and most of all the damage it had done to James.

For weeks, she struggled with trying to fix it, and she saw this as a moment to begin to rectify some of her mistakes.

She stopped washing the dishes for a moment and turned to face him, "James, I want you to know the things your mom taught you about Black and Brown people are wrong." she began.

"Oh. I know Ms. Ellis," he said, nodding his head in agreement.

"I hope I can; I mean, your mom can show you the right way to treat people. Race and color have nothing to do with someone's character. It's not natural for people to hate; it's taught, and it's learned." Cassandra continued. "It's not enough to just know it's wrong; you also have to do something about it when you see it."

"Yeah, or you're a part of the problem, too," James said, finishing her sentence.

It seemed that James had also learned a lot about race since becoming friends with Terrell. He regretted mistreating Terrell, but he knew he couldn't ever really make it up to him. So instead, he vowed that he would no longer prejudge people based on the color of their skin. James also committed himself to get to know more about African-American culture. He remembered his social studies teacher saying that in order to have a world-view, you have to embrace views from around the world without prejudging or bias. The best way to remove bias was to spend time with people of other cultures, and in doing so, a person becomes more well-rounded as a person and better able to navigate the world, not just their neighborhood. James was determined to live that way from now on.

Cassandra smiled after they talked, feeling as if she was doing something right with James, even if he didn't know it was her doing it. James still held a tinge of resentment in his heart for Emily, sewing seeds of hatred in him like she did. He hoped for the courage and an opportunity to let Emily know how he truly felt.

DECENNIAL HEADQUARTERS

Dr. Langston walked into the control room as Emily, Ethan, Robert, and George came out of sedation in the observation room.

"Will you email the reports to Internal Affairs?" Dr. Langston asked Dr. Cooper. "They won't leave me alone. Tell them we still have a couple of officers still in the program and three sessions left."

They're getting on my damn nerves, and I wish they'd just trust me to do my job without all this oversight," Dr. Langston complained as the team powered down the computer system that operates the Decennial Program.

Dr. Hughes walked into the observation room and assisted the officers with their headgear and reclining chairs, and pulled Emily to the side.

"Emily, we have observed extremely promising results from you." Dr. Hughes conveyed to Emily. "It appears that your son James has helped you see the unconscious bias that you were not aware of when you started the program. Because of the growth we have seen in you. I am pleased to say you have officially graduated from the Decennial Program. Dr. Langston and the team wanted you to know that."

Emily gave Dr. Hughes a big hug as she smiled quietly and walked away. Emily quickly turned towards Dr. Hughes and said, "I still have lots of work to do in the real world, and I promise you I won't be back."

Emily and Dr. Hughes shared a laugh as Emily left the Decennial building.

Robert, Ethan, and George faintly heard the conversation between Emily and Dr. Hughes but saw the familiar hug and handshake and realized Emily had completed the program.

"I can't believe I'm still in this program," Robert complained as he rubbed his stiff neck.

"I don't really mind that much," Ethan yawned peacefully as he lifted his arms to stretch. "At least I get to see Tasha every day while I'm in there."

George and Robert glared at Ethan's enthusiasm as they brushed past him. Their experiences in the Decennial Program left them feeling more and more hopeless. The session ended, and everyone gathered their things and prepared to leave the building after their wrap-up session with Dr. Hughes.

"I just don't understand why this Malik guy can't catch a break," George said. " It can't be just because he's Black, can it? There's gotta be more to this story. Is a bank even allowed to be racist?" George asked Ethan and Robert right before walking through the doors.

"Well, is a cop allowed to be racist?" Ethan countered, raising an eyebrow as they walked out of the observation room.

Robert and Ethan continued out of the building, but George, stricken by those words, stopped briefly before following them out. Before George could open the door, he heard his name being called from the observation room.

George turned around and saw Dr. Cooper calling his name and waving her hands trying to get his attention. George walked into the observation room where Dr. Langston and his team were assembled.

"George, we have been monitoring your progress in the Decennial Program very closely," Dr. Langston stated. "We have been paying close attention to how you're responding to the situations you have found yourself in through Malik. We debated whether you needed one more session, and Dr. Hughes here thinks you're ready now. What do you think."

"Well, I don't really know what to think. Do I want to spend one more session going through hell? I'd rather not. I will say this." George paused and took a moment to gather his thoughts. "I will say that when I started this program, I resented having to come here. I felt like I was just fine and didn't need a mental adjustment. I never felt like I was racist at all. But I have learned that the reason why I didn't feel like anything was wrong was because I and everything in my world had been insulated with people who look and think just like me, so I never felt like I needed to change anything."

George went on to say, "Once I had to step into Malik's world and see all that he had to deal with, I began to see just how hopeless Black people can feel when everywhere they turn, they have to endure one bad situation after another. No one really wants to, or is able to help, and initially, that made me wonder why Black people aren't better at helping each other? I realized that just like me and my friends, you tend to associate with like-minded people. So, if Malik is broke most of the time, the people in his circle are in the same or a similar situation; and I just don't know how you find hope in that. I thought it was tough being a cop on the streets, but naw being Black on the streets is way worse. I mean probably not for you guys because yall are all educated in stuff," George continued as he quickly looked around the room.

George nervously cleared his throat and explained, "I never thought I would be saying this, but what I experienced as Malik is wrong, and I do truly want to do something to help guys like him, you know the Blacks that are living right and trying to do the right thing. I think sometimes Black people, especially Black men get a bad rap. They get labeled for not being providers, for not being a father to their kids, and so much more, and from what I saw, that just ain't true. Malik was being the best dad he could be, hell he was much better at it than my dad ever was. Why is it that most of how Black's are portrayed in the media is bad? How do you get up expecting to do good in the world when people see you negatively or people are constantly putting you down, not offering any help, taking away every opportunity to better yourself. If your asking me, do I want to do another session like that, the answer is a definitive, Hell naw," George concluded.

Dr. Langston and his team looked at each other in sheer amazement, not just because of what George said, but mainly because he had never been that open to talk before. They had the results from the computers and data charts, but confirming their findings with George's statement was all that they needed to hear.

Dr. Langston sprung up from his chair and extends his hand to George. "George, you have officially completed the Decennial Program. After today you no longer have to report here.

"Remember what you have learned here, George. Make sure you keep a piece of Malik with you. More importantly, share what you learned with others like your friends and family so that the power of what you experienced grows exponentially." Dr. Cooper said to George as she shook his hand.

"I will not forget, trust me, I don't think an experience like that leaves anyone, any time soon," George mentioned.

"I do want to say thank you all. I know I don't talk much. I kinda like my actions to do the talkin' I am sure yall will see me again, but under different circumstances, of course," George said with a big smile on his face.

George turned around and left the observation room, taking one last glance around the place somewhat nostalgically, and then exited the building.

GEORGE MCDUFFIE

As George drove home, he passed the bank that denied his loan when he went into the bank as Malik. He made a U-turn into the parking lot of the bank, wondering if it's possible to prove they denied Malik because he's Black. Inside, he was immediately greeted by a banker, but as Malik, he waited for almost 15 minutes before someone came to assist him.

George applied for the same loan he did as Malik, knowing they had the same salary and credit score. The banker was charming to George, making casual small talk as he typed in George's application. George remembered how rude and testy the banker was when he applied as Malik. Within minutes, George was approved for the loan.

He left the bank without saying a word to the banker.

George finally understood how hard it would be to get ahead when no one wants to help you, and he now understood that the only difference between who he is now and who he was in the program was that as Malik, he was a Black man. A man perceived as not worthy of a loan from the bank.

He sat in his car, regretting all the things he assumed about Black people, especially about them being lazy.

That night, George lay awake and stared up at the ceiling. Snapshots of his misguided ideas and atrocious behaviors filled him with guilt and regret that kept him writhing in anguish. He had so many reasons to feel guilt, including his unjust shooting of Avery Brooks. A myriad of thoughts rushed in like a tidal wave. He wondered why he ever thought it was okay to shoot to kill someone, especially a kid. He remembered how dismissive he'd been after shooting him; now, he was eternally thankful that he hadn't killed him.

How could he even begin to rectify the mistakes he'd made? He wondered. He knew he couldn't ever give Avery the ability to walk again, but he could do something to express his remorse.

That same week, George liquidated the entirety of his 401k and all of his other retirement plans and began to make arrangements to create a scholarship in Avery Brooks' name. He wanted the funds from the scholarship to go to Black students who were directly impacted by violence at the hands of law enforcement officers. It wasn't enough to make amends with Avery or his family, but he felt it was a start. He named the scholarship "Books for Brooks."

Once George established the scholarship fund, he felt like the next step for him was to meet with Brooks family in person. He rehearsed a million times what he would say if he ever had the opportunity to speak directly to them, and each time he would botch it in his head. After realizing he just would have to set up a meeting and go from there, even if it didn't go perfectly, he knew he had to at least give it a try.

Avery Brooks' family reluctantly agreed to meet with George after he established the scholarship. The last time that they saw him, George was unapologetic and apathetic.

George was nervous as he sat down with the Brooks family. Seeing their pain and sorrow sobered him even more and made his heart feel like someone was wringing it, like a wet shirt. He noticed Avery especially, whose eyes reminded him of Samuel's--which made his heart even heavier with emotion as he struggled to speak.

"I'd like to begin by making it clear that I don't deserve your forgiveness," he choked.

"You damn right you don't." Avery's mother snapped, still reeling with pain. Mr. Brooks rubbed her back as tears of anger and grief flooded her eyes.

"I took something away from you that I can never return." George continued, his voice shaking. "I wake up every day and regret the choice that I made. I was careless and heartless--and exhibited unconscious bias, something I didn't know at the time." George confessed as a tear descended down his cheek. "Still, there's no excuse for my behavior." George turned and looked directly at Avery. "Avery, I'm so sorry. I could spend the rest of my life trying to make up for what I did, and it wouldn't be enough," he said, his voice thick with emotion as he glanced back to Mr. and Mrs. Brooks.

"Avery has always been a wonderful kid. I didn't create the scholarship just for show. I looked into his record at school and in the community, and I was inspired. You've got a great son, and this scholarship will help other kids be as great as him."

"I'm so sorry," he finished, holding back tears. They all stare at George cautiously.

"I forgive you," Avery uttered from his wheelchair.

Everyone's eyes turned to Avery in shock. George never expected to be forgiven, and judging by their shocked looks, his parents didn't expect him to say that, either.

Mr. and Mrs. Brooks watched, stunned, as Avery motioned for a hug from George. Their faces softened as Avery and George engaged in an emotional embrace. George cried deeply but silently as Mr.and Mrs. Brooks leaned down for a group embrace. George suddenly found that he felt one hundred pounds lighter after letting go of an immense amount of guilt and emotion that he had been carrying for some time.

After gaining the Brooks' family's forgiveness, George was inspired to keep fighting for racial justice. He reported the bank manager for racially profiling Black and Brown clients, which led to a full investigation of the bank. The bank fired the manager and launched an initiative requiring employees to complete diversity training programs, and established a fund to help to destroy economic disparities between White and Black people.

The "Books for Brooks" scholarship garnered national attention, and George was invited to appear on several news broadcasts to talk about his journey. At one such broadcast he fidgeted nervously as the production assistant adjusted his microphone—a bead of sweat formed on his forehead. "You're on in three, two, one," he whispered as George dabbed his sweat away with a handkerchief.

As the interview began, the reporter started by praising George for creating a scholarship in Avery's name. She went on about how inspiring and uplifting his story was.

"I don't deserve any praise or appreciation for creating the scholarship," George emphasized. "Avery Brooks deserves all of the praise and the recognition. He is probably one of the most honorable persons I've ever met. He inspired me to be a better man, and I'm only sorry it took this unfortunate incident to bring about a change of heart in me. I shot that young man, and it was uncalled for. I can't give him back the use of his limbs, but I can try to bring awareness and attempt to reform our policing tactics here in America," he concluded remorsefully.

The reporter asked George a series of questions about how he decided to create the scholarship as well as spearheading the investigation into several bank's lending practices. George revealed that by participating in the Decennial Program, he came away from it with a newfound understanding and appreciation for the Black community and the things they encounter at the hands of racist ideas and practices that make up systemic racism.

"I have to admit. I thought the Decennial Program was just another ploy to get people to 'think' the police were actually interested in reform. But the program immersed each of us fully into the life of another person. That kind of experience gives you a new perspective," George expressed.

"That's just remarkable," The reporter said. "You make it sound so real."

"Oh, it was real alright." George laughed. "I lived life as a Black man in America, and it changed my entire outlook on life. Now, I have the utmost respect for Black Americans and the things they've had to endure as a result of White supremacy and the many trap doors that have been purposely and strategically laid out so that they just can't get ahead in life," he continued. "Every White person should experience the Decennial Program, especially people like that racist bank manager, and people like the person I was. I'm just glad I was able to participate in the program. It truly changed my life," he said, looking directly into the camera.

"They say you can't teach an old dog new tricks. People are stuck in their ways, and I get it. But, I say you're never too old to change; it's never too late to decide to do better, and I'm just glad the Brooks family was able to see my sincere desire to change and seek forgiveness. I've become a better man because of this, and I hope we all seek to better understand one another in this country. There's a great deal of healing to be done around the idea of racism and White supremacy," George concluded confidently.

"I couldn't have said it better myself," the reporter commented. "That's all the time we have today. Thank you for talking with us and sharing your powerful message."

EMILY CAMPBELL

As Emily arrived home, she was greeted by James, who was waiting for her in the living room. Usually, she returned from the Decennial Program still feeling groggy and irritable; this time, she felt a sense of peace and clarity.

"Hey, Mom, can I talk to you about something serious?" James asked.

"Sure, what's up?" Emily replied as she tossed her purse on the coffee table and sat on the couch, waiting for James to begin.

"Mom, I need to be honest with you about something, and it's kinda hard to say," he paused as if he were thinking about his words very carefully. "I have been spending a lot of time with my Black teammate Terrell and his mom. I have been to his house many times for dinner and just to hang out, mostly. Mom Terrell's family is nothing like you said Black people are. I actually enjoy hanging out with him more than some of my other friends." he explained.

Emily was stunned by his bluntness but remained silent so he could continue.

"I think about the things you taught me about Black people, and when I do, it makes me angry. I used to treat Black people like shit because of you, and I used to walk around like I was better than them, just because I was White and they were Black. You taught me that I was always right, and they were always wrong, and that's just not right." he went on.

Emily looked down shamefully. She didn't even bother to correct his profanity because she knew he was right. She hadn't realized the degree to which she'd damaged James, but she wanted to fix it.

"I'm - I'm embarrassed." he stuttered, starting to get emotional. "I've hated myself for mistreating Black people, especially Terrel, but I did it because of what you taught me, Mom," he said as his face started to become flushed.

She had never seen James this emotional before. She could tell that he had been feeling that way for quite some time. It broke her heart to see him hurting because of something that was her fault, and the guilt overwhelmed her.

"I'm so, so sorry, Son," Emily said as her voice cracked with emotion. "There's no excuse, except that I didn't know any better myself. I gave you what I got from my folks," a tear fell down her face. "I was teaching you to be hateful, and that's not the kind of mom I want to be." Emily's tears were gushing and rushing down her face, and she didn't attempt to hide her shame, "I'm so sorry, baby," Emily reached for James, gathering him in a tight hug as she rubbed his back. She was delighted to have been able to see that James seemed to experience a lot of growth, on his own, as well.

CHAPTER 18

SESSION IX. YEAR NINE

DECENNIAL CONTROL ROOM

Dr. Langston's team found themselves transfixed to the television in the control room as George McDuffie gave another interview about the scholarship he created.

After the interview ended, Dr. Cooper picked up the remote and clicked off the television.

"Good for him. George has made wonderful progress, and his story is bringing a lot of awareness to our program," Dr. Cooper mentioned.

"Yeah, I thought he was gonna be one of the last two standing," Tyrese complained playfully. "Now I owe Dr. Hughes $20!"

"You're betting on our cohorts?" Dr. Langston sternly questioned Tyrese as he entered the room.

Tyrese looked around like a deer caught in the headlights before replying, "Uhh, no. Of course not," he stammered unconvincingly.

"Please see to it that our guests are okay, Dr. Cooper," Dr. Langston stated as he picked up a thick file from his desk. "I am heading to the conference room. Another one of our cohorts is ready to graduate."

Ethan, Robert, and Roger shift slowly in their seats, waking up from another session.

"I bet I'll make it out before Rob does," Roger said jokingly to Ethan as he unloosed the chin strap on this helmet.

"Yeah, whatever," Robert grunted as he stretched his back. "How many more times do I have to do this damn thing, anyway?"

"You've completed nine sessions; the final session is next month, Robert," Dr. Cooper cautioned. "It's up to you to make the change," she reminded them all as they prepared to leave the observation room.

"Ethan, Dr. Langston would like to see you in the conference room," Dr. Cooper said as she motioned Ethan to follow her.

Ethan cautiously entered the conference room and saw Dr. Langston seated across the table from him with a stack of folders and slowly took a seat.

"Ethan Jenkins Jr., when you came into our program, you had a clear disdain for Black people, and perhaps it was inherited honestly from your father, Captain Jenkins. However, since you entered the program even as early as the first session, we have been noticing slight differences in your brainwaves," Dr. Langston mentioned showing a chart of squiggly lines in multiple colors to Ethan.

"Those squiggly lines represent emotional stimulation, as you can see these gray lines become more pronounced and eventually go from grey to red," Dr. Cooper explained.

"Do you know what that represents?" Dr. Cooper asked Ethan.

"I don't have a clue. I was never good at science growing up. Doc, what does all this colorful shit have to do with me?" Ethan asked gruffly.

"Ding-Ding-Ding. I'm glad you asked the million-dollar question, Ethan," Dr. Langston said as he stood up. "Those red lines show that your mind has become totally different from when you started. Initially, your ability to be empathetic and or sympathetic towards others was showing up in a dark shade of grey. Through each session, we started observing progress. That Tasha girl has helped you to see Black people differently and not just her, all Black people.

"Wait a minute, you can tell all of that from a piece of paper,'" Ethan questioned in disbelief.

"I know you have been trying to hide how you really feel outwardly, but inwardly the graphs pick up everything, and they don't lie, and they're never wrong," Dr. Cooper said.

"What we're saying here, Ethan is although you took a different path from your fellow officer's, you achieved the same result. You have completed the Decennial Program.

After today you no longer have to report back here," Dr. Langston continued.

"So what your saying is I'm free to go, and I don't have to do any more of this simulation stuff?" Ethan asked excitedly.

"Yes, that's correct," Dr. Cooper acknowledged.

"So I'm free, really; yall not just pullin' my leg, are you?" Ethan cautiously asked.

"Free to be, all that you can be," Dr. Langston chimed in, trying to inject humor, unsuccessfully.

Ethan quickly stood and shook both Dr. Langston's and Dr. Cooper's hands vigorously and darted out the door, so they didn't change their minds.

'I can honestly say that I have never seen a White boy run that fast," Dr. Langston said jokingly, only to be met with a prune face from Dr. Cooper. After a short pause, they both burst into laughter.

ETHAN JENKINS JR.

Ethan hurried out of the Decennial building. He rushed to Meechie's Cafe in an effort to catch Tasha before her shift ended. He felt like the coffee shop was the best place to approach Tasha because Jamal and Tasha had so much history there. Not only was it the place he met Tasha for the first time, but it had been where they shared so many heartfelt moments. It was the one place Ethan, as Jamal, allowed himself to be vulnerable. The last time Ethan and Tasha crossed paths was at the riots, where he had made an absolute fool of himself. He was eager but nervous to see her again. Just as he pulled up to the coffee shop, he received a phone call from Emily.

Ethan and Emily hadn't spoken much since they hooked up after that night of drinking at the bar. He debated whether or not he should answer the phone. He was so preoccupied with his thoughts of Tasha.

"Hey Emily," he said quickly, holding his phone to his ear.

Emily invited Ethan out for drinks. As Emily finished talking, Ethan stared at the coffee shop a few feet away and realized that he wasn't even tempted to meet up with Emily.

"Umm, I don't think so. I've got other plans tonight," Ethan said, spotting Tasha through the coffee shop window. "Maybe some other time, though, okay? Gotta go. Bye," Ethan hung up without waiting to hear Emily's reply. He watched Tasha for a moment longer before heading inside; her beauty mesmerized him, whether he was Jamal or Ethan.

The bell on the coffee shop door rang as Ethan stepped inside. Ethan couldn't help but note how weird it was to him that Meechies coffee shop had become so familiar and comforting. It was his sanctuary as Jamal. The shop was empty, except for a couple at a table in the back booth talking in hushed tones, holding hands. Ethan thought to himself how much he wanted to do that with Tasha as himself one day.

"I'll be right with you," Tasha said over her shoulder as she made drinks for the couple at the table.

Ethan waited patiently, trying to decide what to say when she came to wait on him. He wondered if she would remember him from the riots. A part of him hoped she didn't, so that they could have a fresh start.

"How may I help y-," She paused as she turned around, immediately recognizing Ethan.

"Before you say anything, let me explain. I'm not a stalker or anything like that. Please, will you give me five minutes to explain?"

Tasha looked at him suspiciously before walking behind the counter to ask a coworker to cover for her for a few minutes. She walked back to Ethan's table and sat in the chair opposite him. Tasha's body was noticeably unsettled, as if she would jump up and run at any moment. She perched on the very edge of her seat, her eyes darting around the room distrustfully.

After a few moments of silence, Tasha cleared her throat loudly.

"Well, are you gonna explain? I don't have all day, and you asked for five minutes. You've blown through one of them already just sitting here," Tasha snapped.

Ethan opened his mouth to speak, but no words came out. "I have to get back to work," Tasha said as she stood up from her seat.

"Tasha, please wait! There's an explanation, but I can't say it's a very believable one," Ethan pled. Tasha slid back down into her seat hesitantly.

"This is gonna sound so fucking weird," he said, mostly to himself. Tasha raised her eyebrows and waited for him to continue.

"My name is Ethan Jenkins Jr., and I was participating in a project called the Decennial Program; my name was Jamal Edwards, and I would meet you right here every morning to get my mother's coffee. As I would come here every day, I found myself falling in love with you," he explained. Tasha looked him up and down with her brows furrowed in confusion.

"This is a waste of time," she scoffed, standing to leave again.

"Your name is Tasha Butler, you have been working at Meechie's Cafe for three and a half years, you are an activist that is heavily involved in your community, you're allergic to peanuts or any other nuts for that matter, you have this amazingly adorable giggle when someone is flirting with you, you don't easily trust men because of your past, you got your heart broken by your ex the day before Valentine's day and that's why you don't like Valentine's day to this day."

After a moment's reflection, she turned back to the table and slowly sat back down.

"How do you know those things about me?" Tasha asked inquisitively.

"Because I *am* Jamal. I know it's hard to believe, but hear me out," he desperately explained.

She signaled with her hands for him to continue.

"I got into trouble a few months back for police brutality, and they put me in the Decennial Program. It's like a simulation where I had to live my life as a Black person, as Jamal. I have spent a lot of time getting to know you in this very Cafe. We have had numerous conversations in this very booth. I have spent a lot of time getting to know everything I could about you. I started off being mostly intrigued by your beauty, but the more I got to know you, the more I found myself wanting to know even more about you. I know it sounds like a bad sci-fi episode, but I promise you, it's real," Ethan revealed.

"The feelings that Jamal had and that I now have are also real."

"You're Jamal?" she asked, confused.

"Yes," Ethan sighed.

"When I was Jamal, I convinced you to give Ethan a chance. I told you that he'd be crazy not to fall for a girl with eyes as beautiful as yours," he said as he gazed into Tasha's almond-shaped brown eyes, which were widening in surprise as he spoke.

Tasha looked deeply into Ethan's eyes and briefly saw Jamal's tenderness.

"Oh, my God," she said, realizing that Ethan was telling the truth. "You're Jamal," she affirmed.

"I'm Ethan," he said lovingly. "I've been in a constant state of agony, wondering whether you would understand. I'm just happy you know now," he said, feeling a weight lifted off of his shoulders.

"What the fuck is this?" Tasha asked hollowly, throwing her towel down onto the table. " I trusted you. I confided in you as Jamal. I have no idea who you are or what to trust," she exclaimed. "This is bullshit! I feel like you misled me the whole time!"

"Tasha, no. It's not like that," Ethan explained, trying to calm her down.

"You're White, and you're a cop...a cop who got busted for police brutality, at that?! This is so fucked up," she continued. "Man, I would have never, ever, ever, dated you if I'd known who you were," she emphasized.

Although Ethan assumed that Tasha didn't date White men, it hurt him to hear her say it to his face. He looked down at the table, dejected.

"You think I don't know that?" he countered. "I know that I'm White, and you're Black. And I know a whole lot of people don't wanna see us together. But you wanna know something, Tasha? I don't care. I'm in love with you, and I want you to give me a chance to show you I'm not the same guy who went into the Decennial Program. That experience changed me, Tasha. I don't look like the same guy, but I'm the same guy who has been in here every day trying to get you to fall as deeply in love with me as I am with you. I know how much I love you, and I now know love knows no color." he finished.

"Love knows no color?" She scoffed. "That's easy to say when you're White, You could never understand what it's really like being Black."

"You're right, Tasha. I'll never fully understand," he agreed. "But I will walk proudly with you on my arm, and I'll fight with anyone that gets in the way of that," he declared. "Please, Tasha," he begged as he held her hands in his own. "Give us a chance. Let me prove myself to you."

There were several moments of silence as Tasha contemplated what she had just heard. The seconds felt like hours as Ethan waited for her response.

Tasha reflected on the connection that she had with Jamal and all of the playful, flirtatious moments they spent laughing and talking, but her heart was torn.

"I don't know," she sighed as she pulled her hands away. "I can't give you an answer right now," Tasha replied.

Ethan's heart dropped into his stomach. He was disappointed that she didn't say yes, but hopeful because she didn't say no.

"I'd wait forever for you, Tasha. Take as much time as you need. I'm not going anywhere," Ethan promised.

Without a word, Tasha stood and walked behind the counter. Ethan watched her go, unable to tear his eyes away.

Ethan slowly got up and left the coffee shop, wishing he could possibly turn back into Jamal for just a few moments. Although he was desperate for an answer, he didn't want to pressure her into giving him a chance before she was ready.

The days seemed longer as Ethan waited, and he began to think that Tasha would never respond. The anxiety became tortuous, and it overcame Ethan. After waiting for many long weeks, Ethan decided to just show up at the coffee shop, mentally preparing himself for an answer from Tasha, whether it be good or bad.

When Tasha looked up and saw Ethan standing in the doorway, her heart skipped a beat. She was happily surprised but masked her emotions with a straight face. She didn't plan on ever talking to Ethan again. Not because she didn't want to, but because she didn't know what to say. Her mind had been playing tug of war, trying to decide if she could forgive Ethan enough to really get to know him. When she got a moment, she walked over to where he was standing.

"Hey, Tasha, I know I told you I would give you time, but I couldn't wait any longer. I had to come see you," Ethan began. "I know that you have had a lot to think about, but I can't get you out of my head. I think about you every day. I got the feeling that you didn't want to talk to me, but I'd hate myself every day if I didn't give it one more shot." he expressed passionately.

"Just let me take you on one date. Just one," Ethan pleaded. "If you never want to talk to me again after that, then.,." he paused. "Then I'll be heartbroken, I would understand, or try to understand, but I will leave you alone," he admitted. "One shot?" he begged as he held his breath.

A small crowd of Tasha's coworkers gathered around to see what was going on. They looked at Tasha, anxiously waiting for her response. She had confided in one or two of them seeking advice. She had no idea what to make of the whole scenario. Tasha's coworkers were aware of her feelings for Ethan, and they were hoping she'd say yes to him. After a moment of thought, Tasha finally opened her mouth to respond.

"Okay," she said as Ethan finally breathed a sigh of relief. "You get one chance. One," she said reluctantly, holding up one finger.

Ethan smiled from ear to ear, celebrating internally. "You won't regret it. I swear," Ethan vowed excitedly. "I'll pick you up tomorrow night at 7 pm sharp." He smiled as he seemingly glided out of the coffee shop with joy. "Finally!" he exclaimed to himself.

"I told you he would come back for you," One of Tasha's coworkers said teasingly. "What did I say? Let him go, and if he's really yours, he will come back."

"That boy loves you," another coworker said as she playfully bumped into Tasha.

"Shut up," she smiled. "These drinks aren't gonna make themselves," Tasha said jovially as she got back to work.

Tasha was ecstatic that Ethan came to see her, although she would never admit it aloud. She had determined that she was going to let fate decide their future. If he never returned, she would put Ethan and Jamal out of her mind, forever. If he returned, it would prove that his words were sincere.

Tasha made up her mind the moment Ethan entered the door, but she wanted to make him sweat a bit, a penance for putting her in such a topsy-turvy situation.

The next night, Ethan arrived at Tasha's place at 7 o'clock, sharp. He stepped out of a chauffeured-driven black town car holding a dozen red roses for Tasha. He was wearing a white button-down shirt with the cuffs turned up and the top two buttons undone, deep navy slacks, and navy blue dress shoes. He wanted to look his best for Tasha in case this was the only chance he would ever have with her.

Ethan watched in awe as Tasha cascaded down the stairs in front of her brownstone apartment. Her silky white dress clung to her body as the breeze blew by. Her natural, dark brown curls and coils were gathered in an elegant updo, complementing her delicate features. Ethan already knew that Tasha was gorgeous, but seeing her dressed to the nines was captivating.

"Wow," he breathed as he took her hand. "I don't know how it's possible, but you get more beautiful every time I look at you," he said as he admired her. Tasha smiled and looked away bashfully as Ethan guided her into the town car.

Ethan planned an extraordinary, romantic date for the two of them. The date began at an elegant waterfront restaurant, looking out over the rippling waves and underneath the onlooking stars. Warm romantic candlelight illuminated their table as they laughed and talked.

After dinner, the driver picked them up and drove them to a quaint jazz lounge. The lighting in the lounge was dimmed such that it created the perfect romantic ambiance. Ethan strategically reserved a small table in the corner that would cause them to have to snuggle closely together. They sipped red wine and listened to a string quartet play romantic jazz melodies for several hours.

Neither of them wanted the night to end, so after leaving the lounge, they took a stroll along the boardwalk, hand in hand. As they strolled to the end of the boardwalk, there was a horse-drawn carriage waiting for them.

"Oh my goodness. Ethan!" Tasha squealed happily. "I can't believe you did all of this," she smiled as they rode off on an enchanted journey through the park.

At the end of the evening, Ethan escorted Tasha up the stairs of her brownstone. "I had an amazing time," he said as they arrived at her front door. "I hope you did too."

"Tonight was better than anything I imagined," Tasha said as she smiled. Tasha's response made Ethan's heart swell. Ethan was head over heels for Tasha, and it seemed she was finally starting to let her walls down again.

"Can I see you again sometime?" Ethan asked, trying to hide his nervousness.

"I'd love that," Tasha said as she bit her lip. She wasn't ready to admit it, but she was starting to like Ethan more than she expected, or wanted to. She never envisioned herself dating a White man, let alone a policeman. There was just something about Ethan that made her forget about her reservations, the rest of the world, and their opinions. She knew the scrutiny would come if she chose to go forward with the plan to see him again, but she would cross that proverbial bridge when she got there.

After a brief awkward silence, Ethan wondered if he should go in for a kiss.

"Goodnight," Tasha said softly as she opened her front door slowly, secretly hoping that he would make a move. Ethan saw his window of opportunity closing and decided to step closer to Tasha. He held her face in his hands as he softly caressed her cheek with his thumb and leaned in for a kiss.

Ethan thought he heard fireworks explode in the distance as he pressed his lips to hers. For a moment, time seemed to stop, lending its ears to their beating hearts.

"Wow," Tasha said as they pull away, at a loss for words to describe the moment they shared.

"Goodnight," Ethan said as he made his way down the steps and back to the town car, still entranced from their electric kiss. He wanted to jump and click his heels. His heart seemed to beat a mile a minute as the car swept through the twinkling city streets. Adrenaline rushed through Ethan's body in a way he never felt before. At that moment, Ethan knew he would do anything to keep that feeling alive.

CHAPTER 19

SESSION X. YEAR TEN

DECENNIAL OBSERVATION ROOM

As Robert Whitmore and Roger Simms entered the observation room in the Decennial building, Robert looked around the room at the empty stations where his colleagues once sat. He was one of only two participants left in the program, which gave Robert a bit of a nervous feeling in his stomach. Knowing he hadn't performed well enough to be dismissed made him wonder what he was doing wrong. He knew if Dr. Langston's team didn't see reform in this session, he would face prison time. Trying not to think about it, he prepared himself to enter into the program for what he would hope to be the last time, one way or the other.

Roger seemed to be unphased by the significance of this being the tenth and final session. He refused to allow himself to take the program seriously.

"Before you two get strapped in," Dr. Lansgton began, glancing at his clipboard, as he and the rest of the team approached Roger's station. "We'd like to talk to you about your progress in the program."

"Or lack thereof," Tyrese chimed in. Dr. Cooper and Dr. Hughes glared at Tyrese before nudging him to be quiet.

"Roger, do you know why you're still in the program?" Dr. Langston asked.

"No, not really. I feel like I'm doing what I'm supposed to be doing, not sure what more you all want from me," Roger mumbled.

"I see," Dr. Cooper said as she raised her clipboard and wrote a few notes before walking away from Roger's chair and towards Robert's.

Dr. Langston and his team walked over to Robert's station. "Robert, this is session 10 of the Decennial program, the final session. Do you know why you are still here, when most of your comrades have completed the program?" Dr. Langston asked inquisitively.

Robert paused for a moment of reflection. He had never really been good at articulating his thoughts, but he wanted to make sure they understood what he was trying to say. "I've learned so much in these past months," he began slowly. "This world is cruel and unjust. Black people are treated like they're guilty the moment most law enforcement officers roll up on the scene, and that ain't right," he continued.

"I feel like I'm still here because I do know I am holdin' on to a bit of me that is still a little hesitant of letting go of some deep-rooted stuff. I used to bend the law- Ahh hell, I used to break the law to punish people that I decided were guilty, and it didn't matter if they were, in the eyes of the law or not," Robert confessed. "I didn't see that as a problem, and I certainly wasn't ready to admit fault."

"Are you ready now?" Dr. Coopers asked.

"I am," Robert said, nodding his head slowly. "I know that I have been a big part of the problem, and so are other people who see the world the way I do—the way I did."

"That's precisely why we are sending you into session ten, Robert. Not because you have to, but with what we see in our data, we believe one more session will really help you in ways we just can't explain; you just have to experience. Our data is extremely accurate, and one more session will allow you to reach a deeper level of understanding. Robert, we believe you have the potential to be a catalyst for change in a lot of people. You have the potential to really make a difference with helping Black people get the justice they deserve in this country, starting with Wesley," Dr. Langston explained.

"There is some real good that you can do, and we believe one more session will prove that," Dr. Cooper said as she gently patted Robert's hand.

"I think I'm ready. I know I'm ready to get Wesley the justice he deserves. So, let's do this!"

Robert swallowed his pills and leaned back in his recliner, beginning the Decennial Program's final session.

WESLEY ROBERTS

Wesley had been in solitary confinement for more days than he could count, and he'd lost his sense of time. The days and nights were the same. He was starting to go insane, staring at the wall for hours at a time.

Seemingly out of the blue, the door to the padded cell was opened, and two officers entered and stood him on his feet. They handcuffed him and escorted him to the warden's office.

It had been weeks since Wesley had seen any light, so the brightness of the fluorescent lamp above the warden's desk made him squint until his eyes adjusted. He looked around the room as an officer removed his cuffs. That's when he noticed Pierce Ramsey, standing in the far left corner of the room.

"Wesley Roberts, It's a pleasure to meet you. I'm Pierce Ramsey," Ramsey said, reaching out to shake Wesley's hand. "I wish we were meeting under better circumstances, but I do believe I have some good news for you."

"What's going on?" Wesley asked, rubbing his sore wrists.

"Internal Affairs has brought charges against the officers that arrested you," the Warden began. "As it turns out, they've been dirty for years, planting evidence and making unlawful arrests."

"We're currently in the process of investigating and possibly overturning every case those two have worked on since they joined the force," Ramsey continued. "I wanted to deliver the news in person, Mr. Roberts. You're a free man. On behalf of the entire police department, you have our sincerest apologies, Sir."

Wesley couldn't believe what he was hearing. He thought he might be hallucinating from spending so much time in solitary confinement. "I'm going home? I'm just... free to go?" He hedged.

"Yes, Mr. Roberts. You've been exonerated. You are free to go, and this unfortunate incident will be expunged from your record. Once again, I am so sorry," Ramsey apologized.

When Wesley walked out of the prison gates a few hours later, he just stood outside, feeling the sun on his face. It was the first time he'd stood outside those gates in years. He didn't even know how to express the joy that he felt. He knelt and felt the green grass. Being surrounded by gray concrete walls for so long made the world appear alive and in technicolor. He let out a gleeful laugh as it sunk in that he was finally a free man.

DECENNIAL CONTROL ROOM

"How amazing was that?" Dr. Hughes said, astounded as she watched Wesley's journey on the main monitor.

"Robert was definitely the most stubborn of all the officers." Dr. Cooper added. They both turn around when they hear Tyrese sniffle in the corner.

"Tyrese, are you crying, man?" Dr. Hughes asked, surprised.

"Yeah, Tyrese, what happened to, 'Oh, how could you cry for them?" Dr. Cooper mocked.

"Man, shut up," he said as he sniffled again and wiped a tear from his eye.

"This one hit differently. This kinda shit has happened to people I know. They have their whole lives taken from them, and most of them never see justice served," he shared. "It's just nice to see someone was able to get justice, you know?"

"Well said, Tyrese," Dr. Langston added. "That's why the Decennial Program exists; we've changed the lives of nine of the ten officers forever. We're creating a better police force, one session, and one officer at a time." Dr. Langston mentioned as the doctors exited the control room to join Robert and Roger as they came out of the final session.

"Well, Robert, it gives me great pleasure to say you did it. You have successfully completed the tenth and final session of the Decennial Program," Dr. Langston stated as he walked towards Robert to shake his hand.

"Thank you," Robert said to Dr. Langston and his team as he removed his headgear. "I wouldn't say it's been nice, but it's been life-changing," he chuckled as he shook the hands of every member of Dr. Langston's team.

"Likewise," Dr. Langston said jokingly. "I wish you the best, Robert."

Before he turned to leave, Robert stopped to hug Dr. Langston, giving him a friendly pat on the back. Dr. Langston was initially shocked and not sure how to respond. Eventually, Dr. Langston accepted Robert's kindness and returned Robert's gesture with a hug and pat on the shoulder. Dr. Langston and his team watched as Robert left the building.

ROBERT WHITMORE

When Robert left the Decennial Program, he reported straight to Jameson's office. He marched in, removed his badge, and slid it across the desk. Puzzled by Robert's decision, Jameson asked him what was going on. Jameson wanted to know why Robert was quitting the police department.

"When I joined the force, I vowed to protect and serve the people of this city. But that's not what I did around here. We only provided protection and service to the people that we deemed worthy of it. That's not right. I don't wanna be a part of that injustice anymore. Consider this my resignation," Robert declared before walking out of Jameson's office.

After everything he'd experienced as Wesley, Robert was ready to leave law enforcement behind him. He was ready to start a new chapter of his life. He was already feeling like a better man with each passing day. He still wrestled with the trauma he had experienced as Wesley. Nightmares of prison life still haunted his mind at night from time to time.

Robert began writing in a journal, expressing the fears and guilt and the lessons he learned while in the Decennial Program. Eventually, he filled the pages of his journal and turned it into a book. He titled it "When I Walked In Your Shoes" and dedicated the book to Wesley Roberts.

He began selling the book locally, and it eventually gained the attention of Fortune Publishing Group. Soon, Robert's book was in almost every bookstore in America, and it was flying off the shelves. People were skeptical about whether the events actually happened the way he said they had. Some people accused him of making up the entire story. Nevertheless, the more people talked, the more popular the book became.

Robert went on a book tour to promote "When I Walked in Your Shoes," and thousands of people showed up to get their copy signed by him. Robert was determined not to let his success go to his head.

At one of his book signings, he announced that he was going to donate a substantial portion of the proceeds of his book to The National Minority Coalition, a non-profit organization. Robert chose the National Minority Coalition because it was dedicated to creating positive images of all minority groups, especially the African-American community, as well as focusing on furthering diversity and inclusion in corporate America. Two things Robert believed could make a big difference when it came to race relations in America.

Robert went on to explain that he chose the National Minority Coalition because he agreed with the fact that if minority groups were represented better in the media instead of mostly being vilified, then perhaps people would see minorities differently and treat them differently.

During all of Robert's book signings and interviews, he made it a point to wear a T-shirt he received from the National Minority Coalition. It was a Black T-shirt with white lettering that said, "I Give a Buck about Racism, I supportNMC.org." *SupportNMC.org* was the non-profit's website. He felt like N.M.C. had a clear and simple mission: if enough people just gave one dollar a month to the organization, then it would obtain the budget to film, produce and distribute positive images, videos, and stories on a nationwide level, and that would make a significant difference in the way minorities are viewed in America.

His announcement propelled the book to further success. Robert was invited to appear on many national television shows to discuss his experiences as Wesley. He maintained that the Decennial Program was real and that it had, in fact, changed who he was as a person.

"Robert, can you tell us a little bit about your experience inside the program?" One TV host asked as she leaned in, eager for his answer.

"When people have conversations about race, many people often ask, 'What if the roles were reversed?' Robert began. "That's what the Decennial Program does. You step into the body of a Black American, but with your own mind," he explained. "You experience the world from their perspective, and it forces you to come to terms with some really horrible things that Black Americans have to deal with on a daily basis. I had to accept the fact that there are two Americas, still to this day. I never realized it because I never saw it, and you know what they say, 'Out of sight, out of mind' so naturally not seeing it, I never had to deal with the reality of the other America."

"As a White man, it was easy for me to ignore racism. It was easy to feel like I'm better than others because that's how I am treated—like I'm better. But, when I became Wesley, I was wrongfully imprisoned and treated like downright scum; it opened my eyes. I was the same person internally, but simply because I looked different, I got treated so much worse. This is the system racism creates and perpetuates," he explained. "I just want to take a moment to thank Dr. Langston and his team for creating this program that's gonna make the world a better place. I think every police force across this nation should make it mandatory for all of its officers to undergo this program."

The studio audience erupted in cheer and roared with applause. Robert's story was inspirational and gave hope that American's could change for the better. The host thanked Robert for sharing his journey with the nation, and the camera panned out as it faded to Black.

Pierce Ramsey smiled and nodded his head in admiration as he turned off the television in his office that was airing Robert's interview.

Between George and Robert's interviews, Ramsey had seen such immense success from the Decennial Program. What he initially thought was a long shot turned out to be one of his best decisions. Now, Ramsey was happy to greenlight the furthering of Dr. Langston's program. He dialed Dr. Langston's number as he raised the phone up to his ear.

"Dr. Langston, I'd like to meet with you again and go over some details about Phase Two," Ramsey said, leaning back in his chair.

CHAPTER 20

DECENNIAL'S FUTURE

DECENNIAL CONFERENCE ROOM

Dr. Langston and his team sat at the large oak table in the conference room of the Decennial building preparing for a series of meetings. Dr. Cooper picks up the phone on the table and dials the receptionist at the front desk, "Send in Roger Simms. We are ready to meet with him now."

Roger sauntered into the conference room with his usual nonchalant demeanor. "Why am I here? I thought we didn't have to come here anymore. I thought the program was over," Roger exclaimed.

Dr. Langston looked sternly at Roger, "Roger Simms, you were sentenced to go through the Decennial Program because you attacked a group of protesters that were dismantling a statue of a Confederate officer. You've gone on the record as saying you admire, is that correct?" Dr. Langston asked while thumbing through Roger's file.

"Yes, that is why I was sent here. I thought it was bullshit then, and I still think it's bullshit allowing people to tear down all the history of our great nation. People that risked their lives so that we have the freedoms we enjoy today," Robert briefly paused and muttered under his breath with a sinister smirk on his face., "well, at least some of us." Roger then continued, "I just think people need to respect history, is all."

"So, you still don't think you did anything wrong, or if you could get that day back, do things a bit differently," Dr. Cooper asked. "You used excessive force, and your actions incited a riot that resulted in several injuries and one casualty."

"Like I said then, I will say now. They committed a crime, so I did what an officer is supposed to do. I attempted to restore the scene to order. They have to obey the law. That's my job to uphold the law. A society without law and order, hell ain't no society at all," Roger continued.

"Roger, are you aware that of all of your fellow officer's you're the only one who did not respond to any of the simulations in a positive manner?" Dr. Langston asserted.

"No, how on earth could I know what they were going through? All I know is I had to endure my own shit and the shitty Black life of the guy you sent me into as Sean Roberts. I hated going through that. Didn't see the point in all of it. I still look at Black people the same way. I just now have confirmation of what I always believed about Black people. So should I be thanking you fine folks for that? I'm not sure," Roger said sarcastically.

"Roger, you are the only one who didn't successfully complete the Decennial Program, and you know why? It's because of this," Dr. Langston barked as he pointed in Roger's direction showing Roger's lack of effort that was clear in his body language and his conversation.

"Our data revealed your brainwaves never wavered from the first day you came here," Dr. Cooper divulged as she glanced through his charts. "We had done hundreds of test cases before you all started in this program, and do you know how many people we can say come out of it completely unchanged? Well, there's you. Less than one percent of the population will go through an extensive program like this and not be affected at all. Congratulations, you are an anomaly."

Just as Dr. Copper concluded her statement, Ramsey walked into the conference room almost on cue with an armed guard.

Ramsey took a quick look at Roger and said, " Roger Simms, we have the conclusive data that showed you did not satisfactorily complete the Decennial Program, and therefore, you will be remanded to a state prison to complete your sentencing.

The guard stood Roger up and put handcuffs on him, and escorted Roger out of the conference room.

"Well, now that that is done, we have other matters to discuss," Ramsey gleefully stated as he took a seat at the conference table, opposite of Dr. Langston and his team.

Ramsey motioned for Jameson and the various department heads of the police community to join them in the conference room.

Dr. Langston initiated the meeting by presenting extensive findings and the program's initial results.

After Dr. Langston's team had given their full report and showcased their final results, Ramsey, who was already impressed, now seemed astonished.

Dr. Langston smiled, gratified that his hard work was paying off at last.

Tyrese pulled up footage of the officers. The initial scenes display each officer engaging in biased activity or hate speech. Then footage from months later was displayed, footage from the officers and how they were interacting with the community after the Decennial Program. The scenes illustrated the same officers responding to different scenarios with justice and decency. The presentation showed the officers' journey and growth from session one to each of their final sessions, marking the moment they realized the error of their ways. Each of the officers faced their prejudices and biases head-on and responded positively to the program.

"This is amazing," Ramsey pronounced. "This could change how police departments deal with prejudice in law enforcement," he said to Jameson, who was surprised by the program's success. Dr. Langston knew that Jameson was expecting the program to fail.

"This can change how we deal with prejudice in our society, overall," Dr. Langston suggested. "The Decennial

Program doesn't have to stop at law enforcement; this can benefit anyone," he added as he slid Ramsey each officers' folder and final results.

"I have to admit," Tyrese began. "After all the setbacks, I didn't think that we'd ever get here," he confessed.

"How can you be so sure that they're not just playing along to get out of your little program?" Jameson asked.

"Jameson," Ramsey scoffed. "There are mountains of evidence supporting the officer's growth," he motioned to all of the files and the video footage on the screen.

Jameson scowled, folding his arms across his narrow chest. Langston frowned back from across the conference table.

"Jameson, truth be told, this program should have been approved when I first presented it to your department years ago," Dr. Langston asserted. "It's frustrating to see Jameson remaining obstinate when there was clear evidence that the program worked. We could have saved some lives and changed some lives sooner."

Ramsey leaned and whispered something indistinctly to Jameson as Dr. Langston's team looked around at each other in confusion.

"What are they saying?" Tyrese whispered loudly to Dr. Cooper and Dr. Hughes. They both shrugged their shoulders as they all stared across the table, waiting to hear from Jameson and Ramsey. Jameson leaned back over towards Ramsey, nodding his head reluctantly in agreement with Ramsey.

Ramsey smiled and rose from his seat as he began to address Dr. Langston and his team.

"Dr. Langston, we were very pleased with the findings that your team had presented. The reports you supplied were conclusive as well as comprehensive. We have been monitoring this research, and it has definitely been beneficial to our officers. We want you to continue to expand your program on a greater scale." Ramsey announced. Ramsey's smile was wide as he slid Dr. Langston a check for 10 million dollars.

Dr. Langston's team gathered around Dr. Langston as they glanced down at all of the 0's on the check.

"You're funding us?" Dr. Cooper asked, astonishingly.

Dr. Langston held the check-up and smirked happily as Tyrese and Dr. Cooper celebrated with a high five, and Dr. Hughes cried a single tear of joy.

"Let's put this program into full swing!" Ramsey exclaimed. "What's next?"

"Well, we have been looking at the headlines in the news, and we believe we have our next round of cohorts lined up," Dr. Langston said.

"More officers?" Ramsey questioned.

"No, this time, we have ten new candidates from ten different walks of life," Dr. Hughes chimed in.

"It seems that racial injustice doesn't just happen on the police force." Dr. Langston uttered as everyone laughed.

Support the

 NATIONAL MINORITY
COALITION

HELP US CREATE
POSITIVE IMAGES,
STORIES, AND VIDEOS
THAT CHANGE THE WAY
MINORITIES ARE
VIEWED IN AMERICA.

Go to: SupportNMC.org

Be Part of the

SOLUTION
Donate $1 a month

ABOUT THE AUTHOR

Max Fortune is the Executive Director of the National Minority Coalition (supportnmc.org), which is a nonprofit organization that focuses on creating positive images and stories of all minority groups as well as working to increase diversity and inclusion in the corporate world.

He is also the President and CEO of Fortune Publishing Group, a publishing company specializing in helping authors get their books published quickly and affordably. Being an author, Max Fortune wanted to provide an all-in-one solution for other authors who wish to self-publish their books with ease.

Max Fortune has written and published four books of his own, has ghostwritten numerous books for other authors in many different genres, but specializes in writing self-help books and memoirs, and has published hundreds of books for other authors.

Max's first book was "Success: The Blueprint to Achieving Your Dreams and Goals," a book written to provide a blueprint to achieving any dream or goal that you want to achieve.

"Get Rich in Your Niche" is a book written for business owners who wish to grow their business, focusing on building your business brand by marketing in your niche.

"How to Publish a Book and Make a Fortune," which is a book written for aspiring authors as well as seasoned writers, illustrating how to plan, write, publish, pay for, and market your book.

Max Fortune is also an accomplished book coach who has coached many authors on writing their own books in 90 days or less and offers a book coaching course on BookWritingUniversity.com.

Max Fortune has also written, filmed, and produced a sports documentary titled "Unfinished Business: The Story of the Undefeated Howard Lions."

OTHER BOOKS BY
MAX FORTUNE

SUCCESS: THE BLUEPRINT TO ACHIEVING YOUR DREAMS AND GOALS, A BOOK WRITTEN TO PROVIDE A BLUEPRINT TO ACHIEVING ANY DREAM OR GOAL THAT YOU WANT TO ACHIEVE

AVAILABLE ON

DECENNIALBOOK.COM

BARNES&NOBLE

amazon

OTHER BOOKS BY
MAX FORTUNE

GET RICH IN YOUR NICHE IS A BOOK WRITTEN FOR BUSINESS OWNERS WHO WISH TO GROW THEIR BUSINESS, FOCUSING ON BUILDING YOUR BUSINESS BRAND BY MARKETING IN YOUR NICHE

AVAILABLE ON

OTHER BOOKS BY
MAX FORTUNE

HOW TO PUBLISH A BOOK AND MAKE A FORTUNE IS A
BOOK WRITTEN FOR ASPIRING AUTHORS AS WELL AS
SEASONED WRITERS, ILLUSTRATING HOW TO PLAN,
WRITE, PUBLISH, PAY FOR, AND MARKET YOUR BOOK

AVAILABLE ON

DECENNIALBOOK.COM

BARNES&NOBLE

amazon